DEAD FISH

Ruth Carrington is the pen-name, for this series, of crime and thriller writer Michael Hartland. In writing the Alison Hope novels, he has been grateful for advice from many people who work in the police and the courts. Several judges and barristers – often women in a man's world like Alison – were particularly helpful in sharing their experience. So were some of their clients. *Dead Fish* is being adapted for television.

DEAD FISH

An Alison Hope Mystery

RUTH CARRINGTON

FOURTH ESTATE • *London*

First published in Great Britain in 1998 by
Fourth Estate Limited
6 Salem Road
London W2 4BU

1 3 5 7 9 10 8 6 4 2

A catalogue record for this book is available from
the British Library.

ISBN 1-85702-877-5

Typeset by
Vitaset, Paddock Wood, Kent

Printed in Great Britain by
Clays Ltd, St Ives plc, Bungay, Suffolk

For Lesley
with love

The author offers warm thanks for their help to John Ardern, lately Courts Administrator for Devon & Cornwall, and his colleagues on the Western Circuit; and to his editors, Caroline Upcher and Kate Goodhart.

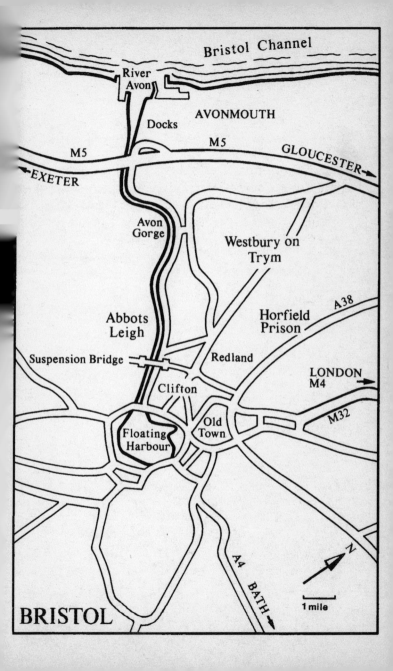

1

For a moment Quinn panicked. The house, *his* house, was on fire. He stopped the car abruptly, leapt out and started to run, his feet slithering on the gravel. But then he saw it was just that light blazed from every window. None of the curtains had been closed. There were several cars at the side of the building and brilliant white arc lamps made it daylight in the garden. He had left the place locked and dark. What the hell was going on?

It was a long driveway for a house in a suburban street; he was panting and his legs started to slow. He swayed unsteadily as he cut across the lawn, still spongy underfoot after the rain, suddenly feeling the exhaustion of three days' continuous driving. He needed to sleep, to get away from it all for a few hours. The front door was half open and he stumbled inside. The familiar white-painted hall, oval mirror over a rosewood table on the left, broad Edwardian staircase rising on the right. A uni-formed policeman emerged from a door carrying a large cardboard box, glanced curiously at Quinn and vanished outside. There were sounds of people everywhere.

A man in his fifties appeared in another doorway, tall, worn grey suit. He looked astonished, but recovered quickly. 'Dr Quinn?'

Quinn nodded, his head spinning.

'Dr *Geoffrey* Quinn?'

'Yes.' It was as if somebody else were speaking. Nothing mattered except that he needed to stop running, lie down, switch off. A pain was piercing through his temples, so sharp that he almost cried out, and his sight was blurred: bands of bright, flickering light dazzled his eyes.

The man pushed past him, slammed the door shut and stood against it. He held up a small plastic-covered card, but Quinn could not read it. 'I am Chief Superintendent Manning. Geoffrey Quinn, I am arresting you on suspicion that between the sixth and ninth days of this month you murdered your wife, Nicola Quinn, and your two children, Jessica and Thomas.' Suddenly uniformed police were pouring into the confined space, surrounding him. He felt his wrists seized and handcuffs snapped round them. He was shackled between two constables. 'You do not have to say anything. But it may harm your defence if you do not mention, when questioned, something which you later rely on in court. Anything you do say may be given in evidence. Do you understand?'

Quinn did *not* understand. He was too confused to speak. It was a nightmare. The whole three days had been unreal. The haggard man driving like a madman was somebody else. He would wake up and the agony would stop. He was hustled out into his own drive, into a white police car, and driven away.

Manning stood and watched the car go, red brake lights glowing as it reached the road, disappearing as it turned left towards the suspension bridge. He returned to the kitchen and went down the brick steps to the cellar. It was lit by two temporary spotlights on metal stands. Frank, his sergeant, and the pathologist were still kneeling in front of the boiler. It was a French wood-burner for the central heating: a steel cylinder five feet long, mounted on two piers of concrete blocks. It had taken hours to cool down before they could get inside.

Now the round door was open and a litter of ash, charred cloth and bones covered the sheet of blue polythene spread on the floor. 'That was Quinn,' said Manning. 'I've arrested him.'

Frank jerked and turned round with an expression of astonishment, his face and shirt smeared with ash. 'You *arrested* 'im, sir? Wasn't that a bit hasty? No questioning? No evidence?'

Manning gestured at the polythene sheet with his shoe. 'What the hell do you think all this is?'

'But what do we do if 'e's got a decent alibi?'

'Let him go again. Caught me on the hop, walking in like that. Like seeing a bloody ghost. I over-reacted – but he's our man, no sweat, there's no one else involved. I'll let him stew for a few hours then go down the nick and hammer the bastard.'

3

The pathologist stopped putting pieces of bone into clear plastic bags with a pair of forceps, labelling each meticulously. 'I thought he'd turn up, you know.'

'Not *here*, surely? I thought he'd be miles away, out of the country by now.'

'Bet he never left Bristol.'

Manning sighed and sat down on a dusty box. 'So the body was burning about three days?'

'Yes, and with all that fat there must have been one hell of a lot of greasy white smoke going up the chimney – I'm surprised no one noticed.'

'They did.' Frank was a laconic Yorkshireman. 'But ther' a load of toffee-nosed gits round 'ere, keep therselves t'therselves. Neighbours just thought wife 'ad left 'im so 'e was livin' on Indian takeaways.'

The doctor picked up a charred skull. 'It has to be her, Peter. The jaw and teeth have survived and I'll get her dental records. I'm sure they'll match, but I can do a DNA test if necessary.' He stood up and stretched, a small man in his thirties: blue shirt and brown cords, cherubic face, gold half-moon spectacles. His eyes said that he had seen it all, but had an opaque look that suggested it had not left him untouched. 'This thing's efficient – might get one myself, I'm thinking of going over to wood – but it's not a cremation oven. The skeleton's in bits but more or less complete.' He pointed to a length of thick bone, splintered at the end. 'This is a femur, as you can see, largely intact but the legs have been broken at the knee – with a hammer I'd say – to get

4

her into the furnace.'

'What do you think happened?'

'Not easy to say without a body. But I'd guess they had a row upstairs in the kitchen and he hit her. She fell down the steps and broke her neck.' He picked up a floppy length of vertabrae and matched it with another. 'There are also minor injuries to the skull. We found some traces of hair on the third step up. That fall killed her. If he'd had any sense, he'd have called an ambulance and said it was an accident. But he panicked and decided to get rid of the body. God knows why – that's for you to find out.'

'He'll have to go before the magistrates to get a remand, Alec. Hope he'll come clean as soon as I question him – but if he doesn't, is there anything else to tie him in? Apart from it being *his* wife dead in *his* cellar?'

'Which isn't a bad start, you know ... but we're sweeping the whole place for forensics. There are some bloodstains on the boiler door. Haven't done any tests yet, but they look only a day or two old. If they're his—'

'Can you match them, if we get him to give a sample?"

'Of course.'

'OK, it's enough to hold him. They had two kids, you know.' Manning's eyebrows rose questioningly. 'What the devil's happened to *them*? We've dug up half the garden, but no trace.'

'Maybe he's hidden the bodies out in the woods? Or they're alive and he's taken them somewhere

5

safe? You've just seen him, Peter. Is he crackers?'

'Barking.'

The doctor shrugged, pulling on his jacket. 'Then maybe he took them out too?'

'You reckon? Poor little bastards.'

'Poor all of them, I'd say.' He gestured upstairs. 'Nice gaff, this.' Manning knew the pathologist lived alone somewhere out in Somerset. 'A family could be very happy here. Wonder what went wrong?'

2

Quinn could remember little of the next few days. At the police station he was driven into a darkened yard and hustled up concrete steps, his head covered in a blanket. He didn't *want* his head covered, and there was nobody to see anyway, but he supposed the police were all conditioned by seeing real murders on the television news. They left him alone in a cell for what seemed like hours. He crouched awkwardly on the edge of the narrow metal bed, unable to bring himself to touch the thin mattress and threadbare blanket that stank of another man's urine.

His mind was in turmoil. He thought his brain would burst from the hammer-blows of fear and anger and confusion. He did not much care that Nikki was dead, nor even that a faceless detective in a grey suit thought he had killed her. The faces that mattered were those of Jessica and Tom. He could see them floating in and out of focus through the mist of tears that clouded his eyes, not innocent and laughing as he remembered, but twisted in terror. *Were they dead*? The thought was too full of pain to bear. *No, they had to be alive*. Whoever killed their mother had taken them away. Someone had to find them. *He* had to find them. There was no one else. He hammered on the cell door until the judas opened and a face glowered through the small square opening. 'Yes?'

Quinn was almost too distraught to find the words. 'I must ... I must see someone in authority. Quickly. It's my children, you see, they're in danger ... kidnapped, taken away ... must be terrified ... if you don't go after them it may be too late. Could you ... please ... I must see someone *now*.'

'Give it a rest, Quinn. You'll be questioned soon enough.'

'No, you don't understand. It's my *children*. I'm worried about my children. I must see someone *now*, they're in danger – for God's sake, *do* something!'

'Use the bell if you want anything else.' The judas snapped shut.

Quinn stared in disbelief. They didn't believe him. Thought he was a killer, thought he was mad. He started to smash his fist on the door again, simultaneously pressing his other hand on the bell-push beside it. He could hear the long, continuous ring at the end of the corridor. This time the whole door swung open and two officers stood there in short-sleeved shirts, one with a sergeant's chevrons on his shoulder flaps. 'For fuck's sake stop this racket! There are people here trying to sleep.'

'I *must* see someone in authority – it's my kids, I don't know what's happened to them, they must be frightened and in danger.'

'I said *shut up*!' The sergeant stepped towards him threateningly. 'Save that for the guv'nor, Quinn. Just chuck it now, lie down, get some sleep, you're going to need it tomorrow.' Quinn had always thought of the police as helpful people, broadly on his side: it came as a shock to realise that they were his enemies, and tough-looking enemies at that.

'*Sleep*? How the hell d'you think I can sleep?' Quinn was suddenly shaking with emotion, his voice rising. 'There are two children in danger out there – I want to know what's being done to find them. I'm their *father*, can't you understand?'

'Yeah, yeah, we all believe you. Give it a rest, Quinn, save it for the morning.'

'No, you don't understand!' He tried to push past them, out into the corridor. 'For God's sake, this is *serious*.' When they grabbed him, he struggled and struck out wildly. His fist connected with soft tissue, there was the splintering of bone and shriek of pain.

'Shit! You stupid bastard! *Hold him.*' The sergeant's nose was pouring blood, staining his white shirt. Another figure appeared, hands were grasping at Quinn's arms, he kicked out, felt a heavy blow over his kidneys and a knee slamming up into his groin. As he caught his breath and doubled up, he felt the hard steel of handcuffs snapped around his wrists, strong fingers were at his throat, there was a sharp pain in the side of his neck, his head swam and he lost consciousness.

When he woke there was a throbbing in his temples and his mouth felt very dry. He realised that they had put him out with the 'sleeper' – pressure on the carotid artery in the neck – but they must also have injected him with a sedative. His wrists were free again – he still had his watch and was lucid enough to see that he had been asleep for ten hours. The urine-soaked blanket had been replaced with a clean red one.

Geoffrey Quinn was no coward. He had faced disaster and threats more than once in his life; and survived. He had kept his head above water even in the last six months, though they had taken him to the brink. But now he was scared, bloody scared. Less than a day ago he had been a doctor, a respected figure, free. Now he was not only locked in a cell, the men and women on the other side of that door had already convicted him of murder, of killing his own wife and children. They despised him, they had beaten him up and sedated him without his consent. If he told them the truth they would disbelieve him.

It took Quinn a matter of seconds to see the future only too clearly, and it was terrifying. No one had the slightest intention of looking for Jess and Tom. And their father was on a conveyer belt to a lifetime in a cell like this. There was no point asking for help here. He sat on the edge of the bed with his head in his hands, eyes shut, close to weeping but trying to fight off the waves of self-pity and despair. Eventually he knew what had to be done – he must get to someone on the outside as quickly as he could.

An hour later, he was taken to an interview room and the man in the grey suit introduced himself again as Chief Superintendent Manning. They sat on hard chairs at a modern table surfaced in sapele veneer. The room was brightly lit but had no windows. Two uniformed officers in shirt-sleeves stood with arms folded in the corners. Did they think he was dangerous? But he was already adjusting, there was no point being shocked or intimidated. They were the enemy; he must keep calm and watch every word. A woman in civilian clothes joined them at the table. 'This is Detective Inspector Curzon.' There were no preliminaries. Manning switched on a cassette-recorder and started to speak into it. 'Bristol Central police station, fourteen hundred hours on the tenth of September. Present are—'

'Just a minute.' Quinn was surprised by how firm he sounded. 'I'm not prepared to answer any questions without my lawyer here.'

Manning sighed and switched off the recorder. 'Very well. That is your right. Who is your solicitor?'

'I don't have one yet.'

'You don't *have* one yet?' The same jeering tone that the men who beat him up last night had used. 'You've had nearly twelve hours to do something about that. You're not here for a motoring offence, you know.'

'*You* know perfectly well I was unconscious in a

11

cell for nearly all of that time.'

Manning had a smooth, young-looking face, though with his silver-grey hair Quinn put him at over fifty. 'Is that true?' Manning addressed one of the constables standing in a corner.

'Yes, sir.'

'I should have been told.' His eyes flashed angrily, then he turned to Quinn with an emollient half-smile. *Remember he is the enemy.*

'OK – I'm going to charge you with murder in an hour's time unless we've started your interview by then. Would you like us to get the duty solicitor? Or you can make one telephone call.'

Quinn was escorted along a corridor by the two silent constables, seeing daylight for the first time since his arrest, through windows looking down on yellow buses crossing the centre of the city. It was sunny outside. One of the escorts opened the door of a tiny office and indicated a telephone on the desk. Both of them stood inside the door watching him; there was to be no privacy.

He sat down, trying to ignore them, and puzzled who to phone. He didn't know any lawyers, nor did he have any intimate friends. It was ludicrous; or it would be if he wasn't facing a murder charge. Who on earth *did* you ring in this situation? He couldn't bring himself to call the surgery and ask one of his partners for help. They'd have heard by now; they'd pretend to be supportive, but they'd believe he was guilty. Everyone else would too. Husbands were always killing wives, or wives husbands. He was well known to have a shaky marriage, so they probably wouldn't even be that surprised. He picked up the phone, hesitated, then put it down again.

This was ridiculous. All he needed was someone to get a lawyer down here, a good one. Bill was the man. He worked at the head office of a small building society and moved in the city's financial and legal circles. Bill would know who to go to – and he was, come to think of it, the nearest thing Quinn had to a friend. Bill Taylor was a neighbour in Abbots Leigh; they were not close friends, but shared the ownership of a small sailing cruiser. It was really no more than a business arrangement and the boat was rarely used by either of them, but Quinn could not think of anyone else. 'May I have a telephone directory?' He looked up Bill's office number and keyed it firmly.

A switchboard operator answered and Quinn asked for Taylor. Seconds later a classy female voice said: 'Managing Director's office.'

Quinn had not known Bill was quite so grand these days. 'Could I speak to Mr Taylor, please? My name's Quinn.'

'May I tell him what it's about?'

'It – it's a personal call.'

'Very well, Mr Quinn.'

After a long pause, there was a man's voice. 'Bill Taylor, can I help you?'

'It's Geoff Quinn.' There was a loud silence.

13

'God, Geoff, where are you?'

'I'm at the Central police station. I'm under arrest. I need a bloody good lawyer. Can you help?'

'Yes, Geoff. It was on the news this morning. I – I'm really sorry, of course I'll help, but how – do you want me to come over? I'm only a few minutes' walk away.'

'I didn't do it, Bill. The whole thing's some sort of ghastly mistake.' He suddenly felt last night's panic again, and was close to tears.

'Of course it is, Geoff.' He almost sounded as if he meant it. 'I didn't think for one minute … Look, I'll come over.'

'Could you come later? What I really need now is a lawyer – they want to start questioning me. Do you know anybody?'

'They say Roger Dixon is the best solicitor in town and there's a woman barrister he often briefs in – for this sort of thing. Would you like me to phone him?'

'Yes, please. Say I need someone down here right away. And, Bill—'

'Geoff?'

'Tell him I *didn't* do it.'

'Yes, I'll tell him that. You bet I will.'

Quinn stood up, feeling shaky but slightly better. 'My lawyer will be here soon and I'm not prepared to speak to anyone until he is. OK?'

The constable nodded. 'Then we'll take you back to the cells to wait for him.' He hesitated and Quinn thought he was about to add 'sir', but instead he slipped a handcuff round Quinn's wrist, shackling them together as they walked down the corridor to curious eyes. Even in Bristol Central, murder wasn't an everyday occurrence.

Taylor arrived forty minutes later, a short insigni-ficant-looking man with thinning red hair; but not without courage. Quinn was cheered to learn later that Taylor had behaved like a friend ready to stand up and be counted. Since he was Quinn's *only* friend to stand up and be counted, it mattered a lot. After forty-five years of obscure respectability, Bill Taylor had announced to his secretary where he was going, so it was all over the building society headquarters in minutes, then strode across the centre of the city with Roger Dixon, two pinstriped caricatures, up the steps and into the main door of the Central police station.

Unfortunately, once inside, Taylor was forbidden to see Quinn, but Dixon was conducted through a door that locked automatically behind him. 'I insist on seeing my client at once.' He addressed the corridor generally, as if speaking directly to each of the six people in it.

A constable came forward. 'And you are?'

'Mr Dixon, Dr Quinn's solicitor.'

'I'm the custody officer; I'll check with the guv'nor.'

Ten minutes later Dixon entered the cell and Quinn looked up to see a tall, fair-haired young man, handsome in a boyish way, exuding confidence.

'I'm Roger Dixon,' he smiled. 'You're not on your own any more.'

Geoffrey Quinn gasped in relief and burst into tears.

3

By the time Alison Hope was retained to defend him, Quinn had been moved to Horfield prison. He had been locked up for six weeks and when he came into the interview room his face had a grey, jail pallor. Horfield was an old prison, brick walls painted muddy pea-green and the only window barred and high up. Most of the light came from a flickering fluorescent tube. The man might have been a doctor with the biggest practice in Avonmouth, she thought, but now he looked defeated. No, worse than that, crushed, destroyed before he had even come to trial. He was wearing a striped prison shirt under the jacket of the crumpled suit he must have been in when they arrested him. They'd taken away his tie and shoe-laces. She knew he was on the hospital wing, where – as with anyone charged with murder – they'd be checking on him every fifteen minutes. Enough to drive even the most stable prisoner to screaming paranoia. 'Please sit down.' She gave an encouraging smile.

They sat each side of the table, its grimy plastic top covered in the brown rings left by styrofoam beakers of instant coffee. Quinn raised his head slowly and looked at her: he saw a small, vital woman in her thirties, a mass of wild, black curls, lightly-tanned skin and flashing brown eyes. 'I'm Alison Hope. I'm a barrister. I've been asked to represent you, if you want me.' She had a strong Aberdonian accent.

'Yes.' Some hidden corner of his brain said that despair was addictive and this might be his last chance not to drown in it. But was this woman genuine? Could he trust her? 'Bill Taylor said you'd be coming. Why has it taken so long?'

Alison gestured at the young man sitting at the third side of the table. 'Your solicitor, Roger Dixon here, was there when the police interviewed you. That's how the system works. Now he's asked me to represent you in court.'

'OK.' Quinn met her eyes for the first time. She was shocked. She knew that he was only forty-one and could see that he hadn't been bad looking. Good bone structure – he would have been handsome ten years ago. But now the face was gaunt and his eyes sunken like an old man's. They stared at her from deep sockets, the white showing red veins and partly bloodshot. The depth of pain and fear in them was terrifying. 'I've been told you're good, even the screws say so. But get rid of him.' He nodded towards Dixon. 'The berk who just sat there while the police walked all over me and hasn't been seen since, even though I've asked for him every day.' He paused with an expression of slight surprise, as if he'd broken through a crust, managed to make a decision for the first time in six weeks.

Alison sighed. She understood. Dixon was a smooth young man who put himself about a lot in the city's clubs, projecting the image of a successful lawyer. But in the profession he was well-known to be slipshod. She glanced sideways at him and his boyish features coloured. 'Pressure of work, you know,' he muttered.

Yes, she knew. But the man was on a murder charge; and now his anger boiled over. '*Pressure of work*? For Christ's sake! Have either of you the slightest idea what it's like being in here? Someone's murdered my wife and taken away my children. I've been wrongly arrested. I'm locked in a cell twenty-three hours a day because they've put me on Rule 43. I keep having to see some mad psychiatrist who's convinced I killed my children and wants to put me on hypnotic drugs. I haven't seen my supposed lawyer for a month, but I *have* been held down by four screws and injected with sedatives.'

'That's wrong and we'll certainly lodge a protest with the governor.' But she was not surprised; they must see him as a serious suicide risk. 'Do you have another solicitor you'd like to act for you, Dr Quinn?'

'Not really. The last time I used a lawyer was to buy my house.'

She frowned. 'Well, it's not for me to choose your solicitor and I think it would be helpful if Mr Dixon stays and takes a few notes today. Then he will ask the senior partner of his firm to come and see you, tomorrow, and he will provide you with someone else, if that's what you want – or recommend another firm all together.' Dixon seemed about to protest, but saw the set of her jaw and stayed silent. 'Is that OK, Roger?' He nodded angrily.

Quinn's mouth gave a bitter smile. 'Thanks.' He hesitated. 'Is this place bugged?'

It was a question she often asked herself. 'No. No one's listening.' She wished she was certain. 'You can be straight with me.'

'Can I?' The tormented eyes continued to stare through her. 'It's the children I'm worried about. Jessica and Tom.' The words echoed hollow in the bare room. 'I'm so bloody scared for them and no one's *doing* anything.'

Roger Dixon joined in for the first time. 'The police believe they're dead, Dr Quinn.' He paused pointedly. 'What do *you* think has happened to them?'

Quinn reared back and raised his arm as if he were going to hit him. 'How the hell can I know?' His voice rose in anger and a face appeared at the window in the door. 'Locked in here? They must be bloody terrified, and the only person in the world who cares about them is me – I think of them every second, I lie awake at night, pouring with sweat in the dark. But I can't *do* anything – sometimes I think I'm going mad.'

After the outburst he suddenly deflated. A few tears trickled from those gaunt eye sockets and he made no effort to wipe them away. He turned to Alison, his voice a whisper. 'Do *you* think they're dead too? Like Nikki?'

'I don't know, Geoff. May I call you Geoff? I wish to God I did. I know the police *are* looking for them.' Or at least for their bodies. 'As soon as I leave here I'll find out what's going on.' She changed the subject gently. 'Look, I know it's the children that are on your mind, but can we just go back to the beginning?' Alison crossed her legs under the black skirt and pulled a notebook from her handbag. She met his eyes and was again shocked by the sheer pain in them. She wasn't quite sure she believed him, but if his story were true the last six weeks must have been unbearable. 'Your wife has been murdered. Did you kill her?'

He seemed about to explode again, but swallowed and answered matter-of-factly. 'No, of course not.'

'Right. Then why was her partly dismembered body left burning in the boiler in your basement while you disappeared for three days?'

'I've no idea.' She studied his face but saw only fear and confusion. He covered it with his hands and his shoulders shook. 'It's like some kind of nightmare.'

'No idea? You've no idea *at all* who might have killed her?'

'No, I don't.'

'Very well. Now, I don't want to distress you, but I must also ask: did you kill the children?'

21

'No! I just told you.'

'You don't think they are dead too?'

'I can't face that.' His eyes pleaded with her for reassurance. 'But no – somehow I feel they're still alive.'

'Why do you feel that, Geoff?'

There was still strength in that tormented face, despite the fear, the drugs, the guilt, the interminable hours of solitary confinement. 'I love them both very much, I can't explain how much … I think I'd, well, *know* if they were dead. It would be as if part of me had died. I'd just know.'

'And if they're alive, what do you think has happened to them?'

He shook his head in defeat. 'I don't know. I just don't know. I've never been so scared in all my life. I just want to get out and find them, hold them, tell them they're safe.'

'Yes, well there isn't much chance of that at the moment.' She sounded very crisp and Scots as she turned the page of her pad. 'I think you'd better tell me the story from the beginning, don't you? There *was* a beginning, wasn't there?'

'I suppose so.' He gave a rueful half smile. She should have guessed he'd be on Rule 43 – he was a suspected nonce, a child killer – they'd keep him in solitary to protect him from the other prisoners. No wonder he had come so close to the edge, but now he was catching a little of her determined confidence.

'Well?' They sat in silence. A screw's face

appeared at the window again, mouthing 'Are you finished?' She had only booked the room for forty-five minutes but she waved him away. 'Look, Geoff,' she said at last. 'I really do want to help, but I need some facts to understand what happened.' She put her hand on his reassuringly. 'Your wife *is* dead. That's for sure. I believe you didn't kill her, but how did you get on when she was alive?'

'Badly.'

'Always?'

'No, not always. It was OK until about three years ago; then Nikki got frustrated and fed up.'

Alison smiled encouragingly. 'Why, Geoff? What happened? Or didn't happen?'

He was starting to weep again, not much, just a trace. 'I barely noticed to begin with. I suppose I was working all the time, not home much, always tired.' He shrugged. 'I think she found the children a drag, she found me a drag, we never went out.'

'Did you have rows?'

'Yes, but it was more of a cold war. She started to go out without saying where she was going, acting secretively, coming back late. I wondered if she was having an affair – you must have seen it all before.'

'Sure, but it doesn't always end like this.' She met his eyes questioningly.

'I didn't bloody well kill her.'

'No. We've established that. But *someone* did. To defend you sensibly I'm going to have to find out who – and what happened to your children. When did you last see them all?' She sighed inwardly. It was all very well showing him boundless confidence, that was a professional necessity, but even she was starting to feel defeated.

'Three days before they arrested me.'

'What time of day?'

'In the morning. About eight. The children were having breakfast, watching telly in the kitchen and I was leaving for work.'

'Did you always leave about eight?'

'No, I was late – I usually went about half seven, got to the surgery by eight.'

'Uh-huh. So?'

'I was in a hurry to get away. Nikki was shouting – she wanted me to get home early so she could go out with some girlfriends. I thought she meant with some bloke and said I didn't know how late evening surgery would end. We had a row.'

'You had a row?'

'Yes.'

'Did you hit her?'

'Of course not. We just shouted at each other until I walked out and slammed the door.'

'The police found some of your blood on the door of the boiler. They matched it from a sample you gave.'

'I know.'

'They say it was recent, consistent with the time Nikki died. They say you cut yourself when you were getting rid of her body.'

'I know. It's rubbish.'

'Well, how *did* it get there?'

'I cut my hand chopping some kindling.'

'When?'

'I can't remember, maybe a day or two before Nikki vanished."

'OK, Geoff.' She sighed. 'So you went to work?'

'Where else?'

'Did you phone home during the day? To make things up? Or continue the battle?'

'No. But I got home at about seven in the evening.'

'Was that early?'

'Oh yes, especially for a Friday.'

'And what did you find?'

'The house was locked up and Nikki had gone. So had the children.'

'Did she leave a note?'

'No. Nothing.'

'But she'd taken clothes and things?'

'Yes. Clothes, make-up, the kids' Walkmans. Everything you'd need for a few days away.'

'But you'd no idea where she had gone?'

'I thought she'd walked out – she'd done it before – and gone to a holiday cottage her parents gave us in Dorset. I drove down there straightaway, there's no phone.'

Alison stopped writing. 'If your marriage was so bloody, why did you bother? Weren't you glad to see the back of her?'

'I didn't want to lose the children – and I was worried they'd be confused and frightened.'

She nodded. 'OK. So you drove to Dorset, but she wasn't there?'

'No. It was all locked up and I felt a complete prick. It had been a long week, I was knackered, it was pitch dark and pouring with rain. I'd also forgotten the keys. Anyway, I broke a window, crawled in and fell asleep. I left about five in the morning.'

'Back to Bristol?'

'No. By then I was sure Nikki had gone to her sister's – they live out on the Yorkshire Moors, north of Pickering.'

'That must be over three hundred miles – did you phone to check?'

'No, I wanted to walk in when she wasn't expecting me, take the children home, tell her we were through, that I'd had it up to here.'

'You were angry?'

'I was furious, spitting blood. This selfish bitch had spent most of our married life whinging and griping while living a style of life that most people would give their right arm for. I was to blame, of course, working all the time, never there, though I didn't seem to have much choice. But her selfishness and self-obsession had finally got to me. Yes, I was angry.'

'Are you sure you didn't see her again? Attack her?'

He bridled, then shook his head. 'No. If I *had* found her I can't say what might have happened, but when I got to Yorkshire after driving for seven hours, she wasn't there. Her sister hadn't seen or heard from her for a fortnight, that's what she said anyway.'

'And then?'

'Nikki had obviously been talking to Kate about what a bastard I was. She didn't even offer me a cup of tea. I was too tired to drive back and stayed the night up there.'

'Where?'

'In a lay-by.'

'And you arrived back in Bristol on Monday evening, when you were arrested?' Quinn nodded. 'But that doesn't fit, Geoff. If you'd driven straight back, you'd have got home on Sunday evening. So why was it twenty-four hours later?'

4

Alison Hope left Horfield with relief. It was a miserable place and, even after ten years in and out of prisons, she never got used to the pervasive smell of stale cabbage, sweaty bodies and piss. Her car was in a nearby side street. Today it had not been vandalised.

She drove back into the city through heavy traffic. It was raining hard. The windscreen rapidly misted up and the wipers could not keep pace with the volume of water. At least it would wash the layers of dirt off the old XJS; so far as she could remember it was bright red underneath. Not for the first time, she thought of going back to London, to the real bar, the glamorous bar, the well-paid bar. What the devil was she doing, stuck in the provinces defending a no-hoper like Quinn who didn't seem to care that he was facing a lifetime in that brick shithouse?

But the rain stopped as she passed the Royal Fort, a dying sun came out and the old town was spread below her. It must have looked like that when the Cabots sailed for Nova Scotia and a new world: the clustering spires and towers of so many churches, sandstone glowing in soft evening light. The court she appeared in almost daily was in the maze of narrow streets they protected; once the harbour had reached into their midst and the spires would have been mixed up with masts and sails. The two rooms she rented for her chambers were in John Street, looking out over the disused graveyard of another medieval church that had not survived the blitz. She knew it was ridiculous, but she loved every inch of it.

She turned under the arch of the old city gate, bright with the stone figures of saints picked out in blue and red and gold, and parked in her precious single space down a cobbled alley at the back of the office. And why shouldn't she love this mellow place that had taken her in when she ran away? Away from the Temple and Fleet Street and Fulham Road, from the waves of humiliation that still made her shudder, from the pain that had almost broken her. How tragic they had all said, with mocking eyes she could never bear to meet again. No, she owed a lot to this city and the people with whom she had made a new life. And this *was* the real bar she told herself fiercely. Real people. Real crime. She yawned. Real exhaustion. She had been up at six to get to a case in Gloucester and now it was eight in the evening. Alison pushed open the back door and ran upstairs to pick up her papers for the morning. There were thirteen message slips on her desk and it took half an hour to deal with them.

When she finally drove home by the river, along

the bottom of the Avon Gorge and under the flood-lit suspension bridge, she reflected how like a village this city could feel. Up there on the left, in the gloomy woods that topped the rock face, was Quinn's home. At the end of the gorge lay the sea and Avonmouth, where he had practised. She sighed and also reflected that just at the moment she wanted nothing so much as a wife. Someone waiting for her with a hot meal, tender loving care, bed. But the flat overlooking Clifton Down would be silent and empty. She couldn't be bothered to cook – maybe she'd pick up a takeaway.

But she didn't and at nine o'clock wearily climbed the six steps to her shared front door, eight feet high, burgher-black with a heavy brass knocker and tatty line of bell-pushes at the side. The flat was half the ground floor of a once grand merchant's house, but it was neither silent nor empty. As she turned the key and dumped her leaden case on the floor, the lights were on and Mozart and garlic flooded from the kitchen. There was an extravagant bunch of roses in a bucket on the floor.

'George!' She burst out laughing as a bearded face appeared from a doorway and a man twice her size and well over six feet tall followed it. 'What on earth are *you* doing here? For once it's lovely to see you.' She did not protest as he folded her in his arms.

'Ungrateful wench.' He had a booming voice in between kisses. 'Spurned, derided, but I cannot abandon you to this cruel world, you wilful child.'

'*Scourged*, derided,' she corrected, a little ashamed that she felt so surprised to hear him quoting Chesterton and 'The Donkey', or rather at her underlying assumption that she knew about stuff like that and he didn't. 'But I'm not into that kind of thing and I'm *not* a child, George, I'm fat and thirty-two. Hey!' She laughed again as he picked her up bodily and carried her into the living-room. 'Oh, I *am* pleased you're here. It's been a bloody day.' He sat in an armchair and she curled up on his lap like a cat, looking up into his face with half-closed eyes. 'I'm sorry, George. I was horrible. I don't deserve all this.' She smiled as he stroked her face and reached up to kiss him. It was all slightly unreal.

That was the trouble. George was always unreal, a mad addiction. The passionate Alison of the night loved this flamboyant oaf, always just a whisker ahead of bankruptcy and, for all she knew, jail. He was the most intriguing – and kindest – man she would ever meet. Then the feminist Alison of the day told her sternly that she could manage perfectly well as a woman alone. She had her own home, her own money, her own career, there could be discreet lovers. One day she would decide. One day she would grow up.

'No, you don't deserve it. Never darken my doorstep again, you said, or rather screamed.' His mouth smiled slightly among the fair-to-grey whiskers.

'That was two days ago.'

'It was unwarranted, my girl.' George Kristianssen

31

always boomed, except in bed. 'I have come to seek amends.'

'*You've* come—' She bit the words back. 'We'll talk about it later – can I have a bath first? What's cooking out there? It smells terrific.'

'Roast pheasant, with most of the trimmings. Avocado overflowing with prawns to start. Claret *chambreing* in the kitchen. There's time for a bath. Shall I scrub your back?'

She looked doubtful. 'You're supposed to be in disgrace. But you could massage it gently – you know how it aches when I've been on the go all day.'

She lay back in the warm water, sipping a glass of wine. George sat in the rocking chair – it was a huge Edwardian bathroom – and she did not invite him to join her. It would do him good to wait for full rehabilitation, but she hoped her breasts were peeping provocatively through the scented foam. 'Will you stay tonight?' They had never lived together for more than a few days without falling out and George had his own place a mile away in Redland.

'If you want me, Alison Hope, I shall, as always, be honoured.' His eyes crinkled. 'I'm sorry, too.'

She closed her eyes as he ran more hot water into the bath. 'There's a lot to be said for rows if you can make up like this, you know. You were drunk as a skunk, George, and I was *so* embarrassed. The Medico-Legal Society is a *vairy ser-rious* gathering.'

She rolled her 'r's to sound sternly Aberdonian. 'The Infirmary's senior common room, for Christ's sake, distinguished speaker, High Court judges present, civilised buffet. I bet no one's *ever* got pissed there before.'

He gave a great roar of laughter. 'Do them good to meet a peasant for a change.'

'Not if the peasant is my guest, thank you very much. You knocked a bottle of Chablis over Mr Justice Lawrence, the joke about the well-hung donkey was definitely unsuitable and I had to hold you up when we left. You must *never* do it again, George, or we are definitely through. You've put back my chances of becoming a QC by about twenty years.'

'Does it matter?' He looked humble.

'Of course it bloody matters! For one thing I can charge more and that may help if I'm ever daft enough to succumb to your raffish charms.' She raised her right leg elegantly and dangled it over the edge of the bath – she had good calves and the chunky top half was lost in the suds – as he refilled her glass.

'Will you marry me, flower?' He asked most days.

'No, I won't.' A grey cat squeezed through the narrow gap where the door was not quite closed and seemed to nod in approval. Large, long-haired and scruffy, Hamish had been Alison's closest companion for twelve years: he was the only creature who really understood her. He ignored George and leapt cautiously onto the side of the

33

bath; Alison stroked him and he started to purr loudly.

'Shall I serve dinner?' He held out a large blue bath sheet and his pupils enlarged dangerously as she stepped out, dripping and covered in foam. 'You're beautiful, Ally.'

'And you're a dirty old man.' But inside it made her glow as he folded the towel round her and she put her arms round his neck to kiss him. 'But I'm glad you came back.' Hamish looked away disdainfully.

Early next morning they walked George's dog briskly across the downs. The Airedale was as scruffy as his master and known as Wedgie – after Wedgwood Benn, for George was a lifetime Labour supporter. When they could see the gorge and the suspension bridge, Alison jerked her head towards the dark woods above the cliff on the other side. 'My new client comes from over there, in Abbots Leigh.'

'What's he called?'

'Quinn. Dr Geoffrey Quinn.'

'Drugs again?'

'No, murder. His wife and maybe two kids.'

'Nasty. Did he do it?'

'He says not, George, I have to believe him.'

'But that's not the same as—'

'OK – I half believe he's guilty. The other half says he's potty. He's shell-shocked, hardly able to speak and has nothing to offer except that Nikki –

his wife – had been behaving oddly and had some dark secret to hide.'

'What dark secret?'

'Ah well, there words fail him and he doesn't know. Really helpful, eh?'

'You don't want the case, Ally?'

She laughed quietly. 'Right on, George. No, I like to win and this bugger's already inured to a lifetime in jail. It's hopeless.'

'You've said that before – and won.'

'This time I haven't got a hope a hell.'

'Then give it up, kid – go with the flow.'

She shook her head. 'Only dead fish go with the flow, George.'

Twelve hours later she was driving back into the city when her carphone buzzed. She hesitated before picking it up, partly because the XJS was sandwiched between two juggernauts and she needed two hands to survive, partly because the bloody thing never brought good news. But it was George. 'You OK, darlin'?'

'Am I late, George? I'm cooking for *you* tonight.'

'How very kind, ma'am. But meet me at the Port of Call first. I made an interesting discovery today, something we need to discuss.'

The little pub was just off the Down, near Blackboy Hill: cosy, beamed, full of tobacco smoke. Despite occasional invasions by bottom-pinching rugger players, it was one of her favourites. George was on his second pint and she had a whisky. 'OK, what's the word on the street?'

'Don't I get a kiss?'

'No. I'm still working.'

'We are *both* working,' he smiled, pointedly. 'Your man Quinn.' The bearded face vanished behind the bottom of his tankard as he drained it. 'May I have another?'

Irritably she went to the bar and returned with a foaming mug. 'Now cut the crap, George. It's been a long, long day.'

'Ah, yes. Dr Quinn. I made a few enquiries today – discreetly, of course.'

'You shouldn't have, George. I may need help later, but just now I can't afford to pay and it could get confusing.'

'Sometimes you need a keeper, Ally. You needn't worry – you weren't mentioned. I just thought I recognised Quinn's name, then I happened to have lunch with my old friend Eli Friedmann.'

'Friedmann? The fence?'

'The distinguished goldsmith and jeweller.'

She gave a snort. 'Anyway – what did he have to say?'

'Ah.' George rubbed his nose with a forefinger meaningfully. 'You mean I know somethin' you don't, darlin'?'

'Unlikely as it may seem, yes.' The smoke under the low ceiling was starting to sting her eyes and she was getting annoyed.

'Old Friedmann has a long memory. Did you know your doctor was a bit of a local hero eight years ago?'

'No. He looks completely washed up now.'

'Neither he nor this useless solicitor have mentioned the Boniface case?'

'What the hell's the Boniface case?'

'Let's go for a ride, darlin'.'

'Where to?'

'Avonmouth.'

'What *for*, George? For God's sake cut the mystery, I don't need it tonight.'

'Just trust me.'

'We'll go in my car, then. You're well over and I don't want to end up on a slab.' She gave a sideways smile as he put a huge arm round her and absent-mindedly fondled a breast. 'Sorry, that was uncalled for – I *do* trust you, George.'

George had never possessed a car. They left his Ford Transit van outside the pub and she drove north, across the black expanse of the Down, through the twinkling lights of Stoke Bishop to the river. Alison turned into Portway and gunned the old Jaguar along by the Avon. It was low tide and there was nothing but a dark expanse of mud on her left, the glowing windows of a few houses on the right. Avonmouth lay at the end of the estuary, where the river met the sea. They passed a wall of corrugated metal, the high side of a feed mill, and following George's instructions, she turned into the looming, dark shapes of the warehouses. The docks were feeling the pinch these days and there were only three ships to be seen, masts and funnels floodlit above the buildings. Alison slowed down. 'Where to now, guv?'

'Straight down St Andrews Road and turn left when I say.' They passed a long line of oil storage tanks, flat and round like draughts on a monster board. A man with a peaked cap and an Alsatian was patrolling the boundary fence topped with razor wire. When she turned off the road, the car bounced across rail tracks, then her headlights bit into empty darkness. The jagged outlines of derelict buildings glinted in the moonlight like broken glass. They gave way to saltings that stretched desolate to the sea, with spiky marram grass twisting in the breeze.

'Stop here, Ally.'

They were by a long brick shed, all its windows smashed, door hanging by one hinge. As she locked the car, the wind was icy on her face. She shivered. 'Why are we here, George? It's horrible.' She put her head inside the shed. 'God, it must be used by methies: stinks of spirit and pee.'

She shivered more when she saw how serious his face had become in the thin grey shafts from the moon. 'Quinn should have told you he was called here at night eight years ago. He was first on the scene. A man was bleeding to death after being shot and his girlfriend had been raped. He did a good job until the ambulance arrived. She lived.'

'The man didn't?'

'No. It was a gangland killing. The Mr Big down

38

here then was called Simon Boniface – a misnomer if ever there was one. Ugly brute, came from Birmingham. Into everything – drugs, protection, prostitution, extortion, even simple old burglary, but only silver and works of art. The Old Bill could never pin anything on him and he became quite a folk hero. Flash lifestyle, like a soccer star. Had a big Southfork bungalow at Severn Beach, attracted a crowd when he appeared at charity functions – he was into that, I suppose it gave him a kick, a kind of two fingers to the establishment.'

'Who was the man he killed?'

'Bloke called Jevanjee, another crook. But Boniface was here first. Jevanjee was stepping on his feet, pinching his territory.'

The voice on the phone at the surgery sounded very, very scared. It was a girl, screaming, close to hysteria, wouldn't give a name. 'Is two people, bad accident, dying. Please come!'

'What sort of accident? And where are you?' Quinn was taking the call himself. It was eight at night and the receptionist had long gone home.

She was so terrified her voice was distorted, but he could just about make out that she was in a shed on the dirt road opposite a disused petrol station. 'OK, I've got that. Have you called an ambulance? Dialled 999?'

The jerky voice went up several octaves. 'Just come!' The line went dead.

Quinn sighed and dialled 999 himself, asking for an ambulance and the police, then reluctantly set out for the saltings. He knew it would take a while for either to come and it was bandit country down there. As he was searching for the turning in the dusk, a white Mercedes sped down the track in a hail of chippings. It almost hit him as it bounced onto the tarmac, skidding wildly like a car in a bad B movie, and roared off towards the motorway.

In the long empty building, a girl was writhing on the concrete floor, whimpering painfully. She was still wearing a white blouse, but her other clothes had been ripped off; her brown legs and groin were smeared with blood. A man lay face down in the corner, motionless, a dark red puddle spreading under his body. Quinn checked the pulse and breathing, then ran his fingers tentatively under the bullet holes in the jacket. The wounds in the man's back were extensive. When he lifted the body, the exiting bullets had torn most of the chest away and he felt his hands sticky with blood. There was nothing for him to do there.

The girl moaned as Quinn knelt by her. There was a bullet wound seeping blood from her shoulder and she jerked and shrieked with pain when he touched it. 'I'm sorry. Try to keep still, it will hurt less. I'll give you a shot of painkiller, but first try to tell me where it hurts.'

The soft dark eyes looked up at him, full of pain but flickering with other emotions. Hatred? Shame? 'My vagina, everything there. They raped me, four of them.' She groaned as he opened the case he had brought from the Rover. He had ampoules of morphine for accidents in the docks and filled a disposable syringe. 'And my shoulder.' She groaned again. 'Please – it hurts so much! Is Ahmed dead?'

'He's badly injured, I'm afraid.'

'Don't lie to me. They put out his eyes with broken bottles, cut off his prick and shot him. He's dead – right?'

'Yes, he's dead.'

'I'm glad. He was screaming like an animal … they hurt him so much, jeering at him when he begged them to stop. I felt so humiliated and angry. They were enjoying his pain so much they forgot me – I crawled into the kitchen and there was a phone.' Quinn could hear sirens approaching. 'They tried to shoot me too but I dodged them. They ran away. The bastards. The bastards!'

The door burst open and a paramedic ran in, orange reflective top flapping over his green uniform.

5

'God, it's freezing out there.' They were back in the car and Alison had driven down to the mud at the edge of the sea. The Bristol Channel stretched away in darkness to the lights of Cardiff on the other side. The sputtering red navigation lamp of an oil tanker was moving slowly into the dock entrance on their left. George's face was lit by the blue glow from the dashboard. 'What happened?'

'Jevanjee was dead, his girlfriend recovered after a hysterectomy. She was only nineteen and so defiled she couldn't get a husband in the Asian community. A year later she committed suicide.'

'Poor kid.'

'But Quinn identified Boniface and his friends from the Mercedes. After years of cocking a snook at the law Boniface was arrested. Quinn was the star witness at his trial.'

'He was found guilty?'

'Yes. Of murder. Boniface paid for the best briefs in the country. He could certainly afford it. But Quinn's evidence clinched it. He went down for life with a recommendation he should serve twenty-five years, had to be held down by four screws in the dock, swearing vengeance on everybody.'

'He can't do much harm while he's inside, can he?'

'He's not inside. Not any more. Boniface was in the maximum security wing at Durham but they agreed to move him to Parkhurst on the Isle of Wight. That's max-secure, too, and his old mum would find it easier for visits. The van moving him was in collision with a truck, the two escorting screws were beaten silly and Boniface vanished.'

'When?'

'Three months ago. Hasn't been seen since.'

'Is he here, in Bristol?'

'I reckon he was on a plane within hours, to somewhere he couldn't be extradited. Maybe Northern Cyprus – his family were Turkish Cypriots. But he's still rich and can buy anything he wants. He has a lot to be bitter about. He loved his role as a kind of local Robin Hood – being convicted was a real body blow.'

'You mean … No, George …'

'The word is Boniface swore to get Quinn – and the QC who prosecuted, the trial judge and a copper called Brigham, the DI who nailed him. Brigham's dead, had a heart attack years ago. Don't know about the others.'

'No – it's too unreal.'

'What's unreal about wanting revenge? You ever read the Old Testament?'

'It's nonsense, George, like something out of a cowboy film.'

'Boniface was nothing if not a cowboy.'

'It *was* kind of you to find out, love, but honestly I can't believe there's any connection. It's such a long time ago … and if Quinn felt threatened, wouldn't he have told me right at the start?' George looked doubtful and shook his head. 'All the same, it's odd that he hasn't mentioned it at all. That line about the last time he saw a lawyer was when he bought his house. Bloody liar – what the hell is he playing at?'

He nodded vigorously. 'Just so, Ally. Maybe your client has something he needs to hide even from his own barrister? You sure you want this case? Can't you chuck it?'

'No – the old cab rank principle. I've damn well got it now, whether I like it or not.' She started the engine and turned the car round.

Alison was in her chambers by eight next morning. She walked to the window and threw it open. The tiny graveyard outside always had a tranquil feel to it, large square tombs covered in moss, shafts of sunlight brightening the shadows between them. She had two hours before court and perched on the window seat, summoning the energy to open a file.

The office was quite big, furnished with a cluttered desk, brown leather Chesterfield and two matching armchairs. She had painted the walls Wedgwood blue, with some framed legal cartoons. In a desperately conservative profession, it was designed to show that she was an advocate to be trusted, even if she was a woman.

Wearily she opened the thin green folder that was all she had so far on Geoffrey Quinn. The useless Dixon had, in fact, assembled a few pieces of paper before being fired. Most of it was predictable and not much help. Quinn came from a working-class family in Norwich. There had been a driving mother and all three children had done well for her. One a doctor, a brother who ran his own building firm, a sister who was a social worker. Correction: *director* of social services in a huge London Borough.

She flicked through the untidy mix of typed sheets and scribbled notes of phone calls. He'd gone to grammar school, then straight to read medicine at St Thomas's in London. A year's VSO in Ghana. Brilliant hospital career. Houseman. Registrar. Then to the Bristol Royal Infirmary as a Senior Registrar, on the escalator to be a consultant in orthopaedics. A surgeon.

So why the devil had he copped out and gone into general practice? It seemed to coincide with his marriage to Nikki ten years ago. Nicola Gardiner, only daughter of an old Bristol family. There was a faded photograph. She was a stunner. A tall girl, she must have been nearly six foot. Pretty, with dark wavy hair not unlike Alison's own, but much more expensively cut, plenty up top, long legs. It made you sick.

She sighed. If she was a copper she'd have arrested him too. It looked so clear cut. *Had* he flipped his lid and broken her neck? If so, the sooner Alison knew the truth the better. Might she

45

still be able to bargain it back to manslaughter? He'd probably closed the door on that by destroying the body and running away. On the other hand, if his story was *true* there was a great deal to be explained. She had to find someone else. Someone with a motive. Someone who hated Quinn. She didn't believe George's way-out theory – but why should anyone *else* hate Quinn? It was the dullest, most worthy life she'd ever come across. Most of her clients were paid-up villains. This was different. So why wasn't he being straight with her? But it was too early to confront him with the past. She had to win his confidence first.

Bill Taylor came at twelve. She had been wanting to meet him since she had first been asked to represent Quinn; and he had responded at once when Duncan, the clerk she shared with eight other barristers, telephoned. 'I'd be happy to talk to Miss Hope at my office, at my club in Clifton or at her chambers, whichever she prefers. When would be convenient?'

He knocked on the door, smiling diffidently as the church clocks all around were striking the hour. Alison smiled back. 'Thank you for coming, Mr Taylor. Please sit down.' Duncan brought coffee and Alison studied Taylor briefly, settling into the other armchair. He was not tall, about five foot six, and his red hair was thinning; but he had an open, unlined, honest face. She knew from her notes that he was about forty-five, the son of a taxi driver who'd grown up on one of the city's roughest council estates, but he'd joined the building society as a clerk the day he left school and, thirty years on, here he was: its managing director and a member of the Clifton Club. The restrained suit, light grey with a neat stripe, was beautifully cut and must have set him back seven or eight hundred. The man had made it in a big way.

'Dr Quinn's solicitor ought to be here,' she explained. 'But he's been held up – in any case, I think he may be handing over to someone more experienced.'

Taylor shrugged. 'Yes, I know a bit about the arcana of your two professions, Miss Hope, but I'm quite happy to talk if you are. Geoff's in a mess and I guess you've no time to waste.'

'No, to be honest I haven't.' She skimmed the file for a few moments. 'How well do you know my client, Mr Taylor?'

'Bill, please. I was Bill as an office boy thirty years ago and since I'm still in the same place it's kind of stuck.'

'Bill, then.' She looked at him questioningly, still waiting for an answer.

'Not well, I suppose, but we met six or seven years ago – we both belong to a sailing club in Portishead.'

'Dinghy sailing?'

'Yes, Scorpions, Mirrors, that kind of thing. Later, we bought a small yacht between us for inshore cruising and shared its upkeep.'

'Could you both afford it?'

'Good lord, yes. She was only a twenty-two-footer with two berths, second-hand and pretty tatty; we paid six thousand for her. She was called *Black Falcon* when we bought her and we kept the name, though to be honest *Lame Duck* would have been more like it. The trouble was we were both working long hours and she hardly ever got used. She's moored at West Bay, near Bridport in Dorset, and I haven't been down there for at least three months.'

'Did you ever sail her together?'

'A few times when we first bought her, but not lately, no. If one of us wanted to use her, we just rang the other to clear it.'

Alison rested her notepad on the arm of the chair. 'So let me be quite clear – how often did you actually meet Dr Quinn?'

'I suppose every one or two months. We used to meet more often, dinghy sailing on the Bristol Channel, but he hasn't been for a couple of years.'

'Do *you* still go?'

'Oh, yes. But Geoff and I went on meeting regularly – at my club or a pub near the office, just to sort out the practicalities of the boat – mooring fees, repairs and all that.'

'You didn't go to each other's houses?'

'In the past, yes, quite often in fact, but then things changed.'

'In what way?'

'I guess we got together as two couples to begin

with.' He hesitated. 'My wife died three years ago.'

'I'm sorry.'

He nodded. 'She had cancer, it was bloody rough, fortunately we have no children. But anyway, for your purposes I saw a bit less of Geoff after that.'

'And nothing of his family?'

Taylor shook his head. 'A little, but not much.'

'How did Geoff get on with Nikki?'

'As I say, I haven't really seen much to know lately.' He hesitated again. 'I'd say Geoff was a lot less happy in his marriage than he had been.'

'Why?'

'Just a feeling from the way he spoke about it – I think he was bored with Nikki and she was fed up with him, always at work or too tired to be any sort of real companion. It's a common enough story.'

'Did he kill her?'

'No, not Geoff, I can't imagine it.' Taylor met her eyes firmly, but she thought it was the answer of a decent man, a loyal friend: in his heart he wasn't so sure.

'People do crazy things when they're angry or confused, Bill. Why not Geoff?'

'Just a gut feeling, I suppose. I can't see Geoff being violent towards anyone. And then there's the children …'

'What about the children, Bill?'

'Well, I can't believe they aren't dead too. I mean, no one who isn't completely potty is going to go to all that trouble to destroy the mother's body, then carry off two howling kids, are they?'

'Probably not.'

'Geoff loved those children. Jess and Tom meant everything to him, he loved them as a father in a way I guess he could never love an adult. He's incapable of harming them in any way, let alone killing them, I'm absolutely certain of that.'

'Tell me about them.'

'Jessica was nine, I think. Rather serious, very like her dad. Tom was seven, handsome little fellow, going to be tall and good-looking like his mother. Despite the strains between Geoff and Nikki, they seemed happy enough on the few occasions I saw them. Nikki was discontented with everything else, but she was a good mother – and very close to her children.'

Alison made another note. 'Thanks for your help, Bill. You'll be a character witness when we come to trial?'

'Of course.'

At two she went back to the prison, driving into rain again as she weaved through the mean streets around it. The usual routine. Knock on the wicket in the main gate, sign in, down endless pea-green corridors, through locked grilles, following the duty screw with his keys clanking at his belt.

Quinn came into the interview room with downcast eyes, wearing exactly the same clothes as before. He looked slightly defensive. Perhaps he already sensed that she was less sympathetic, though she had decided not to mention Boniface and Jevanjee yet. 'Let's forget two days ago,' she said abruptly. 'Today I want the truth. Before you say anything, let's be clear what the police are saying. That you had a row and hit your wife, who fell down the cellar steps and broke her neck. Her neck was certainly broken – I've been to the mortuary and seen the bones that came out of the boiler. Maybe you didn't hit her, she lunged at you and slipped? Then you panicked.' He started to splutter, but she held up her hand. 'Let me finish, Geoff, I've done this before and you haven't. Then you panicked. Now – if it *was* something like that, the sooner you tell me the better. They might reduce the charge to manslaughter. You'd go to jail, but not for so long.' She stood up and walked round to stand next to him, resting her hand on his shoulder. 'Think before you answer.'

The harrowed face looked up at her, wounded, angry but with a hint of despair. 'Is that what you believe? You too?'

'Just the truth, Geoff. I need it to help you.'

He shook his head. No tears this time. No open emotion, though he was obviously going though hell inside. 'No. Nothing like that. It was as I told you. When I last saw them, they were all alive.'

'You're *sure*, Geoff? Alive? *All* of them?'

'Yes.'

She sat down again and took out a lined pad. 'OK. I believe you. But unless we can point to someone else, the jury won't.'

'What do you mean?'

'I mean you're the obvious candidate. *Your* wife, dead in *your* home. If someone else killed her, who? Why? You must have *some* idea, surely? Do you have any enemies? Did she?'

'None that I know of.'

'Try again. I don't believe you've got to forty-one without falling out with *anyone*.' He stared at her blankly. 'Or have you ever had contact with anyone involved in crime … even if it was only petty crime?'

'No, I can't think of anything.'

Why was he lying? 'Nothing? Well, keep on thinking. Think *hard*, Geoff – I'll be in again tomorrow. What about Nikki?'

He shook his head again. 'So far as I know, everyone except me liked her. She didn't *do* anything to make enemies. She was busy at home with the children, secretary of the PTA at their school.' He stared dully at the table, his fingers drumming nervously. 'I wish I could be more help.'

'Frankly, so do I. The other day you said that in the last six months, maybe a year, she was up to something, keeping something from you?'

'Yes.'

'Were you still sharing a bed?'

'Usually.'

'Well, didn't you ever *talk* to her about it? Challenge her outright?'

'She just laughed at me.'

'She wouldn't tell you?'

'She laughed and said I was paranoid. Losing my

52

marbles. I sometimes felt inclined to agree with her.'

'And had you no theories of your own?'

'I thought she was having an affair.'

'But she denied it?'

'Yes. Emphatically.'

Alison stood up and stretched. 'But it all centres on Nikki, and her great secret, doesn't it? So let's go right back to the beginning. Ten years ago, when you first met Nikki – what happened?'

Nicola Gardiner was bored. At twenty-three she was too old to be spending a weekend with her parents, even on their yacht. They had driven down from Bristol on Friday evening, an hour and a half on the motorway to Exeter, then along sideroads to Starcross.

The boat was a Westerly thirty-footer, capable of sleeping six and reaching the Mediterranean, though it rarely left the sheltered sweep of the Exe estuary where it was moored. But on Saturday morning they sailed down the Devon coast and dropped anchor in the Dart, just below the red brick of the naval college. It was a dazzling June day, warm enough to sunbathe, so when the others went ashore she stretched out on the cabin roof in a minute bikini that showed off her slim figure brilliantly. Pity there was no one around to see it.

Nikki lay dozing in the hot sun, wishing that her life was less of a mess. Only daughter of a prosperous accountant, she knew she had been thoroughly spoilt. She had idled her way through one of Bristol's classier independent schools, then turned three years at the poly-technic into one long party, getting laid at satisfactory intervals. After failing her degree in sociology, she had a couple of grotty jobs in market research. But for a whole year now she had managed to avoid work of any kind.

Her father provided an allowance that wasn't bad and had just replaced her sports car. He paid the rent on a small flat in Redland. Her mother dropped heavy hints about careers and husbands, but the first bored her stiff and the second eluded her. Tom had been OK – already a partner in one of the city's older estate agencies, but neither of them had tried enough to make it work. He had drifted away, leaving her fancy free. In some ways it was the life of Reilly, but even for Nikki it was not quite enough. She wanted some sort of life of her own.

The fact that she was pregnant had come as a shock and she knew she would have to do something about that bloody soon. It must have been at the rugby club party, a crappy ten-minute screw in James's car with seat-belt buckles digging into her back. He didn't want to know afterwards and she didn't much care. She could get an abortion. Perhaps she should go abroad. She sighed and closed her eyes. The sun blazed red through the skin of her eyelids, but faded gradually to purple and black as she drifted into sleep.

The splashing of the tender woke her. She heard it bump against the stern. 'Look who we met in Dartmouth!' Nikki opened her eyes as the woman scrambled aboard, fat in her black slacks and orange sailing jacket. It was her mother, that dreadful cultivated bray. Her father was out of sight, but two young men were bobbing up and down. She knew Robert, one of her father's assistants, a complete wanker. The other man, now pulling himself aboard, was tall and good-looking. A narrow, intelligent face with a lock of prematurely greying hair that made him look rather distinguished.

She sat up as he smiled. 'Hi, I'm Geoff. You must be Nikki?' She felt him appreciating her body and crooked up one leg provocatively. There was some real electricity about this one. Nicola's life had made her nothing if not cynical, but he was different to the bores she was used to.

The next hour passed quickly. They lounged in the cockpit with a bottle of wine and she discovered that Geoff was a doctor. As she had hoped, he suggested dinner in Dartmouth and her parents smilingly said they would sooner stay on board. The two men had come down to look at a boat Robert was thinking of buying. It had turned out to be a wreck and they had been about to drive back when they met her mother on the quay. It worked out brilliantly. Robert would still drive home; he had a wife and two children under three expecting him. Geoff was persuaded to stay and return with the Gardiners on Sunday night.

By eight o'clock she was eyeing the intriguing young doctor across a candle-lit table in the Carved Angel. He didn't seem to notice her desperate efforts to remember how to hold a semi-intellectual conversation and she was mesmerised by his confident manner. He made her laugh. He obviously fancied her. Back on the yacht they clung to each other naked for a long time and she didn't mind that they ended up sleeping in separate narrow bunks. When *they made love she didn't want her parents in the next cabin; she was going to shout and twist and abandon herself to every last second of sensation. It was the one thing she was really good at.*

6

'What happened then?' Alison stopped taking notes, thinking how far he had spiralled from the June idyll to the bare interview room.

Quinn shrugged. 'The usual kind of thing. Back in Bristol I took her out. She didn't seem to mind that I spent so much time in the hospital – I think she found the whole doctoring thing glamorous. She'd only seen it on telly, of course, she never knew the reality: the crushed limbs from a car crash, the pain, the vomit, the stress and the never-ending bloody exhaustion.'

'Were you in love with her?'

'I've asked myself that a thousand times. Mostly in the last six months. Yes, I think I was. She was absolutely beautiful, full of life.' He looked around at the pea-green paint under the fluorescent tube, wrinkling his nose. 'It's hard to explain to another woman, particularly in here.'

'Try.'

'I'd spent fifteen years making it as a surgeon, never time for much outside it. There'd been girls, of course, mostly randy nurses. But nothing like this.' He looked embarrassed. 'It must sound ridiculous, but I really had lived a very thin life. I'd been working my butt off making a career ever since the bloody eleven plus, but suddenly it was coming right. All the sacrifices … I loved her – it was like a fairy tale. The successful doctor and the adoring woman who made love like a tigress. I thought we had everything.'

'You got married after four months?'

He nodded. 'I think I knew we were deceiving ourselves before then, but I pushed it away. The day came – quite a grand affair at the church in the village where her parents lived, marquee on the lawn. My mother was over the moon.'

'What about your father?'

'He was dead.'

'I'm sorry. But why did you go through with it?'

'I suppose I thought it would work out. We bought the house in Abbots Leigh with a crippling mortgage. She was expecting the baby – not mine, of course – within a couple of months and seemed as keen as I was on having a home and family.' He gave a thin smile. 'At least it made a change from living in hospital flats.'

'When did it start to go wrong?'

'Almost at once. Nikki lost the baby, was plunged into depression and started to cry every time I went to work.'

'Is that why you changed to general practice?'

'Basically, yes. I failed to get a couple of consultant jobs and it was clear we'd have to move away if I was to find one. She didn't want to, clung

58

to her mother, who was a lot more help than I expected.'

'Wasn't that, well, a sacrifice? You'd been set on it for so long? You were almost there?'

'Of course it was a fucking sacrifice. I felt I'd failed, but I didn't seem to have much choice.'

'But, Geoff, that was ten years ago. If it was such a bloody marriage, how come you stuck it so long?'

'It wasn't so bloody then. In fact it came together when Jess was born, then Tom. Nikki was a good mother and the next bit wasn't bad at all – we rubbed along happily enough.' He paused, with a slight smile.

'Go on,' she encouraged, gently.

'I was just thinking that the sun always seems to be shining when I remember those early years … I used to get more weekends off then and we often took the children down to the cottage in Dorset, went sailing, that kind of thing. Tom and Jess brought us together.'

'When did it start to go wrong again?'

'Even in the good times, Nikki resented me working so much, but I suppose the cracks started to show when the children went to school and she had more time to get bored. The real problems started three or four years ago.'

'Was she still good with the children?'

Quinn thought for a while. 'No, I suppose she wasn't. She did still love them, of course, and took an interest in school and all that, but she didn't want to be bothered with looking after them.'

'Did you have someone to help with that?'

'Yes, Nikki found a series of au pairs, the last was a young woman from Bosnia.'

'Called?'

'Vesna Vasiljevic.'

'How the hell do you spell that?'

'V, a, s, i, l, j, e, v, i, c.'

'Was she here as a refugee?'

'She said so, but it wasn't quite true. In fact, she'd come on a tourist visa and just stayed, hadn't claimed asylum or anything. In the eyes of the authorities, she was here illegally and I thought it was all a bit dodgy, but she lived with us and the children loved her. She wasn't a girl – about thirty, I'd say, earthy and pleasant and didn't mind Nikki's tantrums. Having her around helped to keep us all sane these last twelve months.'

'Geoff, you weren't …?'

He gave a thin smile. 'No, I wasn't, though the thought did cross my mind when Nikki was being particularly vile. Vesna was a good-looking piece, not pretty but striking – angular face, long black hair, flashing dark eyes. Wild and romantic, like a gypsy.'

'And where is she now?'

'No idea at all. There was a crackdown on illegals in the city a few months back and the police arrested about twenty – I think they were deported. Vesna got the wind up and went off to find a job in London, where she thought she'd be less visible.'

'And you don't have her new address?'

He shook his head. 'No, I don't think we heard

from her again. I wasn't really expecting to. She'd helped us out and we'd helped her, but she *was* a non-person, no National Insurance number, no papers, didn't officially exist. I guess she just wanted to vanish.'

'So until a couple of months ago, Vesna was looking after the children and Nikki was up to something? You thought she was having an affair?'

'Yes, I did – but she insisted she wasn't.'

'Well, she would, wouldn't she?'

'Maybe she was telling the truth?'

'But she was keeping *something* from you?'

'Oh yes, and she *loved* it. Seeing me confused and frustrated. Nikki's great secret.'

Alison nodded. 'Nikki's great secret – but you really have *no* idea what it was?'

'I wish to God I did. It might just explain why I'm banged up in here.'

'And in all those years, Geoff, you never thought of trying for a consultancy again?'

'No.' His eyes were hollow, shifty and frightened again. 'No, I didn't.'

In London Alison might have had to drive for an hour or more to consult the police officer in charge of a case. In Bristol, she only had to walk a couple of hundred yards – from her chambers, across Quay Street to the Central nick. She had doubts about approaching Manning directly, but the whole case was becoming so bizarre … and could it do any harm?

Manning was known to be unstuffy and had agreed to see her at once when she phoned. His office could have belonged to a bank manager, except that it was larger and had a map showing the city's police districts on the wall. Come to think of it, he *looked* like a bank manager – neat grey suit, dark-blue silk tie. His reading glasses rested among papers on a large desk. It was hard to imagine him as a copper at all. 'Please take a seat, Miss Hope.' He was keeping it formal, which was fair enough when she was defending a man he had charged with murder. 'What can I do for you?'

'I've been spending a good deal of time talking to Dr Quinn, Chief Superintendent.'

'Of course.' He met her eyes across the desk, showing no emotion. He wasn't hostile, but nor did he look over-friendly.

'I was wondering whether you are still working on the case?'

'So far as I'm concerned, Miss Hope, our job is completed. We've made our report to the Crown Prosecution Service and your client has been sent for trial. His case is not complicated and will be heard the next time a High Court judge sits – within a month or two, I hope.'

'Are you *convinced* of his guilt?'

'I should not have charged him otherwise.'

Alison looked beyond him, through the window. The street was full of buses and other traffic, but no sound came through the double-glazing. 'No, I do understand that, but I'm bound to say I'm

62

convinced that he is innocent.'

'That is your professional duty, Miss Hope.'

'Don't you have *any* doubts, Chief Superintendent?'

Manning swung round in his chair and looked out of the window away from her. 'Off the record – and this part of our conversation is not taking place as far as I am concerned – he might not have *planned* to kill her, but I am in no doubt that he did cause her death, and then tried to destroy the body in a thoroughly criminal way. The charge is the correct one.'

'But he denies that and, if it wasn't an accident, he had no *motive*. Whereas his involvement in the prosecution of Simon Boniface eight years ago left others with powerful motives to harm both Quinn and his family.'

Manning gave a patronising smile. 'I worked on that case too, you know, and I'm aware that Boniface has escaped from custody. If you're trying to suggest there's some connection with the death of Quinn's wife, I can only say you're in the realms of fantasy. Forget it, Miss Hope. Do your best for your client – put in one of those pleas in mitigation you're so good at, like for that fraudster the other day.' There was just the beginning of a sharp edge to his tone. 'I worked for the best part of five years on that case, Miss Hope.'

The message hung in the silence between them. Eventually she said: 'I'm sorry, I was simply doing the job I'm paid for, and I'm only doing that now. It may not be Boniface and the Jevanjee murder, but I really *do* believe that someone other than Dr Quinn is involved. I'm asking you to make some more enquiries, in the interest of natural justice. That's all.'

Manning laughed. 'For heaven's sake, Miss Hope, we're on different sides. You must do what you deem right for Quinn's defence. I have done all I believe necessary to close the case. If you discover any information on criminal matters – and I am not impressed by the nonsense you are hinting at today – you have a duty to report it and you may rest assured it will be treated seriously, very seriously.'

Pompous arsehole, she thought. Aloud, she said: 'I still believe your investigation should be continuing, you know. By assuming Dr Quinn is guilty, you may be letting others guilty of his wife's murder – and perhaps of much else – go free.'

Manning stood up and pointed to a large square board by the door. 'Miss Hope, just for the record, I'm a copper who's served in every rank from Constable to Chief Super and I'm two years off retirement. I'm not making a name any more and you know damn well that I'm not in the business of putting innocent people behind bars. But this city is ridden with serious crime – there are thirty major ongoing cases on that chart, and I'm handling them *all*. For God's sake, I haven't the men or resources to do your job as well. In my book, Quinn's guilty and what you're suggesting just muddies the water. If some of your colleagues were sitting in that chair

I'd suspect they were trying to do so deliberately.'

'I'm doing nothing of the kind!'

'I don't suggest you are, Miss Hope.'

'If I bring you evidence, will you consider it?'

'If it's new, criminal and serious, of course. But your client is going for trial and there's no question of changing that.'

'What about the children, for heaven's sake? They're only seven and nine and they've been missing for weeks!'

'Your client is not charged with their murder, Miss Hope, only that of his wife.'

'But are you still *looking* for them?'

'Of course we are, Miss Hope, or at least for their bodies.'

'You believe they are dead?'

'I'm quite certain they are dead, but they are not included in the charge.'

'But you *are* still looking for them? Seriously?'

He sighed. 'Don't you follow the local media? We've appealed for help in the press, on local radio and the regional television news – and we've received a number of leads from the public. None of which, I'm afraid, has come to anything. But we'll find them. We always do, you know, even if it takes a year or two.'

Five minutes later she was back on the pavement, dodging through the traffic back to her chambers. She shouldn't have gone – it had been a waste of time. Manning would do nothing more – and if he couldn't find Quinn's children with a whole police force at his disposal, neither realistically could she. She would just have to concentrate on producing everything she could to defend Quinn in court. Could she convince a jury? It looked increasingly unlikely.

She met George early that evening, in a pub on the quayside. In fact they hardly ever met in the evening *without* going to a pub – maybe that was why Alison's erratic jogging had so little physical effect. After thirty-two years, she was reconciled to being pear-shaped, but she did sometimes wish her breasts were a *little* bigger and her chunky thighs just a *little* slimmer.

The Llandoger Trow was one of the oldest inns in Bristol, by the harbour in the heart of the city. It rarely saw ships these days, except boats giving trips round the harbour and motor cruisers, but it still had a nautical feel. It was a sunny evening so they sat outside, alone by the water, and she fumed about Quinn.

George Kristianssen could be the pits. Drunk, oafish, socially inept and lacking civilised graces. He could also be kind, good in bed and startlingly wise. It would take a lifetime to make him out – perhaps that was the attraction. Tonight he was on top form and she thought how different he might be if he hadn't left school at fifteen: a decent haircut and he could make a better lawyer than she. 'What's Quinn hiding, George? What can be so dreadful that he's keeping quiet about it even now, when he faces a lifetime in jail? When he needs me?' Alison was drinking a pint of Guinness, not as a feminist gesture but because she liked it. 'Drugs, money, fraud? What could put him even deeper in the shit than he is already, if it came out?'

'Something that would make him more likely to be convicted? Or to stay in jail longer if he is?'

'But you say the Boniface case made him a local hero? It doesn't make any sense.'

'Maybe we're making too much of it, darlin'? Maybe it just hasn't occurred to him that it's relevant? Maybe I was wrong?'

'Stuff. You don't believe that.'

'It seemed important when Friedmann mentioned it, but maybe it's a blind alley.'

'And then the solicitors haven't done nearly enough – I've got so little to go on. I went to see Manning but as far as he's concerned the case is closed; he doesn't want to know about anything that complicates it, so we'll just have to do his job for him. They've even moved Quinn to Marychurch today, a bloody ten-mile drive out of the city, *really* convenient. At least Horfield was close.' She wrinkled her nose and coughed as he lit a roll-up. 'And Quinn's in such a bloody state. Half the time he sits in his cell staring at the wall like a zombie. Even when he tries, his memory's shot to bits. He's lost a whole day in the weekend of the murder, when he was driving round the country. I need some help, George. Have you got time? Usual terms.'

He sank his pint. 'You wish me to go down into the bazaars, ma'am?' His booming voice carried to some passers-by who looked at them curiously. 'Among the great unwashed? The Great Game?'

When she was honest with herself, his booming was the one thing that really got to her. It was so bloody phoney. The real George wasn't like that at all. 'Give it a rest, George. Don't tell the whole world.'

'Seventeen-fifty an hour plus expenses. Special cut rate. That's if there are funds to pay – if not, I'll do it just for your body, sweetheart.'

They left the pub at nine, walking arm-in-arm across the cobbles towards King Street. It was dark now and pools of light rippled on the water under cast-iron lamps. A group of teenage boys were aimlessly kicking Coca-Cola cans in the gutter, radiating suppressed violence; well-dressed couples strolling past the Old Vic avoided them warily.

As they reached the car, Alison saw an *Evening Post* billboard that made her catch her breath. She bought the paper and they read the front page under a street-lamp by the car. 'Why the fuck do I have to find out like this,' she hissed furiously. 'It's like a nightmare.'

The front page story was brief. Just a photograph of a rough grave in woodland and a brief account of the discovery of the remains of two children by a council worker. It was in Leigh Woods, a few minutes from Quinn's house. She looked at George miserably. 'Manning didn't even mention it. I suppose it has to be them?'

'It's not the Princes in the Tower, kid.'

'Then I guess it's all over bar the shouting. Three bodies and no alibi is pretty conclusive. Oh, *shit*.' She had seen the parking ticket taped to the window in a plastic bag. 'I thought I *could* park here?'

Silently George nodded at the temporary police cones by the kerb. 'Sorry, Ally. I didn't see them either.'

'Ah, well, it always comes in threes.' The carphone buzzed. 'I don't believe it!'

'Leave it, love, let's go home.'

'No.' She picked up the receiver. 'Alison Hope.' Her body stiffened as she listened. 'How is he?' George could not hear what was being said, but she wasn't enjoying it. 'I see, I'll come straight over.'

She turned to him. 'That was one of the assistant governors at Marychurch. Quinn's tried to top himself.'

'How?'

'Sharpened up a piece of metal from his bed and slashed a wrist. He was left alone in his cell for at least six hours, may have been bleeding all that time. He was unconscious when they found him.'

'Could he know about the children?'

'I don't think so. He didn't mention it and I was with him only this morning. And he was more positive and cheerful then. I *can't* believe he tried to kill himself an hour or two later. It doesn't make sense. Oh God, George.'

They sat silently in the car. 'You're not going to get him off now, Ally.'

'No – but suddenly I believe his story. This whole thing stinks.'

7

Alison drove fast through the empty streets. It had started to rain hard, pounding on the car roof, and the road surface glistened with sheets of water. George lay back in the bucket seat beside her, craggy bearded face outlined by the street-lamps. They drove in silence and she smiled to herself – what an odd relationship it was. She hadn't met him at work, but in a fit of public spirit when she had joined the Samaritans three years earlier. He was there at the training sessions in a draughty church hall, standing out like a block of unsmoothed granite among the middle-class do-gooders. The beard was unkempt and he wore a cloth cap and scruffy anorak. He looked like a down-at-heel market-trader. No one except her spoke to him when the instant coffee came round.

But when it came to discussion of befriending the suicidal and despairing, he was the most intelligent and compassionate person in the room. In the pub afterwards she discovered that he had once been a merchant seaman, had studied by correspondence for his mate's and master's tickets, ending as the captain of a freighter until the recession made him redundant. Somehow he had never married, never really had a home, never quite made a career. His freighter had been more of a tramp steamer, a rust-bucket plying to forgotten ports in Latin America; he was used to rough and ready seamen, he drank like a fish, he could take care of himself in dark alleys. Like Alison, he knew prison cells – but in George's case as an inmate, usually short-term but all round the world.

Now he was a freelance private investigator; as she'd discovered in the robing-room, one of the best in the business. As the weeks passed, and they graduated to answering the phone and talking to 'clients' in the Samaritans centre, she learnt that he had been born in Hotwells, son of a Norwegian seaman he had never known. His mother told him before her death that they had lived together between his voyages and intended to marry. She thought he had not deserted her, but been torpedoed in 1944; she had adopted his surname and given it to George.

Although he was twenty years older, Alison was not conscious of it. She felt comfortable with him and he was the first – the only – person she had ever told about the months of wretchedness that had brought her to Bristol. He became a dear, understanding and protective but platonic friend, until they day they were both sacked from the Samaritans. They had been on night duty, where you slept at the centre to answer the calls, and George had made them both tea in the morning.

The director had been shocked to find him perched on a bunk that contained an obviously naked Alison between its sheets and drawn the wrong conclusion. But they went quietly and became lovers for real later the same day. It seemed a waste not to.

She smiled at the memory, but they were leaving the city, driving through the darkness of empty fields, stopping at a floodlit red-brick gatehouse and it was back to reality.

As it turned out, going to the remand centre was a waste of time. Alison left after an angry interview with the governor and ten minutes sitting by the bed containing Geoffrey Quinn's unconscious body. He was on a saline drip and had been heavily sedated. He was so still, his face white and drawn, that if his chest had not been rising and falling she would have thought him dead.

Apart from his bandaged wrists, his head had a gauze dressing over a shaved patch to one side at the back. When she asked the screw minding the prison hospital about this, he just shrugged. 'Dunno, love. I wasn't on duty when they brought 'im in. You better ask the doc. Maybe Quinn collapsed as he lost blood and banged 'is 'ead?' Pigs might fly, she thought.

The governor received her irritably. Stooped, defeated and bald, he must have been close to retirement; the eyes in his pasty face were opaque and uninterested. One of the screws had warned her that he had been called from home when

Quinn was discovered, on his way to the theatre. 'All very regrettable, Miss Hope.' He sat on the edge of his chair behind a cluttered desk, like a greyhound straining at the trap although he wouldn't make the final curtain now. 'But I gather he'll survive.'

'It was a suicide attempt?'

'Obviously.'

'Are you quite sure, Governor? He seemed perfectly stable when I saw him this morning. *Both* wrists slashed so badly? That wound on his head? Did he creep up behind and knock himself out?'

The man's small moustache bristled. 'What are you suggesting, Miss Hope?'

'I'm asking a question, Governor, that's all. Could those injuries have been inflicted by someone else? Someone who didn't want Quinn to stand trial?'

He stood abruptly. 'That's an absurd accusation! This is a secure establishment and Quinn is a prisoner on remand for a murder charge, kept in solitary for his own protection. He could not be safer than he is in here. He tried to kill himself – which, in his situation, is hardly surprising, however much we offer him by way of help and support.'

Alison was about to ask what possible support anyone had been giving the broken man she had watched disintegrating in the past weeks, but bit the words back. She might still need this bastard's co-operation and the whole system was hardly his fault. She nodded and smiled. 'Thank you, Governor.' She was not going to let him get to her. She turned to go. 'There's just one thing …?'

'Yes?'

'I believe Quinn was left bleeding for several hours?' The governor stared her out but did not reply. 'When I thought standing orders were for anyone on a murder charge – and therefore a suicide risk – to be checked every fifteen minutes?'

He looked embarrassed. 'Normally, yes.'

'What do you mean "normally"?'

'It's normal for three or four weeks, Miss Hope, but Quinn had been in custody for more than two months without harming himself.' He shrugged. 'We decided that regular surveillance was no longer necessary. We are *very* short-staffed, you know.'

The next morning she too felt almost suicidal. The bodies discovered in Leigh Woods had turned out to be fifty years old, the skeletons of two children missing since the war who had probably been the victims of a mad woman hanged for a string of child murders in 1946. That was a relief, but otherwise the case was a disaster, there seemed nothing she could do for Quinn and it wouldn't do much for her reputation either. Why, oh why, had she ever taken it on? Roger Dixon alone should have been enough to put her off. She had been an idiot.

She went over to the Crown Court in Small Street like a sleepwalker, barely aware of what she was doing, glad there was something to push Quinn to the back of her mind. Routine rapidly took over. She pulled on her gown, clutching the tiresome wig and her brief, and knocked on the locked door leading to the warren of cells under the building.

The Dutchman in the bare concrete space, lit only by a lamp behind thick glass in the ceiling, was about forty, neatly dressed in an expensive leather jacket. He had been convicted two days ago of master-minding an operation to smuggle a million pounds' worth of cocaine. She had lost that one, too. All that remained was her plea in mitigation and the sentence. She knew that he was already a millionaire and part of her said that he thoroughly deserved the long stretch he stood to get. But she would do her best.

They said goodbye in the same cell half an hour later. He had been given eight years. 'Good luck, Mr Meerburg,' she smiled, warmly. God, he was a jammy bastard. He'd be back to all that loot in four years at most. 'I'm glad it worked out not too badly.'

'Thank you, Miss Hope. Your bill will be paid by the end of the week.' So for a fortnight she would be living on drug money. Ah, well.

Up in the robing-room she pushed her wig and gown into the bluebag and left it hanging up. The room was spartan. White-painted cupboards round the walls, a few cane chairs, a chipped mahogany table. Alison was just about to leave when two other barristers came in, roaring with laughter. One was young and she didn't know him, the other was an old friend, Ernest, who had started late after being an inspector in the police, invalided out when he was injured in a riot. His weather-beaten face grinned broadly. ''Ullo, love.'

'Hi, Ernie. What's the big joke then?'

He looked grave. 'No joke, Alison. Have you not heard the sad news about that old bastard Carswell?' Sir Nicholas, otherwise Mr Justice Carswell, was possibly the most unpopular judge on the High Court bench. Arrogant, obtuse, insulting.

She paused at the door. 'No. But you're going to tell me, aren't you?'

Ernie winked at his companion. 'D'you think I should, Alec? Strong stuff for a delicate young thing, eh?'

'You patronising old git.' She sat down firmly on the table, crossed her legs and stuck out her jaw. 'Get on with it, big boy. I eat people like you for breakfast.'

'Alas, Sir Nicholas died early today.'

Her face changed. 'Oh, I'm sorry. He wasn't my favourite but it must be sad for his family.'

'More than sad, young Alison.' Ernie wagged his finger at her sternly. If he wasn't so lovely she'd have kicked his balls for being such an MCP. 'Mr Justice Carswell was found at four this morning by a nightwatchman patrolling near his apartment in the Temple. Mr Justice Carswell had fallen four storeys from a window, wearing nothing but a garter belt, stockings, ladies' leather boots and a beatific grin alleged to have been induced by LSD.'

Alison stifled a giggle. 'God, how awful.'

'Furthermore, in the said apartment was the body of a woman, a prostitute of middle age. Naked.' Ernie's voice rose orotundly, as if addressing a crowded courtroom. 'Naked, I say. Lying across a bed, her body marked with red weals from a riding crop. Also, alas, deceased.'

'God, how frightfully English. It could never happen in Aberdeen. How did the woman die?'

'Only the post-mortem will say for sure, but the word on the street is a heart attack. She too seems to have been on a hallucinatory drug. Maybe they both got over-excited.' He raised his bushy eyebrows and grinned lasciviously.

'Is this all *true*, Ernie? For heaven's sake, he was a red judge, not some seedy law student. It's dreadful.'

'Nothing but the truth, m'lud.' The old man grinned wickedly. 'Personally I think it's the funniest thing since we found half the Cabinet was flogging tanks to Saddam Hussein. I always knew Carswell was a shit.'

She looked doubtful. 'If you say so. I only appeared before him once and he was horrid, but if you're on the High Court bench and want to get up to something kinky, surely you don't do it in the *Temple*? I was a pupil there and the walls are bloody thin in some of those buildings.'

Ernie was of the generation that could qualify by correspondence and only had to eat twenty-four dinners in the hall of their chosen Inn. 'I wouldn't know, love. It wouldn't surprise me if the Inns of

Court rang to the jangle of chains, howls of pain and cries of ecstasy every night of the week. It is a little outside my personal experience.' He looked at his watch. 'It's lunch-time. Are you coming for a sarnie and a beer?'

The legal profession needs alcohol like a farmer needs rain and she was tempted. 'I'd love to, Ernie, but I've got another case at two and one at three – got to check my briefs.'

He sniggered and she almost hit him.

Back in her room she thought of George and rang him at the office he rented over a branch of Woolworth's, in the suburbs. He had already heard about Mr Justice Carswell. And told her, with some satisfaction, that eight years ago he had been plain Nicholas Carswell QC, practising on the Western Circuit where he had led the prosecution of Simon Boniface.

'I still don't go for it, George.'

'Don't you, darlin'? Now I'm not so sure.'

8

Next morning, Alison's first case was not until ten thirty. On her way into the city, she crossed the suspension bridge and drove towards Quinn's house. It had been raining again. The wet trees by the road shut out the sun and gave the area a dark, gloomy feeling, matching her mood when she thought about Quinn. This wasn't a straight-forward domestic murder, husband and wife locked in hatred: love betrayed, love rejected, love turned into wounds that would never heal. She had seen that many times, but this was new to her. There was something very, very murky behind that body in Quinn's boiler. It was a tiny part of something bigger. She sensed real money and power conceal-ing something – but, dear God, *what* – that could not face the light of day.

Quinn's house was large and double-fronted. Built around the turn of the century, the sandstone looked grey under almost black slates. It stood alone in a half-acre plot, in a street of similar houses. They were all slightly different, half hidden behind high hedges. The street had grass verges and pretended to be a country lane. Peering through Quinn's gate she saw flimsy white tapes still flapping around the excavations to the side. The police had not bothered to take them away.

A woman was walking along the verge, leaning backwards as her yellow Labrador pulled on its chain. She looked curiously at the low red Jaguar. Alison climbed out and smiled. The woman was middle-aged, pretty, wearing a waxed Barbour jacket and headscarf. She did not smile back and looked suspicious. No doubt she was the convenor of the local Neighbourhood Watch. 'Can I help you?' Very cut-glass accent. Challenging. *And who the hell are you?* Definitely not friendly.

'I'm just looking round the area.' Alison tried to sound bright and scatty. 'Thinking of moving and thought Abbots Leigh might be nice. So countryfied but only five minutes from the city.'

'We've been very happy here for thirty years.' The woman continued walking, with Alison trotting beside her. 'There's a footpath to the woods just on the corner, I walk Oscar there most days.'

'Are there many places for sale?'

The woman sized her up. 'Only large family houses,' she said pointedly. 'And people tend to stay, you know. I can't think of anything on the market, but there might not be a board up. People here tend to be discreet.' She could not have sounded more discouraging, but then paused for a second. 'I suppose the house back there might be available shortly.'

'Which one?'

'Where you parked. There was a murder there a couple of months ago. Terrible business. Man cut up his wife and burnt her in a stove. Don't you see the papers?'

'Sorry – I hadn't made the connection.'

The woman shrugged. She was not going to ask Alison in for morning coffee. She'd probably phone the local nick about the suspicious prowler as soon as she was indoors. 'I don't know what happens about these things, but I suppose you don't need a house if you're in prison for the rest of your life.'

'I don't know either, but I'll keep my eyes open for an advert. Thanks for the tip!'

The woman gave a watery smile. She turned into a footpath between high hedges, let the dog off his chain and he bounded away. Alison walked on down the road. All the houses were like that: big, comfortable and expensive. The last one looked particularly expensive. Its front garden was separated from the street by a low stone wall, showing immaculate lawns and a smart frontage. Brass lamps in questionable taste in the porch, a hint of Laura Ashley curtaining at the windows. To each side of the house, a high wall had been built in weathered brick, continuing round to enclose the back garden. Above it she caught a glimpse of a long glass extension – perhaps a swimming pool – and there were double gates to let in cars.

Somebody with a few bob lived there. She wondered who?

*

After a morning of petty crime at the Crown Court, she hurried up the steep hill of Park Street, past the University Tower to a Thai restaurant in Whiteladies Road, near the BBC. She was panting from the climb when she arrived – and slightly nervous of meeting John Forbes. He was the senior partner of Roger Dixon's firm which – apart from the effete Dixon – was one of the oldest and grandest in the city. Alison had really gone ballistic when she phoned to complain, but Forbes had been charming and receptive.

She knew he was nearly sixty, but he did not look it. Alarmingly tall, at least six foot three, the folds of the elegant dark suit seemed to go on for ever, and handsome in a neat sort of way. There was something attractive in the lined face, grey-brown hair and reassuring smile, the gentle old-world courtesy. As they picked at spicy oriental dishes, he came straight to the point. 'I'm sorry Roger made such a cock-up and now it looks so hopeless. If you want to bow out – well, I guess I could find somebody with less of a career to make ...'

'Is that a polite way of saying you want to sack me?'

'Good lord, no. I've taken on Quinn's case myself and you're the best defender in town. I very much want you to go on. It's just that, if it goes the wrong way, I'm old enough to afford a spectacular failure. And so far we – my side of the profession – have let you down.'

'We've *all* let Quinn down. Do you believe he's innocent?'

'I believe what my client tells me. I can't work on any other basis. Nor can you, Alison, I imagine.'

'That isn't what I asked you, John. Just forget the rules for a minute. Do you *really* believe his story?'

Forbes gestured at the white-coated Thai waiter, lurking behind a bamboo screen, 'Two more lagers, please,' and countered with a question. 'Did you know Quinn came round last night?'

Alison shook her head.

'I went to see him straight away. He claims he was attacked just after he'd been moved out to the remand centre. No sooner had he been locked in his cell, than two men in balaclavas came in and knocked him out. That's all he knew until he woke up in the prison hospital.'

'You mean they had the keys to unlock his cell? Two men could march through the jail in balaclavas, get access to a prisoner in solitary, beat him up and fake a suicide attempt? Come off it. I *did* wonder whether someone else might be involved, but not as crudely as that. It's complete balls.'

'Is it? I thought they might just be the same people as the private security guards who'd moved him by van? Not a bad way of getting access if you didn't want him to stand trial.' He met her eyes firmly: he had rather nice eyes, blue with a touch of hazel. 'And if you had the resources for a few bribes ...'

'You mean whoever killed Nikki was rounding it off by taking out Quinn as chief suspect? No trial, and the case is closed? That's quite a *big* conspiracy,

John.' It was the wrong way round, she thought. The older man should be the one reining back *her* outrageous theories. 'Don't you think he *might* just have killed Nikki by mistake, then panicked; and now he's lying through his teeth? It's a whole lot more likely.'

'Of course it is, that's our problem, but in a curious way it doesn't feel to me as if he *is* lying. He's shocked and confused. If his story's true, if he didn't kill her, then the truth is bound to sound pretty far-fetched, isn't it?'

'He's behaving as if he has something to hide or he's completely round the bend.' She filled him in on George's theory about the link with the Boniface trial. 'He still hasn't told me about that. Why the hell not?'

The tall figure twisted on his small and obviously uncomfortable chair and gave a kind of shrug. 'Maybe he didn't think it was relevant? He *did* tell Roger about it, it's in the notes. They're a bit of a mess, but it's there if you search. I think I can see him being so depressed and confused he wouldn't mention it again. Unless George's vendetta theory is correct, and I'm sure it's not, it's not really part of this murder, is it?'

'It wasn't quite like that. I asked him outright if he's ever come across any criminals in the past. He lied to me. Why?'

'Put yourself in his place, Alison. He could be so anxious, locked up and going potty about what's happened to his kids, that his memory and reactions are terribly confused. I don't believe he's lying now.'

They ended the meal with peeled lychees. 'Tinned, of course,' he laughed. 'I prefer them that way – my daughter gets them fresh from the market, or maybe Sainsbury's, and peeling them's a real bore.' Alison remembered that he was divorced, left alone with two girls who must be late teenagers or even grown up by now. 'By the way, did you know the dead Jevanjee has at least one relative left in town?'

'Yes.' George had discovered it. *There's this uncle, still working here as a doctor. A lot of people thought he was mixed up with his nephew in some way, maybe drugs or arms. Wonder what he could tell us, if we could find a way of twisting his arm? Risky, though, have to go in sideways.* 'You mean his uncle, Dr Anwar Jevanjee? Very respectable, runs a private practice for rich hypochondriacs.'

'I'd like to know more about him. I don't suppose he's anything to do with all this, but I'm curious about what *did* happen eight years ago. If Quinn isn't a murderer, he's mixed up in something nasty – and that's the only time he seems to have fallen among thieves.

On the pavement outside, Forbes offered Alison a lift back. His Daimler Sovereign was parked in a side street and she noticed its number plate. It was less than a year old; he must be making a fortune.

He drove fast up the hill, weaving through side streets until they came out on the Down near the suspension bridge. A file of children on ponies was trotting across the grass. Forbes gestured towards a large yellow sandstone house: very solid, probably built at the turn of the century. 'That's Dr Jevanjee's surgery, the bottom two floors.' He stopped on the side of the road away from the terrace. Through high windows Alison could see a waiting-room with Regency striped wallpaper and a large chandelier. She could imagine the rest: deep armchairs and coffee-tables littered with copies of *Country Life* and *Tatler*.

'Looks respectable enough.'

He shrugged. 'Maybe. The word is that his main skill is prescribing for rich addicts – and supplying a discreet range of drugs that are not prescribable. He's definitely not straight. Of course he may have nothing to do with Quinn …'

She nodded. 'But maybe we should check it out.'

9

Next morning, it was just after seven when George crept out of the flat. Within twenty minutes his white Transit joined the stream of traffic on the motorway making for London.

He drove at about sixty, ignoring the rattles all around him, alone with his thoughts and Radio 2. After a while he turned off the radio. The word was that Simon Boniface had set up his escape while in Durham and was now in Northern Cyprus. The judge who had sentenced him had been living in quiet retirement in the Lake District until a week after Boniface's self-engineered release. Then the brakes on his car had failed as he drove down a mountain road. It had gone out of control, crashed through the parapet of a bridge and spiralled down into the valley below. The judge and his wife had both been killed. The detective who had arrested Boniface had died of a heart attack years ago. That left Quinn and Carswell. Did the theory gel or not?

He knew Alison thought it was all rubbish, but he was still not quite sure. His eyes softened as he thought of her. She had still been asleep when he left, looking young and fresh, almost like a teenager, black curls tumbled on the pillow, smiling as if they were still making love. She was the first woman he had really wanted in his tempestuous life, a small bundle of vitality who always made him, too, feel more alive. After a childhood of extreme poverty and teenage years toughening up as a deckhand, George had come to enjoy living on his wits, knowing he was self-sufficient, needing no one. But Alison was just as exciting and vibrant as the most dramatic parts of his other life. It wasn't only that the slightest touch of her body filled him with warm protectiveness and gave him an Oscar-winning erection; it was being comfortable together yet constantly surprised, having so much to share. Trouble was, he never seemed to get it quite right and she kept running away. He adjusted his flat cap and sighed.

Mr Justice Carswell had lived in west London, in a lane running down to the Thames in Richmond. George parked on Richmond Green, his rusty white van sticking out like a sore thumb among the Rovers and BMWs. He had discarded his anorak for an old blue mac and left his cap on the driving seat before locking up.

It was a sunny day. The square of rough grass, surrounded by trees, elegant houses, a pub, a theatre, could have been the centre of a country town, not one of the most expensive pieces of real estate in the capital. The old British fantasy: a village within twenty minutes of the city centre – not unlike Abbots Leigh. He consulted his *A–Z* and turned down towards the river.

It was a small Georgian house, three storeys, in a short terrace. The windows were heavily net-curtained and a flight of steps ran up to a red front door, bright with gleaming brass knocker and letter-box. All very correct, very *bijou*. George took a deep breath, climbed the steps and looked for a bell-push. There wasn't one, so he used the round brass knocker, two bangs that sounded as if he were trying to smash to door down. He half hoped there would be no one in.

But there was. A woman opened the door: mid-thirties, very pretty, with chestnut hair. She was wearing jeans and a check shirt. She smiled questioningly.

'Is Lady Carswell in, please?'

'I'm Lady Carswell.' Sounded wary: she must have been plagued by journalists. 'What do you want?'

George hid his astonishment and handed over his card. 'I'm a private investigator, Lady Carswell, retained by the lawyers conducting a case in Bristol, I think you might just be able to help me. Not,' he added hastily, 'that you're involved in any way yourself, of course.'

She looked puzzled. 'Are you from a newspaper? If you are, just clear off before I call the police.'

'No, ma'am. I am what I say I am. If you wish you can telephone the chambers of the barrister employing me and confirm that.'

She hesitated. 'Oh, well, you'd better come in.' She turned and led the way into a long room with windows at each end, looking out over the street and a small back garden. It had a cheerful atmosphere, a mixture of chintzy sofas and bright curtains, two handsome Georgian armchairs, covered in deep blue, by the fireplace. As she walked in front of him, George noted that Carswell's wife had a darn good figure.

She turned to face him. 'Look, Mr Kristianssen, I've had a lot of hassle lately and I think you've got a bloody cheek to turn up on my doorstep without the good manners to make an appointment. Let's have the name of this barrister and I'll check your credentials. Then I *may* talk to you.' George handed her Alison's card. 'OK. Please wait out in the garden.' She opened a glass door. 'I don't want you going through my things.' He stepped outside and she closed the door and locked it from the inside.

George sat on a wooden bench studying the weathered wall of yellow-grey London brick, covered in the gnarled branches of an old wisteria. The scent from its blue flowers filled the small paved space. It was ten minutes before she appeared to unlock the door again. 'Right. You can come back in.'

They sat facing each other and she eyed him firmly. 'I've spoken to Miss Hope in Bristol and to the Bar Council who confirm Miss Hope is practising. This meeting must be entirely off the record – you aren't taping it, are you?'

'No, of course not.'

'I suppose I have to accept that and I suppose I can't stop you taking notes – but if you reveal what I say to anyone except your barrister I'll deny we ever met. OK?'

'Certainly, if that is your wish.' George thought he sounded like an undertaker, which was entirely the wrong role for this vivacious woman. 'May I come to the point now?'

'Go ahead.'

'Ten years ago your husband prosecuted a Bristol gangland figure called Simon Boniface – on a variety of charges including murder. Perhaps you remember?'

'I remember very well.' She gave a little smile. 'I was a young solicitor working for the police. That was when I met my late husband.'

His expectations of the meeting rose by five hundred per cent. That had never occurred to him. 'What was your name then, Lady Carswell?'

'Rachel Owen. I was his second wife of course.'

'When did you get married?'

'About a year after that case, when Nick got divorced.'

'You know that Boniface swore to get everyone involved in sending him down for life? Including your husband?'

'Sure – I was there when he was sentenced. He was so violent I felt he really meant it. He was a

92

very nasty piece of work, you know. Jevanjee wasn't the only person he'd taken out like that.'

'Your husband died in curious circumstances, Lady Carswell, so I'm sorry to refer to them.' George paused, but she looked angry rather than distressed. 'Do you believe he was high on drugs and engaged in some kind of, well, bizarre sexual activity when he died?'

'Absolutely not!' There wasn't a hint of embarrassment. Her eyes blazed with fury. 'It's total rubbish and if you're here to pursue that you can get out right now.'

George held up a hand. 'I'm *not* suggesting anything of the kind. I don't believe it either, I'm on your side.'

'You've got a bloody odd way of showing it.'

'I said,' he spelt it out deliberately. 'I – don't – believe – it – either. What do *you* think happened?'

She still looked furious. 'I'm certain he was murdered. God knows how they managed it, but he must have been injected with the drug, stripped when unconscious and chucked out of the window. The woman could have been dead before she even entered the apartment.'

'Who d'you think killed him?'

'Boniface, of course. Revenge. I knew my husband, Mr Kristianssen. I have no intention of going into detail, but believe me, we had a very satisfactory relationship. He was older than me, but he was a terrific man and he still had one hell of a sex drive. I can't conceive of anything he wanted that I didn't provide. I'd dearly love to see whoever did it exposed – it's all been very painful for me, and for our children.' George met her eyes, but there were no tears. 'Nick's dead and we're left a laughing stock. I had to take my youngest away from his prep school, he was being jeered at so much.'

George met her eyes questioningly. 'You really do believe that's what happened? It would be complicated and risky, you know – breaking into your flat in the Temple, getting the woman in, killing her ...'

'But when they'd done that at leisure, Nick would just have opened the front door and walked into an ambush, wouldn't he?'

George nodded. 'I suppose so. But afterwards, when they'd killed him too, how difficult would it be to get out at, say, two in the morning?'

'Not difficult at all. Just climb the wall into Fleet Street or the Embankment. They probably had a car parked nearby.'

'Why do you still have an apartment in the Temple, anyway?'

'Nick took it when we lived in Bristol – he sometimes sat at the Old Bailey and Snaresbrook. If you're thinking it was a clandestine love nest, forget it. It was usually sub-let. We'd only had it back two months and he occasionally slept there when he was working late in London, if I wasn't here for some reason. I still work too. That's all. Now, you've asked quite enough. You know exactly what I think – and I'm sure that is the truth.'

'Thank you for being so frank with me, Lady Carswell. You know Boniface has escaped from custody?'

'Yes, and I'm sure he engineered what happened to Nick.'

'Wouldn't it make more sense to get out of the country as fast as possible? He still had a lot of bird to do.'

'I expect he did. He had the money to hire a plane *and* to get his old cronies to murder my husband.'

'Do you remember Dr Quinn?'

She smiled. 'Of course, he was incredibly brave, giving evidence as he did. He must have known Boniface would be a dangerous enemy.'

George stopped writing and put down his notebook on the arm of the chair. 'Did he have any *choice*? Surely he could have been compelled to testify?'

'In theory, yes. But our great trouble with Boniface was always to find anyone prepared to give evidence against him. Everyone had convenient lapses of memory. We knew he was a big catch – into drugs, protection, big-time burglary. He was as big as the Krays or the Richardsons in London, believe me. People were terrified of him – terrified of being tortured and murdered, simple as that. He had the muscle to do that kind of thing with impunity and they knew it.'

'So Quinn was a big find?'

'Oh, yes. It was a terrific piece of luck that he stumbled into the Jevanjee murder; he was exactly what we needed. A credible professional man who testified without fear or favour. It must have been a great shock to Boniface and his lawyers. And we didn't even have to persuade him.'

George sensed something unspoken. 'What do you mean?'

She shrugged. 'He *must* have been threatened, told they'd get him in some way if he went through with it.'

'But he did? Go through with it, I mean.'

'Absolutely. He also never told us about any threats, which I thought was a bit odd. Other witnesses complained and were given police protection.'

'But he was your *star* witness.'

'Exactly. Boniface would never have been convicted without him.' She paused. 'Quite frankly, Nick was surprised when he won. The rest of the evidence didn't add up to a row of beans, but Quinn clinched it.' She stopped again.

'Go on, please.'

She shook her head. 'It's probably wrong, but it's been puzzling me for years. Quinn saw Jevanjee dead, of course, but he didn't see who killed him. The key point was that he saw Boniface driving away, saw him in the back of his Mercedes.'

'So?'

'It just happened that I was driving back from court in Cardiff that evening. I took the short cut across from the Severn bridge along the back roads to Avonmouth. I was driving through not long before it all happened. There were no street lights working – the defence never seem to have discovered that.'

'You mean Quinn was *lying*?'

'Don't know. Maybe supporting what he believed to be true with a little imagination. But I'm sure he didn't see Boniface, even if the bastard was there.'

'Then why on earth should he say he *did* see him?'

She stood up and walked to the window over-looking the garden, neat chestnut hair shining as it caught the sun. '*We* certainly didn't lean on him or bribe him.'

'Maybe somebody else did? The police?' They faced each other in silence. In the distance George could hear the growl of traffic in Richmond town centre and the house quivered as an airliner descended to nearby Heathrow. 'Did you know Dr Quinn has been arrested on a charge of murder, Lady Carswell?'

She started with genuine astonishment. 'I don't believe it! Who on earth is he supposed to have killed?'

'His wife – and their two children.'

'That's impossible. I got to know him quite well during the trial – he was so inoffensive. It can't be true.'

'Do you think they could be framing him, too – settling the score?'

She looked pensive, and suddenly shivered. 'That man's a psychopath and hates us all. He has every reason to hate Dr Quinn just as much as he hated my husband.'

10

Bill Taylor smiled as he waved Alison to a deep leather armchair in his club, a comfortable Regency house in a curving Clifton terrace. 'Sorry I couldn't get round to your chambers. Would you like a drink?'

'A glass of white wine would be nice.' She looked around at the tobacco-brown masculine surroundings: dark panelled walls, discreet strip lights shining over grimy oil paintings, landscapes and portraits of corpulent burghers. 'I haven't been here before; it's beautiful.'

'Very Old Bristol.' He smiled again, questioningly. 'How are you getting on? Don't suppose there's any good news?'

She shook her head as a waiter in a burgundy coat brought two glasses of wine on a silver salver. 'Have you been to see Geoff?'

'Yes, just after he …' Taylor crossed his legs awkwardly as he hesitated. 'Just after he tried to kill himself. He was in a hell of a state, so drugged it was hard to get through.'

'Do you still believe he's innocent?'

The small man looked a little different from their

first meeting. The crinkly red hair and smooth, round face still gave him an innocent boyishness, but when he leaned forward in the deep chair, mouth, eyes and jaw firm, Alison could see him at the head of his boardroom table. Bill Taylor was nobody's fool. 'Innocent? Yes, of course.' But she knew he longer believed it. 'There's one thing you ought to know, though.'

'What's that, Bill?'

He met her eyes directly. 'It's probably not relevant, but maybe the police … you know?'

'Surely, anything they might discover, I need to know, too.'

'Well, I went down to West Bay at the weekend, to check on the boat. The cabin door had been forced open – the lock broken – and the fuel was much lower than I left it. It was as if the engine had been used, as if she had been taken to sea.'

'Vandals?'

'Nothing had been taken.'

'Had anyone seen her leave the harbour?'

'I asked around, and a couple of fishermen thought that she'd been taken out after dark one night.'

'Recently?'

'The weekend of the murder.'

'So you think Geoff drove to West Bay and …'

'I don't think anything, Alison. In my book, Geoff's not a murderer and someone else has killed his wife and children. This is just a fact I thought you needed to know.'

'D'you have the names of these fishermen?' Silently he handed her a postcard with two names, addresses and phone numbers. 'Tell me, Bill, how sure were they about it being the weekend of the murder?'

'Very sure. The one called John Bartlett had a daughter married that weekend, on the Saturday. He was at his future son-in-law's stag night on the Friday, at one of the pubs by the quay in West Bay. They went on after closing. He stepped out for a breath of air and thought it was our boat he saw leave, chugging out with no sails raised while he was pissing into the water. He says he watched her out through the harbour entrance until she vanished. He thinks she was gone until Sunday night.'

George got back about eight and they compared notes over a takeaway in Alison's flat; and then in bed. He had thought it through and decided that Carswell's attractive wife was, understandably, deceiving herself: the Boniface revenge theory did not work. But he was intrigued by the connection between Quinn and the Jevanjees. He'd asked Joan at the office to look at back numbers of the local papers and spread some old cuttings on the rumpled duvet. Alison picked one up. The dodgy doctor was opening his new clinic. A short man, dwarfed by a high doorway in the mansion on Clifton Down, impeccable in a dark three-piece suit, watch-chain stretched across his waistcoat. He had a high, bald forehead, and metal half-moon spectacles completed the image. 'He looks so phoney he *has* to be a crook.'

'They say he's mixed up in drugs, maybe arms too – some kind of link to politics and terrorism back in India. Haven't got much yet, but I'm looking for a freelance journalist called Hannah something-or-other who's supposed to have been after him for a month or two. They say she got some hard leads.'

Alison yawned and pulled off the T-shirt that was all she was wearing as they lay back against the piled-up pillows. She drew her knees up to her chin, enjoying the delicious sensations of anticipation in her body as she snuggled up to him. 'You're a genius, George, did you know that?' She sighed dreamily as the strong arms enveloped her and the kind, bearded face smiled down. 'But let's leave it till tomorrow ...'

'Sorry, love, was I goin' on a bit?' Then he was looming over her and she closed her eyes as he kissed her.

'No, George ... you were being lovely, you're always lovely ... well, nearly always.' She wriggled with pleasure as he turned her over and began to caress her with long, flowing strokes, all the way down from her neck to her ankles. He had amazingly gentle hands and her hips rose sensuously as she parted her legs and felt his fingers probing deep between her thighs.

Outside it had started to rain and the drops were

rattling against the window, making their warmth and closeness even more precious. Twisting on her back again, she ran her fingernails down his spine, enough to scratch but not to break the skin. When, still kissing him, her fingers travelled on to stroke his scrotum from behind, he almost leapt in her arms, so she did it again and again, driving him wild. She gasped when he seized her wrists and straightened his arms to hold them wide apart above her head. 'God, I love it when you do that.' Arching her spine, she stared up at him with huge eyes, marvelling at his strength as he gripped her, breathing heavily, lips slightly apart, moving in a whisper suddenly so small and vulnerable he could barely hear. 'Darling, darling, George – I love you so much … you won't ever … will you?' Then the fleeting need for reassurance was past and she rolled back on her shoulders, flinging her legs up and round his body. He felt the muscles tightening in her thighs and calves and responded fiercely as she pressed him down, closing her eyes again and crying out as he thrust into her.

They slept secure in each other's arms. The digital clock said it was half past three when George drifted back into consciousness. Alison was lying with her back to him, curled up like a dormouse, and he was still holding her; but when he kissed the nape of her neck, he sensed that she was crying.

It was during her sixth year at the Bar. She had been successful, finding a place in a modest set of chambers in the Temple and charming the clerk – a streetwise East End boy now knocking on sixty – to push her for cases. They had come slowly at first, but meticulous preparation paid off; and once on her feet, after initial nervousness, she began to feel in command in court. She made a name, concentrating on crime – still an unusual choice for a women.

In a profession of old men with puffy claret noses or young men with beer guts and supercilious manners, being a girl had some advantages. Most of them still saw women in a predatory fashion. If you looked passable, as Alison did, they fantasised about getting inside your knickers; and some tried hard – often very hard – to more than fantasise. But they also had to recognise that she was competent *because a third party – judge or jury – made decisions that told them so.*

Walking down Middle Temple Lane that morning, Alison Hope felt almost smug. There was a long way to go yet, but against all the odds she had contrived to become a barrister who was increasingly in demand. She'd cracked it. From now on it was up to her to choose where she wanted to go. First build up the practice and take silk, then – she shrugged to herself, time would tell. But hubris brings it own come-uppance, which was perhaps why she did not see the missing paving-stone where the gas men had been at work. She tripped and fell painfully, grazing both hands. When she stood up, suit smeared with yellow clay, her left ankle was agonising.

She hobbled along to the chemist on Fleet Street, bought an elastic bandage, cleaned herself up in the taxi to Southwark Crown Court and managed to struggle through her case despite the pain. But afterwards she gave up and went home to Fulham, accepting that she would have to take a day or two off. The small terraced house was her first venture into property and it was only six months since she had left a rented flat in Vauxhall. It was the kind of cottage working-men lived in at the turn of the century, now prettied-up in an area that had become gentrified in the last twenty years: a friendly little house, two up and two down, with a sunny walled garden.

It felt odd to be there in daylight during the week but, after a night's sleep, her leg felt less painful and she enjoyed pottering around like a housewife. After two nights she decided to stay at home for one more day and return to work on Friday. She had been meaning to have the shabby nursing-chair repaired ever since she bought it in a junk shop a year ago. Two of its legs were broken and the fabric covering its low seat and spoon-back was torn and dirty; it needed reupholstering. She flicked through the Yellow Pages, made a few calls and put it in the back of her car.

He had a small workshop a mile away, in a mews at the back of a row of shops near the cemetery on Fulham Palace Road, a tall man with broad shoulders and laughing eyes. A shock of black hair, a slightly ridiculous moustache, handsome weatherbeaten face. They sat on a pair of three-legged stools outside in the mews, soaking up the sun and drinking tea from chipped mugs. Yes, of course, he would repair it – he'd do it by Saturday – and he knew an upholsterer who would give her a price for covering it. Somehow they drifted over to the pub, still much as it had been before the war: high mirrors and red plush benches round the walls, brass foot-rail on the floor in front of the bar, dark stained counter and tables.

His name was David. He had been to Cambridge and joined the Diplomatic Service, but dropped out after five years. He didn't want to be part of the establishment, he laughed, felt nearer to real people working with his hands. She remembered a few pieces of new furniture in the workshop. 'Did you make those? They're beautiful.'

On Saturday he brought the nursing-chair back, with two new legs that he had turned and stained to match the existing ones. He had done it with great skill, even inserting a few phoney woodworm holes. He was not quite as tall as she remembered, but she was bowled over by his cheerful flamboyance, his laughter, the shy way he asked if she was busy that evening.

They went to another Victorian pub, then a bistro near Parsons Green. She firmly offered to pay her share, but he wouldn't hear of it. When he dropped her off in his van, full of wood shavings and the smell of varnish, she pleaded that she had to leave for a case in the north early next morning and did not ask him in. It was only too clear what would happen if she did. He kissed her gently.

A week later he brought round the estimate for covering the chair. They went to the same bistro and drank lots of rough red wine. Back in her cottage she sat him in one of her white armchairs and curled up at his feet. It was ridiculous: Balliol, the Temple, six years of a damn good career, complete independence, a free woman but never without admirers. And now she was going to be screwed by an impoverished carpenter with lips that were too thick. Worse, she wasn't doing it just for a good time, she *was actually falling for the bloody man.*

*Next morning she left him asleep – he looked boyish
and she had discovered that he did not snore – and walked
naked to the bedroom window, half hoping he would wake
up and see her standing there. His admiration and cheerful, earthy desire were already waking half-forgotten
sensations of awareness and pride in the better features of
her body. She wanted to please him, but drawing the
curtains on the quiet Fulham street, empty except for a
paper-girl on Sunday morning, she had a serious moment
of doubt. Had a sprained ankle led her to a man she could
genuinely like and respect? A partner who would make
an already very satisfactory life complete? Rubbish – she
just liked his exciting mixture of strength and gentleness.
And, more than any man she had ever known, his body
was beautiful. Those wonderful powerful shoulders that
loomed over her threateningly, dominantly, protectively,
his broad chest, narrow hips, long, strong legs. God, she
loved it when he touched her. For heaven's sake, girl, she
told herself sternly, go and take a cold shower then scrub
the kitchen floor. You can read this stuff in Mills & Boon.
You don't have to live it.*

*So for two months she took it step-by-step, let him
make the running, walking on air but also on eggshells,
waiting for the dream to fade. The trouble was, it didn't.
He moved in and paid his share of the housekeeping, even
though she was plainly earning very much more. She had
lived alone for five years, but felt perfectly comfortable
with David. Sometimes his face came into her mind when
she was on her feet in court; at her desk in the Temple
she looked forward to their evenings together. He was*

107

interested in what she did, curious to find out more, but never intrusive. When she led for the defence in her first murder, he helped out with lots of photocopying and collating over one weekend. Sharing was a new experience; and she enjoyed it.

They went to the cinema or the English National Opera at the Coliseum, drove out into the Sussex countryside at weekends. Sometimes on Saturday they walked by the Thames, only a few hundred yards from her house, along the tow-path to Chiswick and Kew Gardens. They learnt all about each other. David had a widowed mother in Whitstable and had gone to a grammar school in Canterbury. There was a sister somewhere, but Alison never met either of them, although he promised that she would. She took him north one weekend to meet her father in Aberdeen.

11

Alison spent the day in court on a case in Bath. Ten years at the bar had taught her to concentrate her whole mind on a single problem for an hour or two, a day, whatever it took to master facts, structure them and present them in the most favourable light. It was almost like yoga or transcendental meditation – everything else was shut out, even creepy Dr Jevanjee, darling George and impossible bloody Geoffrey Quinn.

On the drive back she had another problem to occupy her. The car started to play up. Every time she stopped in traffic or at lights, the engine stalled. It took long, agonised pulls on the starter to get the damn thing going again. As the electric motor whined, horns behind her blared with impatience and helpful passers-by offered to push her into the verge. She eventually made it, coasting the last hundred yards from the Down to her front door with the engine dead again, sweat running down her back, fuming with anger.

As she pulled herself out of the low bucket seat, she resisted a powerful urge to kick the red metal of the door or drop a lighted match into the petrol tank. Indoors she rang her local back-street garage and Dennis, the mechanical genius who kept her on the road, agreed to come and pick up the Jag first thing in the morning. 'Leave it with me for the day, Miss Hope. It's probably just the starter motor – I'll have her purring again by tea-time.' Alison hoped he could; she loved the beast, but if anything serious went wrong it was always expensive.

She was too tired to concentrate when George phoned. 'More stuff on Dr Jevanjee, flower. Originally from Lahore. Been here twenty years. Very murky reputation. Troubling thing is …'

Alison yawned. 'Tell me, darling.'

'Well, this freelance Hannah Braithwaite was building a file on him.'

'Yes, you said.'

'They say she went and presented him with the evidence before going to a national tabloid. She hasn't been seen since.'

'How d'you mean?'

'Vanished. Empty bedsit in Hotwells. Just gone. She was a woman of forty or so. Lived alone, doesn't seem to have any family, so no one's made any fuss.'

'I don't think I like Jevanjee very much, George.'

'I went round her place and let myself in. No papers. No computer or disks. All very clean.'

Tonight Alison did not want to go to the pub. She wanted to be at home, no one's woman, alone with time to sort out her thoughts. Why the hell was Quinn lying to her? Why had he left the Infirmary on the verge of becoming a consultant? Why had he not told her about the murder of Ahmed Jevanjee in Avonmouth? And what about Jevanjee's crooked uncle? And whatever Nikki had been up to, surely a man who was still living with her would have *some* idea, inkling, suspicion of it?

Shit. It was all too difficult. And George's van had broken down, so reluctantly she walked across to meet him at the Port of Call. It was past nine and turning into a foggy night. The wide expanse of the Down had a sense of isolation, grey bands of mist grabbing at her like ghosts from velvety darkness. She could see the yellow lights of houses flickering in the distance, but when trees swayed in the wind to obscure them, and she heard the gallows-creak of their branches, she felt a sudden sense of menace and, however irrationally, started to walk faster. Soon she was almost running towards the safety of the lights.

It was an unsatisfactory evening. She had too much to drink and it was followed by a long, sleepless night. She was alone in the double bed, tormented by doubts and questions. When at last she fell into restless sleep she was soon woken by rain tapping on the window, then by the sound of footsteps on the pavement outside. At five she lay under the clammy duvet, counting the zebra stripes cast on the ceiling by a street lamp shining through the Venetian blind, and almost got up to start work. But then she drifted back into a deep sleep and was woken with a start at ten past eight. The front door bell was ringing in long bursts. She hadn't heard the alarm at seven. Cursing quietly she leapt out of bed, pulled her kimono over her nakedness and ran out into the hall.

Dennis was on the doorstep, a cheerful Brummy of about forty in clean blue overalls. 'Sorry to disturb you, Miss Hope. Have you got the car keys?'

Alison went back to find them in her kitchen and stood at the door as he started the car. It growled into life after a minute or two on the starter, weaker now after the thrashing she had given the battery yesterday. She watched as he drove away, stalling then starting again jerkily, past the black iron railings in front of the row of solid Edwardian houses, to turn right into the city. It was a sunny morning, the trees full of birdsong. A scruffy sparrow landed by her feet on the steps.

The explosion made her start but was not unduly loud. At first she thought it was the thud of two cars shunting on the road across the Down. Then the blast came crashing back down the street, followed by a rush of hot air, hurling her over like a train bursting from a tunnel. As she rolled down the stone steps, breaking a fingernail as she tried to grab at them, the car vanished in a ball of orange fire, flames clawing at the air, crackling angrily. Her ears stung and her hearing had gone. It was like looking at a silent film. The fireball was topped by a pyre of thick black smoke, flames were spreading to other parked cars and a figure was rolling on the pavement beside it, trying to beat out his blazing clothes. It was the postman.

The next two hours passed in a blur. She ran to the blazing man, but when she reached him, he was dead, his body black, contracted into a foetal position. The eyes stared at her, full of anguished pain and terror that made her stomach turn. She was still kneeling there when the first fire engine arrived. The men in yellow helmets were kind, two of them guiding her away while the others spread out to spray the blaze with foam. She slumped down on the steps, unable to speak, eyes staring ahead with her arms round her knees, unaware that the black kimono had fallen aside to reveal an expanse of broad white thigh. The policeman suddenly towering above her coughed and she stood up, covering herself quickly. 'Shall we go inside, ma'am? Make a nice cup of tea?'

Alison made a brief statement to a detective constable, sitting numbly at her kitchen table while a perky policewoman called Sam made a pot of tea which she poured into mugs already half full with milk and sugar. Alison was too shocked and too grateful to point out that she never drank tea and never put sugar in the coffee she brewed endlessly.

It was only now that reality was hitting her. The whole Quinn thing was not only impossible. It was dangerous. Suddenly, deliberately, someone had tried to kill her. She had barely started to penetrate the truth and they'd tried to *kill* her, as if that were no more than swatting an irritating mosquito; and if the car hadn't played up, they would have succeeded. Someone believed she had knowledge or intentions that were a threat. What made it even more terrifying was that in fact she knew *nothing* – at least nothing that made any sense. She did not even know *why* she was being threatened.

She was also angry – with Quinn, George, John Forbes. She hadn't got into this mess by herself. No, that was grossly unfair – no it bloody wasn't. It wasn't John or George they'd tried to blow up. Perhaps Quinn's story was true and they *had* tried to kill him too … and where the hell did Jevanjee fit in? Somebody out there had something colossal to hide. Enough to kill Nikki Quinn and probably that freelance journalist. Enough to want to screw up Quinn's case, even if it meant another killing, so that other barristers would be warned off, so that it would be endless months before it came to court … months in which they might be able to get to Quinn again, take him out and end the danger. She could still smell the fire: the blazing rubber and petrol and could not get the faces of Dennis and the postman out of her mind. They were both her friends, innocent bystanders, with families who loved them. It was so sad, so unjust. But she was not going to be frightened off. She would not let Quinn down. She would never let anyone down again.

After the first delight in David's admiration and easy laughter, she had, in truth, been cautious. Working daily with crooks had made Alison nobody's fool; she was proud of what she had achieved alone and protective of her freedom and independence. When she had been close to men before, after a time she had always started to feel claustrophobic, trapped, finally irritable, angry and rejecting.

But this time there was a magical quality. She never got bored with David, he demanded only what she freely wanted to give. She was still herself, the tough barrister, but with him her legs sometimes went like jelly – and she loved it. Of course it was partly physical, very physical. That first excitement had not died; it increased until it became a satisfying pastime just to stare out of her window at Fountain Court and imagine the deliciousness of being naked in his arms.

She enjoyed waking before him in the morning, as she usually did, lying there by his warm body, hearing the little sighs as he breathed, smiling to herself in the darkness. That first time would always be precious. She had forgotten to leave any heat on and the bedroom was freezing as they undressed like two white ghosts. Alison turning her back so he could undo her bra. Then she had run downstairs naked to put on the central heating and, back with him, lit the bedside lamp with its yellow-gold shade, pleased that her body looked so tanned in its glow.

God, she had wanted to kiss him, feel his skin on hers. She felt so alive, so desired, as she faced him with open arms, strong brown thighs apart and challenging.

Yes, the sex was good. But in the end what she valued most was the feeling of being wanted in an uncomplicated way: the comfortable intimacy, 'mutual society, help and *comfort', just like it said in the King James Prayer Book. And the lasting knowledge of respect, which tiffs – even a couple of major rows – did nothing to upset. Having David in her life seemed to make her try even harder at the Bar. She started to take him to parties given by fellow barristers, inwardly delighted at the way the women responded to his handsome features and laid-back manner. She even began to think about marriage and children. It had been eight months, and was coming up to Christmas. They were going to spend it together in Fulham. Alison had never felt so happy in her life. You really could have both, if you were lucky – a career and a partner who made you feel like this.*

It was four o'clock before Alison felt able to leave the flat. Her first instinct had been to go to Chief Superintendent Manning. For one thing she needed protection, for another her attempted murder surely put a new slant on the case. But in the end she decided to see Quinn first. Alone. The practice rules made that acceptable if the solicitor, who was supposed to be present, was unavailable. Forbes was unavailable because she wasn't damn well telling him she was going. Anyway, the practice rules were mostly baloney, designed to keep both branches of the profession in well-paid work.

After his suicide attempt, Quinn had been heavily sedated for a week and it had changed him. He was more confident and looked different: for the first time she could see more than the shadow of a handsome and attractive man. She was also very angry with him. She opened her pad on the filthy table and met his eyes without smiling. 'Today is the day we stop pissing about, Geoffrey.' He looked puzzled. 'I told you at the beginning that I could only defend you if you were honest with me.'

'I have been – do you believe I killed them all?'

'No, I believe you're innocent of the murder charge. But why the devil are you concealing so much from me? Things that are bound to be thrown against you in court? I've really had enough – you're coming clean now, today, telling me everything I need to know. Otherwise you can find another barrister.'

He started. 'You can't do that. It's unprofessional.'

'So what? Because you've lied to me I've made enquiries that have upset some very nasty people. They tried to kill me this morning. They put a bomb under my car. A good friend of mine *was* killed. So was a perfectly innocent passer-by.'

'I don't believe you.'

'Then you'd better *start* believing me, Geoff, because it happens to be true – and there are limits even to my devotion to my clients. I've narrowly avoided being blown to bits, so start talking. Why didn't you tell me about the Jevanjee murder eight years ago? Didn't it occur to you that mixing with big-time crime might be relevant to the mess you're in now? Why didn't you tell me about Boniface's trial; or about the threats he made? What the hell *was* Nikki up to in the past year? Don't insult my intelligence by telling me you don't even have a *theory*. You're an intelligent man, not a fool, so what the hell are you playing at?'

He reacted angrily. 'I'm not sure that I know myself. I *did* tell Roger Dixon about the Boniface trial long before you came on the scene. He didn't seem very interested but I assumed he gave you his notes.'

'He did, but you've sat here for hours with me without mentioning it.'

'I thought you didn't think it mattered, wasn't relevant. It's OK for you – you aren't locked in a bloody cell twenty-three hours a day. You aren't breathing foul air that gives you a permanent head-ache, eating crap food that gives you nausea or the shits, turning sub-human and crazy without any-one giving a damn. I'm sorry – I was very shocked when they arrested me, not thinking straight, out of my mind with worry about the children ...'

'It's still the starting point, Geoff.' She looked at him very hard. 'You ought to have told me – parti-cularly if you lied on oath at Boniface's trial.'

'What—?' He looked shocked.

'Well – didn't you?'

'How do you ...?'

'I've been doing my homework, Geoff, like a good lawyer. Pity you're such a lousy client. But it isn't just Boniface and Jevanjee, is it? Or what Nikki was up to? It's something you're hiding from me, isn't it? *That's* the key. Is it to do with leaving the Infirmary ten years ago? Why did it happen, Geoff? You were nearly a consultant, the peak of your

118

profession. What went wrong? Were you sacked for pinching nurses' bottoms or the canteen funds?'

His face sagged, the new confidence suddenly gone. 'I didn't try to kill myself the other day, you do believe that, don't you?'

'Yes, I do.' But in her heart she was not quite sure. 'John told me you said you'd been attacked.'

'I *was* attacked. They tried to kill me. In here. In *prison*.'

'*Who* tried to kill you?'

'I don't know. I truly don't, but they've been threatening me for months. I know it sounds crazy, but I'm not mad, Alison. I honestly don't know who – or why.'

'Don't insult my intelligence again, Geoff. People don't go round threatening you unless you know why – what's the point?'

'They must believe I know something damaging – and that I've shared it with you. They've tried to kill us both now.'

She took a deep breath. She wanted to strangle him. 'But they were unlucky and failed. OK – I'll buy it to be going on with, but I can't defend you on that basis. I need some *facts*.'

'I wish I had them.'

'So do I. Well, let's start with what we *do* know. How were these mysterious enemies threatening you, before you were arrested, I mean? With violence?

He shook his head. 'No.'

'Then with exposure?' He did not meet her eyes;

119

at last she was getting there. 'So you'd better tell me, hadn't you? After all, I'm the only one left on your side and you've come within a whisker of losing me, too.' She reached across the table and took his hand gently. 'Tell me, Geoff, it's not too late and it's the only way.'

12

It was raining in Acton High Street when she left the Magistrates' Court after the short committal of Isaac Madimjaba to the Crown Court. Poor fellow. She could understand how he must have felt when council officials and a bailiff turned up to evict him, his wife and two children from their tower block flat; but the level of injuries he had inflicted with a razor-sharp machete had been horrifying.

She had left her coat in the car, parked on a bomb-site half a mile away, so she dodged into the public library, an unwelcoming Victorian building that looked like a particularly ugly nonconformist chapel, to shelter until the shower stopped. She browsed in the reference section, looking herself up in last year's Bar List. One shelf had a long line of university handbooks and she took down the one for Cambridge. A fat, red book, it was full of lists of fellows, college by college, university departments and their staff, and at the back an alphabetical list of graduates going back to the year dot. No, they weren't all graduates – it was everyone who had been a student – with the date and class of their degree where they had lasted the course. Roberts, David Roberts. But disappointingly he was not there. She went through four whole pages of men and women called Roberts in case he was listed out of order, but no. Ah well, in a list that long they must make mistakes.

She forgot it and the cosy evenings continued, until one evening when they went to a party in Whitehall. It was an office farewell for a college friend who was leaving the Treasury for a job in Brussels, cheap plonk and crisps in an echoing conference room. A junior minister looked in for ten minutes. Afterwards they walked down King Charles Street toward Clive Steps and St James's Park. He gestured at the gates into the Foreign Office courtyard. 'Remember going there for my interviews – very intimidating.'

An alarm bell she did not want to hear rang in her head. Friends from Balliol had applied to the FCO and the civil service. Everyone knew you did the tests and interviews at a modern building belonging to the Civil Service Commission, who recruited everyone whatever their destination. It was at the top of Whitehall, near the theatre. It was supposed to guarantee recruitment without nepotism, departments not doing their own hiring for senior posts. But perhaps there were a few exceptions. She smiled, 'Were you going to be a spy or something – have you been holding out on me?'

'No, darling, just a boring old Third Secretary like all the rest.'

She had to know. She hesitated. She hesitated for a week. A fortnight. How on earth could she bring herself to check up on the man she loved? It wasn't civilised and it didn't matter anyway. But the truth was it did. The facts didn't matter, but she had to restore her trust. She felt devastated when she went to the Temple library and he wasn't in any of the green volumes of the Diplomatic List for the last ten years. He wasn't in the civil service handbooks either. She even foraged through old copies of The Times, which still published a list of those successful in the Foreign Office and Civil Service competitions every year. She studied them with a magnifying glass, but there was no David.

She raged at herself for doing it and somehow felt unclean. Then she raged some more for being taken in. She told herself again and again that he was still handsome, exciting, protective David. He was brilliant at what he did. Without this miasma of silly half-truths and distortions she would still love and respect him. But why, oh why, was everything he had told her about himself a lie? Perhaps he was an orphan, still covering up an empty childhood? Fancifully, she even wondered if he was a spook working for MI5 undercover: then laughed at herself. She knew the reality. She had wanted to entrust herself to a con man or inadequate who in some unfathomable way had invented a fantasy life because he could not face the man he really was. Perhaps he was suffering from real mental illness, though there was no other sign of it. Part of her felt compassion and concern. But there was also apprehension. What dark or terrible secret or fear lay behind it?

Half of her wanted to let it go. Dammit, she'd been naked in his arms often enough and he certainly hadn't felt inadequate then. He hadn't let her down in eight months. She did still want him. Why throw away something that was still working? But the truth was that it had all changed. She screwed up her courage to talk to him, late one evening when they were sitting in front of the fire over a bottle of Burgundy. She had tried to be gentle, understanding, almost flippant.

She regretted it at once. At first he was angry and aggressive, but then his body seemed to shrivel and laughing, warm, strong David had suddenly gone. He stared at her: white and gaunt, his eyes wide with shock and pain. 'I love you, Alison. I've never been so happy.' He didn't apologise or explain and his voice was distant, almost inaudible, lacking all fire. 'Sorry, I didn't mean ... I was going to ... please don't throw it all away.'

She took his hands in hers, stroking them tenderly. 'I love you, too, David, I'm not throwing anything away. Just tell me why, darling. I'm not judging or angry, but we can't have great barriers of secrets between us. You know all about me and I've loved sharing everything with you – my feelings, my fears and hopes, my body.' She laughed, but he did not respond. 'I care about you, David – I only want to understand and just at the moment I don't. I'm confused. Help me, darling.'

But he shook his head abruptly, said nothing: no explanation, no self-pity, no aggression. Eight months of intimacy and trust might never have existed. There was a strained silence, then he pushed her away and stalked out. When she heard the front door slam, she ran after him but the street was already empty. She ran back inside for her keys and drove round to the workshop, but it was locked up. She stayed there for half an hour, then drove back to the house, peering at the road through a mist of tears. She *had mishandled it completely, let him down when he needed her most. She left the front door open, certain that he would come back, and stayed up waiting; she wanted so much to hold and comfort him.*

In the end she fell asleep on the floor and woke up stiffly at about four. Wearily she pulled on her coat and went back to the car, driving shakily through empty streets back to the mews. Before they had met he had lived in a bedsit above the workshop, so maybe he had gone back there after pacing the streets. He must be lonely.

This time the door to the workshop was pulled to, but not locked. When she opened it, moonlight flooded in after her and she shivered in the cold draught. She did not need to put the light on to know that it was David hanging there from the beam, his feet swinging gently above the wood shavings on the floor.

Alison wanted to scream at the ghosts crowding in on her in the silence of the interview room, but dragged herself back to reality. Quinn continued to stare at her. She went on holding his hand. After several minutes, he said: 'This is just between you and me, right? You don't use it unless I agree?'

'OK. If I think it's all that will save you, we'll talk about it.'

'But I have a veto?'

'If that's how you want it.'

'Yes, it is. One reason I've held out on you is that at first I was sure I'd be convicted and get life anyway and I've a gut feeling that what I'm going to tell you wouldn't help. It might make it even worse.'

Alison stiffened, but tried to keep her voice neutral. 'Go on, Geoff.'

'In a nutshell, ten years ago I killed a patient,' he said flatly. 'I was negligent and incompetent and I covered it up with fraud and forgery. That's why I left the Infirmary. I was lucky not to end up in jail then, never mind now.'

There was another screaming silence. 'Go on,' she prompted again.

He sighed. 'It's not easy to face it, even now, even in here … but it wasn't long after Nikki and I married – and it wasn't in Bristol. I was earning a bit extra to pay the mortgage, doing shifts at a local hospital up in Gloucestershire. It's closed now. Should have been then, it was an old workhouse and in a disgusting state. But there were a lot of road accident cases and they kept the theatre going for those and other emergencies.'

The room felt very still, as if time and the footsteps and clatter of the prison all around had suddenly stopped.

'One weekend I was dead on my feet. I think I'd been awake for more than forty-eight hours and I should never have been allowed near a patient. Anyway, a vagrant came into casualty with severe stomach pains and it was obvious he had appendicitis. Said he was called Charlie Brown – not his real name, of course, he was living rough and they make up different identities to cock a snook at the authorities, interfering hospital clerks, the DSS, the wardens of night shelters. Anyway you know all that. So we operated on him within an hour and I got through it all right, even cracked a few jokes to keep the others awake then I went home and slept for twelve hours.'

'What went wrong?'

'They called me back next morning. He had a high temperature, a fever, and was in great pain. I sedated him and he died that afternoon. Then I remembered, suddenly and quite clearly. I'd left a swab inside when I sewed him up. It was full of blood and pus from the appendix, which was close to bursting, and must have infected the whole abdomen.' He gave a grim little smile. 'It was quite a shock.'

'What did you do?'

'I should have come clean.'

'What would have happened if you had?'

'Suspension, a disciplinary hearing. I'd probably have been sacked from the Infirmary, but maybe not struck off the register permanently. I just don't know – anyway, I didn't come clean. I panicked.'

'There must have been a post-mortem?'

'Yes, and correctly carried out by another part-timer. A pathologist from Birmingham on a one-week contract.'

'So how did you keep it quiet?'

'After the PM poor old Charlie was sewn up and the pathologist and I signed the certificates for a cremation. The sad old bugger had no relatives or anything, no one to ask any questions, no one to grieve. Later in the week there was a five-minute committal down at the crem, with just me and the duty priest, then straight into the oven. A worn-out sheet for a shroud and a chipboard coffin.' For a moment Alison's eyes clouded, Quinn's face was not in focus and she struggled to breathe as she remembered standing alone, silent but wanting to scream, before another coffin in a cold crematorium chapel.

There had been no mother in Whitstable. There seemed to be no family of any kind. Since she had found David's body, it was she who dialled 999. A police car and an ambulance arrived. The body was taken to the hospital in Fulham Palace Road and the two uniformed police drove back to Alison's house and took a statement. They were both young, a man and a woman, brisk and not over tactful when they realised she and David had been lovers.

When they drove off, she stayed at home all day, crying. When there were no tears left, she tried to occupy herself by doing the washing, then fell into an armchair and found herself racked with regret and guilt all over again. A policewoman arrived without warning and asked her to go to the hospital to identify David's body. Alison was unprepared and should have put it off, but got into the panda car like an automaton. When she got out she could hardly stand. She was expecting to go into the mortuary, with its walls of refrigerated stretcher cupboards and doors to the dissection rooms. But he was laid out in a small adjoining chapel, tightly wrapped up in sheets to conceal the hideous post-mortem incision she knew was there from his neck to his navel. His throat was badly bruised, his eyes were open and staring; he did not look peaceful. He did not look like anything much: the soul had gone, there was no life there, no David.

'Is that David Roberts?' The young police officer was equally uncomfortable and it came out in a rush. Alison nodded, holding back her tears; and the policewoman hugged her tightly. 'OK, love, sorry we have to do it like this. You're being very brave – would you like a little while on your own with him?'

Alison shook her head. 'No, I don't think so. I thought I would, but he isn't there, is he? There's nothing there, nothing left.'

The inquest was low-key, Alison and the police the only witnesses. The verdict was suicide and the coroner said he was very sorry, almost as if he meant it. There were local press reporters present and the story surfaced in small paragraphs in the nationals. Nothing too visible, but enough to go round the Bar in ten minutes. Her head of chambers was kind: 'Would you like a week or two off, Alison? You've had a dreadful shock and we all feel for you.' Like hell they did: most of them were sniggering behind her back at a story that was almost a classic music hall joke. The career girl seduced by a bum.

Why had he killed himself? Just like that? It made no sense, he had never seemed that unstable. She had mishandled it, threatened something deep inside him, a mistake she would regret for the rest of her life. She felt destroyed, as a woman and as a barrister. And David was still lying in the mortuary waiting for someone to bury him.

Every day brought new discoveries that made it worse.

He owned virtually nothing so the lack of a will did not matter. She obtained his birth certificate, which had only a mother's name, and wrote to her at the address given, in Derby. All it produced was a phone call saying that the woman had probably been a tenant when the house was let in flats up to about twenty years ago. The present owner had never heard of her. She put a couple of small ads in national papers, and several in the Whitstable/Canterbury area, but there was no response. In the end she arranged and paid for a simple cremation, having left it so long it had to be on Christmas Eve or wait until early January. She settled for Christmas Eve, standing alone at Mortlake crematorium while David trundled away through oak doors to the furnace.

Standing outside, still alone, she did not cry. A passer-by would have seen a young woman in black, turning purposefully towards the car-park, jaw set in a determined line, not looking back. She was going to start again. But back in her car, she could not hold back the tears. Had she killed him? Had she killed her own future? And who was he? Who the hell was he? Where had David really come from, what was he trying to escape? It was too hard to bear. The man she had most wanted in her body and her life was already ashes; and she would never know the truth.

13

She pulled herself together; Quinn was still speaking. 'That ended it – social services paid and the evidence was destroyed.'

With an effort, Alison focused on the implications of what he was saying. 'What about the PM report?'

'It was handwritten and left in a sealed envelope, with a covering letter addressed to the hospital secretary. I took a chance and nicked it from the out-tray in the dissection room. That night I simply typed a new report, identical with the original but not referring to the swab. The cause of death was the same – post-operative septicaemia. I forged the signature. It was taking a chance, but I felt quite calm about it. Next morning I simply added the report to the patient's notes and put the file away. I burnt the letter to the secretary pointing out the error. My error.'

'No one found out? What about the pathologist?'

'He never came back. Never asked what happened. He was from Pakistan on a training programme and I hoped he wouldn't be making a career here. I left the notes filed for a month just in case any questions were asked, then one weekend

I removed them, took them home and burnt them. After that I felt pretty safe.'

'No one else knew?'

'No one in the theatre ever said they had noticed me leave the swab in. There must have been a technician about when the PM was done, but he wouldn't necessarily have seen or been told anything. The records had gone and that was what mattered. But I thought if I stayed in the same place there might be gossip; the man had *died*, after all, and it was just possible that some relative might appear. My confidence was destroyed and I didn't trust myself in the theatre any more, so I decided to give up surgery and go to Avonmouth.'

'So that was the end of the story?'

Quinn shook his head with that bitter smile. 'Not quite, Alison. It came back to haunt me two years later, after the Jevanjee murder.'

'What happened?'

'Well, you know how I was called out by Ahmed Jevanjee's girlfriend?'

'Yes.'

'So that wasn't in the script for Jevanjee's killing. He and the girl were both supposed to be left dead. I was an intruder and the following morning I was driving through Avonmouth when my car was flagged down. Two blokes in suits, silk ties, very respectable. We drove to a quiet spot and talked. They weren't particularly threatening and, when they asked me, I told them what I'd seen – after all, I was going to tell the police and put it on public record.'

'Were they Pakistani or Cypriot?'

'Neither so far as I could tell.'

'And?'

'And they told me I'd be paid ten grand if I testified that I'd seen Boniface leaving the scene in the white Mercedes. I told them to go to hell – I knew the background and I *assumed* he was responsible, but he wasn't in that car.'

'How can you be so sure?'

'The streetlights were out, but my headlights raked across the Merc long enough to see the faces of the men inside, all three of them.'

'Three? I thought it was supposed to be four?'

'It was.'

'But Boniface could have driven away earlier on his own?'

'Maybe, but he wasn't leaving in that car just after the murder.'

Another thought occurred to her. 'But why did they need *you*? Didn't the girl testify?'

Quinn shook his head. 'Maybe they were leaning on her, too, but after the murder she had a complete breakdown, a total loss of memory about that evening. By the time of the trial she was sectioned in a psychiatric hospital. She couldn't have been a credible witness.'

'Didn't they threaten you at all?'

'No. They left politely. But a week later there was a brown foolscap envelope waiting for me at the surgery marked Personal & Confidential. Fortunately my secretary hadn't opened it – it was a photocopy of the original post-mortem report, the handwritten one. The fellow must have kept a copy that I'd never known about. God knows why – and I can't imagine how it had got into other hands.'

Alison was asking herself the same question. 'I think *I* can. If he wanted to stay in this country, he probably just kept it as an insurance – something he might use to hold over a potential consultant surgeon if he ever needed a job ... '

'But it was the Jevanjees who blackmailed me.'

'I'm sure news travels in the Pakistani community, particularly among professionals – doctors, lawyers – and it wouldn't be surprising if one of the family heard some gossip and remembered it later, after the murder. They probably used the grapevine to find the pathologist and bought it. He might even have been a relative.'

Quinn nodded. 'The phone calls started that night.'

'Threats?'

'Too true. Calls late at night, always the same voice, cultivated but phoney.'

'Man or woman?'

'A man. He just repeated the message. Ten grand for fingering Boniface, ruin if I didn't.'

'Why didn't you tell the police?'

'For Christ's sake, Alison, what *I'd* done was criminal too. I just sensed they'd thank me warmly and others would see I was struck off and prosecuted. I was a coward, frankly, and a crook.'

'So you gave in?'

'Absolutely. Testified and became a local hero overnight.'

'You had no qualms about sending an innocent man down for life?'

'Don't be absurd. Of course I had qualms, but he was no innocent. He may not have killed Jevanjee – but I'm sure he ordered it and he'd got away with at least a dozen others. He *needed* to be locked up.'

'And they paid you?'

'Yes, ten thousand in used notes. I gave it away anonymously – to the NSPCC and various charities for sick children.'

Alison smiled and stopped writing. 'I'm glad you did that. Then there was silence for eight years?'

'Until six months ago.'

He hesitated and she prompted him. 'What happened?'

'Another brown envelope.'

'Where?'

'At home.'

'Containing?'

'Another photocopy of the PM report; and one of a bank document covering the drawing of ten thousand pounds in large denomination notes.'

'No message?'

'No.'

'Phone calls?'

'No. Nothing. It was uncanny, unnerving. I suppose someone thought it was a threat I would understand – but I had no idea what it was about.'

'You must have had *some* idea?'

'Well, I thought it had to be to do with Nikki. By then I was certain she was up to something, had been for months – out a lot in the evening, sometimes away all night, coming back looking like the cat that's been at the cream. I challenged her outright but she just laughed at me. Told me I was boring, the marriage was over and she'd get a divorce and take me to the cleaners when she was ready. Meanwhile her life was her own. I didn't know what to do.'

'Why didn't you follow her? Use a private dick?'

He stared at her in disbelief. 'I *did* try to follow her once, but I lost her in the traffic down near Floating Harbour. I'm afraid it never occurred to me that civilised people could put private eyes on each other, it just wasn't my style.'

'You'd be surprised how many do … anyway, go on.'

'She was hiding something – I suppose it had to be an affair – but by the time I received the photocopies in the post, there was something else. She was still laughing at me, contemptuous, but she was also *scared*.'

'Of whom? Or what?'

'I don't *know*.' Quinn slumped on the table with his head in his hands and there was a long pause. Alison knew he was weeping. 'Then the late night phone calls started. If I answered, there was silence and whoever it was hung up. When Nikki got them she talked too fast and in a whisper, didn't want me to hear. Someone was threatening her, I'm sure of it.

136

But she wouldn't tell me anything.'

'Why did they send you the copies?'

'I guess they thought Nikki had confided in me, that I knew, so they threatened me too.'

'But you *didn't* know?' He shook his head miserably. 'Didn't you try to talk to her, ask her what was going on, offer to help? Ask if it involved you in some way?'

'I did all that. I asked her if she was having an affair, if she was being threatened. She still just laughed at me. I think that showing she thought I was useless, irrelevant, no longer her man, was the only pleasure she got, kept her going in some twisted way.'

'And you *accepted* that? Didn't you shout and scream, hammer her to come clean?'

'Yes. It made no difference.'

Alison met his eyes very directly. 'Is that *all*, Geoff? You've not missed anything out?'

'No, that's absolutely everything I know. In the last year Nikki was up to something that made somebody really scared, scared enough to kill her. I was too weak to find out what it was before she was dead; I was a wimp and now it's too bloody late.'

It was dark now. A few miles away the houses and cottages in Pill were lighting up. Once Pill had been a village by the mudflats of the Avon, just inland from the sea. Now the M5 bridge soared high above it on thin steel supports like a gigantic grasshopper, the headlamps of cars and juggernauts creating a

137

continuous band of white light arcing in the blackness of the sky.

The police car was drawn up outside a row of council houses that vibrated with the constant roar of traffic overhead. Some children had found the body, trapped in wooden piles under a jetty that ran out across the mud to the river. A solitary policewoman knelt on its edge, reaching down to grip the naked shoulder. She shuddered when she touched it; in her flashlight the flesh was grey-blue and it felt loose, squashy. The abdomen was swollen and smelt horrible, like rotted fish. As she lay flat and peered right underneath she saw that it was a woman. She wondered how long the body had been stuck there, then threw up when she saw that both the head and hands had been cut off.

14

For the first time since she had taken Quinn's case, Alison woke with a clear sense of where they were going. Frustratingly, she also had two days of routine cases, all outside Bristol. She had hired a Rover after her car was destroyed, hoping her insurers would meet the claim before she had to buy a replacement, and now she hit the road to Taunton and then on to Exeter and Truro. The gentle gay schoolmaster in the next flat would feed Hamish. Although she was keen to work through what she now knew, in some ways it was a relief to get right away from the impossible problems of Geoffrey Quinn, not to mention George Kristianssen.

After leaving Marychurch last night, she had spent an hour with George planning his surveillance and enquiries. Then he had taken her out to dinner at one of her favourite restaurants, Muset, in Clifton. It had been a delicious meal, spoilt because he had been drinking heavily before he picked her up at the flat. Usually, she enjoyed the feeling of getting slightly tipsy together, the sensation of warmth and intimacy, collapsing into bed afterwards, laughing then sighing when he touched her, for despite her Presbyterian background Alison had always been electrified by the delicious closeness of skin on skin, the startled wonder she still felt when he entered her.

She really needed him. To reassure her as a woman, to share the breakthrough with Quinn – rapidly becoming the case that could make or break the career she had pursued for ten years – to abandon her body shamelessly to a man she loved and admired. George had swept her into protective arms and given back her confidence and self-respect when she clung to him after David. But last night he had just been pissed, breathing beer fumes over her before she had taken even a sip of wine, grinning inanely, knocking over glasses – glassy-eyed George, so kind, but sometimes so bloody unreliable.

George was sitting at the desk in his scruffy office. It was reached by a staircase from the street, marked by a brass plate:

GK ASSOCIATES
PRIVATE INVESTIGATIONS & SECURITY

Liz, his secretary/receptionist and the two investigators he employed shared the long room that looked over the street. George's cubby-hole was separated from them by a plywood and glass partition.

His hangover was starting to lift and he had a

mournful look, like a dog who has been kicked. One day he would push her too far, perhaps he already had, and she was too precious to lose. He didn't even know where she was staying for the next two nights, so he could not phone and apologise. Anyway, there was Quinn. He looked at the two figures nattering over Gold Blend the other side of the glass. Joan, who had left the Wrens as a petty officer when she was thirty and now found violent abuse on doorsteps relaxing after two years teaching in one of the city's tougher comprehensives; and Pete, fifty, balding and retired from the police. He had dumped a pile of divorce and insurance fraud on them yesterday, but maybe they could fit something else in. He wanted to have done *something* before Alison came back.

But Joan and Pete stonewalled firmly and in the end it was George who went door-stepping in Abbots Leigh that afternoon. He knocked on fifteen doors and learnt nothing useful at all.

Next morning he tried again. God, it was a miserable place – it always seemed to be raining and he was soaked before he had completed six houses. When the deluge stopped, water went on dripping miserably from the branches of the trees and the peak of his flat cap. Passing the small church, St Mary the Virgin, a dull flint and red-brick building with a pretty steeple, he turned in and sheltered in the porch for ten minutes to dry off.

Then on to the next, this time in the imitation

country lane where Quinn had lived. The door was opened by a man in his eighties, wearing a ragged cardigan and carpet slippers. George showed his card. 'Good morning, sir. I am a private investigator working for the lawyers defending your neighbour, Dr Quinn.'

'My daughter's out. You better come back later.' The old man spoke very loudly, as often with the recently deaf. George tried again, but it was hopeless; the man could not hear a word he was saying. 'You a Jehovah's Witness or canvassing for the Lib Dems?' he roared. 'I'm a Tory atheist!' George gave up and retreated down the path. The old boy cackled triumphantly.

Ten minutes later, after trudging up the path to two front doors that nobody answered, he approached a large Edwardian house, set back behind a high hedge and next door to Quinn's. The door was opened by the brisk woman whom Alison had met: the one with a yellow Labrador called Oscar. 'Yes?'

'I am a private investigator,' he explained yet again. 'I'm working for the lawyers defending Dr Quinn, who lived next door to you and is charged with murder. I wonder if I might ask you some questions?'

'What sort of questions?'

'Well, for example, it would help us to know what you may have seen at the time of the alleged murder?' She stared at him unhelpfully and did not reply. 'Were you *here* then, between the fifth and ninth of September?'

'We've already had the police round, you know.' She had a sharp, dismissive way of speaking; he guessed she was always trying to put people down. But she had beautiful skin, clear blue eyes and good auburn hair. As a young woman she must have been a stunner and she was still very pretty. 'Do you have any *right* to ask these questions?'

'Certainly I do, ma'am. But you have the right not to answer.'

'Hmm, well we – my husband and I – were at home on the dates you mentioned. We went out from time to time, of course. He went to his office, I went shopping.'

She made to close the door but George held it firmly. 'Did you know Dr and Mrs Quinn?'

'Not really. People keep themselves to themselves in Abbots Leigh, you know.'

Yes, George's aching feet and empty notebook knew. 'But you saw them coming and going, knew what they looked like?'

'Of course.'

'Could I possibly come in for ten minutes, Mrs … ?'

'Sayers. Rebecca Sayers. Yes, if you must.' She led him into a neat drawing-room, Victorian antiques, some good pictures. 'I can't spare you long.'

'Thank you so much.' George settled awkwardly on the edge of a spindly upright chair. He rolled up his sodden cap and held it in his lap. 'I'd be most grateful if you could think back to those five days and try to recall every movement you saw at the

143

Quinn's house. Every person or vehicle that called there, every person or vehicle that left. Shall we start on the fifth?'

'I shan't be able to help you much, you know, and I've told the police everything I know. I *think* I saw him leave in his car about eight in the morning. Then she took the children to school in their other car at about eight forty-five. I was out for the rest of the day, I'm afraid, and came back after dark.'

'What sort of car did he drive?'

'One of the smaller Peugeots, I think. She had a Volkswagen Golf.'

'And what about the sixth of September?'

'Same routine in the morning, so far as I recall. I don't think anyone came or went at the house after they'd left in the morning and I don't remember her coming back, but I went to visit some friends in the afternoon and was back very late in the evening.'

'OK. The next day was Saturday, wasn't it?'

'If you say so. Shall I get my diary to check?'

'That would be helpful.'

She rummaged among papers on an old roll-top bureau, then went out into the hallway. 'It must be in the kitchen.' George stood as if to stretch his legs and glanced sideways at the bureau, but she was back almost immediately. 'Yes, it was Saturday. Arthur and I came and went at different times, but I don't recall seeing anything at the Quinns'. In fact, I don't recall seeing anything more there until the Monday, when the police arrived.'

'Thank you, Mrs Sayers, you have been most helpful.' George returned to the hall and pulled on his raincoat. 'By the way, did you ever actually *meet* Dr or Mrs Quinn?'

'We passed the time of day. Apart from that no, never.'

'Thank you.' He walked slowly back to the road and along between the green banks and dark trees to the next gate in a high fence. The whole area was so smart he felt desperately out of place. But Rebecca Sayers knew what sort of car Nikki drove, the exact model. And he was certain that the coloured snapshot, half-hidden by a letter from a bank on her bureau, showed Nikki Quinn laughing at some kind of party. Strange, to have a photograph of someone you said you barely knew.

The last house was the posh one, with a high wall and covering swimming pool at the back. The door was opened by a woman in a blue overall, some kind of servant. 'May I help you, sir?'

'Yes, my dear,' boomed George. 'Whose house is this?'

'Mr Alan Mar's, sir.'

'Would you give Mr Mar my card and ask if he could spare me a few minutes?'

'Certainly, sir. Please come in and wait.' George stepped on to the white carpet of a square entrance hall. There was a lot of money in this house. Mar? It rang a bell. Then he appeared, a handsome, square man, about forty, with neat, dark hair. George recognised him: a well-known local businessman who owned a small chain of supermarkets, news-papers and the local radio station.

'Alan Mar.' He held out his hand with a friendly smile. He had a Scots accent. 'How may I help you?'

When George explained, Mar led him back into a large room furnished as an office, looking out over the swimming pool. 'I'll be glad to help in any way I can, Mr Kristianssen.' He gestured George to a modern armchair in black leather and sat down behind the desk. 'To be honest, I've been hoping to God that someone would contact me. I knew Geoff Quinn, a good bloke, and I'm damn sure he isn't a murderer. That's what I told the police too, but the bastards didn't want to know.'

George smiled and relaxed. Maybe he was finally getting somewhere.

15

'Do you find the defendant, Joyce Skinner, guilty or not guilty as charged?'

The foreman of the jury was a farmer, red in the face and sweating in his tweed suit. 'Not guilty, sir.'

Alison breathed a sigh of relief and smiled at the woman in the dock: about her own age, hard-faced and brassy. She was guilty as hell, and Alison knew it, but she had put up a strong defence, sowing doubt and confusion in the minds of the jury, eight men and four women – none too bright, for so many professional people avoided jury service these days.

The judge was telling Mrs Skinner she was discharged and, with a wry grin, Alison wondered whether the county council would take her back to do it all over again. Two years of well-concealed fiddling, stashing away over ten thousand pounds. She was suspended, but it would be difficult for them to fire her now she was officially innocent. Alison crossed the well of the court to shake hands with her client and wish her well, aware that she had impressed the judge and her fellow barristers:

they would admire her professionalism rather than resent her unjust victory.

She left without stopping to chat to anyone else, tossing her gown into its bluebag and hurrying down the steps in front of Truro's modern, white court building. She had done the job, now she wanted to be alone, away from the distractions of the bar mess where the others would dine that evening.

Two or three hours later Alison drove out of the city, along by the Truro River, the few miles to Malpas. Here the water met another creek coming down from Tresillian, and she stopped the car on the high promontory between them. It was dusk and lights were on in the small pub as she struck out, along by the mudflats towards St Clement.

She wished Geoffrey Quinn had not come into her life. It wasn't so much the confusion of the case, though that was infuriating, but that somehow it was forcing her to ask unwelcome questions. Was she really going to spend the rest of her life as a small-time barrister in Bristol? What on earth was she going to do about George? He was a kind and decent man, terrific to sleep with. It was *waking up* that was the problem. She couldn't be totally intimate, totally free, with a man who had to conceal his real nature with all that phoney *bonhomie*. He could be so wise and understanding and gentle, then blow it all by getting hopelessly drunk at just the wrong moment. When other, conventionally civilised men like John Forbes came into her life and obviously appreciated her as a woman, she had to face her doubts. She needed someone *predictable*.

At St Clement it was almost dark, but she could still see the fishing boats lying on their sides on the mud. Yellow lights gleamed in the cottages that stood around the tiny inlet, but outside no one was about. A solitary cat strolled by and there was a smell of woodsmoke. Beyond the mudflats the river was too far away for the water to be heard; she felt cocooned in darkness and silence; still, calm despite the turmoil in her mind. Was that it? Did she have to be alone to cope?

She started to walk back, picking her way through the trees by the white beam of the small torch she had brought from the car, the collar of her Barbour turned up against the cold. She was so confused. Why did she feel such a powerful need for a man in her life? Tonight she would sleep in her hotel alone, but she knew she would sleep more easily if there were strong arms around her.

In Bristol, the bearded man in the flat cap parked outside his block of flats in Redland and ran up the concrete stairs to the first floor. It was a smaller place than Alison's, furnished simply, a little like the ships' cabins that had once been his home. After the ballistic row, he was cold sober and determined to give her the makings of a case to acquit Quinn.

He had visited nearly every house in Abbots

Leigh and learnt almost nothing. Most of their occupants had said they knew nothing of the Quinns. Alan Mar might be helpful, Rebecca Sayers had lied to him. That was the only lead he had. And a gossamer thin one at that … By dropping everything else, he could watch Sayers for a few days, no more. It needed twelve people working three eight-hour shifts but he could make do with eight in two shifts. He had only Pete and Joan in the office, but he knew where to find others. It would cost an arm and a leg and he might never get paid, but if he succeeded it would be worth it. He poured a can of lager and settled down in the old leather armchair beside the phone for a long session with his address book.

At five next morning, he was back in Abbots Leigh. Most of the houses were in darkness, well-concealed behind their fences and hedges. He and the first team of four watchers sat in the back of the Transit, in a lane near the church, their faces lit from below by the blue glow from an electric lantern on the floor. Each had a short-wave radio concealed inside their outer coat. 'There's only one way out of her house – the front gate. All the boundaries butt onto other properties, with good fences. I don't see her creeping out the back. So Pete and Joan will watch the gate, one each side, in their cars. Joan with Dougal and Alice with Pete. Everything here is hidden behind hedges so no one's going to notice you. As I've spent two days and a lot of bloody shoe leather finding out, they keep themselves to themselves in Abbots Leigh.'

'What do we do if she leaves?' Dougal was about thirty, thin-faced, wearing a donkey jacket. 'Christ!' He started to cough; the dog had just farted. George had found Dougal working for a private security firm after ten years in the Paras, half of them on loan to the SAS. He was street-wise and intelligent.

George stroked the dog and it went to sleep again, stretched on the steel floor. 'You follow her, cretin. If she leaves on foot, two of you walk – one in front and one behind, keep in touch by using your radios. The others follow in their car. If she leaves by car, you all go with her. You know how to work. I want to know everywhere she goes and, so far as you can do it, everyone she meets. Anyone she talks to that you can see – in the open or through a window – I want a photograph. You all have cameras and Joan's got the camcorder.'

George left them spread out in the steady rain and drove back to Redland. He had been up all night and took a shower before crawling into bed. It felt very empty. Only a few nights ago Alison had been there, asleep in the few minutes it had taken him to lock the front door and turn out the lights in the flat. Her back had been towards him and her legs drawn up, pushing her bottom back against his groin; she felt soft and warm. She had sighed and stirred when he kissed her sleeping neck and put his arms round her, one hand gently caressing her breasts, but she did not wake and within minutes he too had been asleep.

Tonight it was different. The bed felt cold and empty. He could not lose consciousness and lay awake with his thoughts, black and troubled. It was dawn before he finally drifted off.

16

Alison got back from Cornwall shortly before midnight, so tired that she went to bed without opening the heap of mail on her doormat. In the morning she found that it included a neatly typed report from George, concentrating on Mar and Sayers, with a handwritten PS of abject apology and asking her to meet him for dinner that night. The report was possibly useful, but the steel had entered her soul so far as George was concerned. For all his good points he was an oaf and she had had enough.

Mar sounded interesting and she would have liked to see him straight away, but could not get him on the phone until the afternoon, when she arranged to call at his house at six. She did not want to see George again yet, so she crossed the gorge alone, driving impatiently behind a rusty van. She always found Brunel's suspension bridge dramatic, its narrow roadway dangling between the two rock faces, the plunging drop to the river frighteningly far below. The bridge moved in the wind and crossing it felt almost like flying.

Before setting out, she had phoned John Forbes.

'Hi. What do you know about Alan Mar?'

'Mar? If it's the one from across the gorge you're thinking of, he's well off. Positively loaded. Came south from the Arctic like you, as a young man, and he's been here ever since. Made a modest fortune from supermarkets and local papers. He was married to Lucy King.'

'The Quaker heiress? Tobacco? Chocolate?'

'Just so – I think he worked for her father at one time. She died about a year ago – they'd only been married a few years, skiing accident I think – and I suppose he inherited a few bob. But as far as I know he just lives alone and works bloody hard. No exciting vices. Well-respected in the business community, gives a little to the city charities, but definitely his own man, bit of a loner.'

Mar opened the front door himself. The swimming pool was lit by spotlights under its perspex canopy and she could smell the chlorine through the double doors in Mar's study. The wall at the end of the pool was covered by a gnarled vine on which she could see black grapes. It was all very *Homes & Gardens*.

They sat by the pool, Alison with a malt whisky. 'Glad to see my fellow Scot appreciates the malt.' Mar poured himself one, too. 'So, how can I help you to help Geoff?' Instinctively she felt a little wary. He seemed to be playing a part – because he didn't know how to handle the situation or because he had something to hide?

'How well did you know Dr and Mrs Quinn?'

She was aware that he was examining her legs with approval.

'Not well.' He shrugged. 'They were neighbours. I give the odd party here and they would come over sometimes. Their children came and used the pool with their friends.'

'Did Nikki and Geoff come with them?'

'Sometimes he brought them, sometimes she did. They seemed a pleasant family – and the kids were great. Jess was a pretty girl and becoming a powerful swimmer, very physical and confident. Tom was pretty good, too. They were both well brought up, polite to grown-ups, but full of life and go.' He smiled; perhaps she was too wary – he *did* have a reassuringly straightforward look about him and she felt that he was not lying.

'You told George you were here from the fifth to the ninth of last month, when it all happened?'

'I was. I wasn't watching with a telescope, mark you, but I was around.'

Alison was trying to place his accent – it seemed to be a mixture of Edinburgh and soft Highlands. 'I've got George's notes here,' she said. 'The last time you saw either Geoff or Nikki Quinn was on the Friday.'

'I saw them both leave in the morning. I didn't actually see either of them come back. In the evening I believe I saw a car there when I came home from a trip to Birmingham – about eight in the evening – and I *think* it was his Peugeot. Shortly afterwards, I was upstairs in my bedroom, which is at the front of the house, and I noticed the car drive away. I never saw either of them again before Monday, when the police arrived.'

'Do you know *why* the police came?'

'I believe one of the other neighbours saw smoke pouring out of the chimney while milk was piling up on the doorstep and thought there was something odd about it.'

'Yes, that's more or less what I've been told. George says you thought you saw a van at the house over the weekend?'

'I've been thinking about it, and I'm not a hundred per cent sure any more – maybe it was some other time. But, yes, I *believe* I saw a blue Luton van there on the Saturday morning.'

'You don't remember if there was anything written on its side – or even the registration number, do you?'

'I recall it as plain dark blue. ' He smiled. 'But, I'm afraid I didn't even see the registration number, let alone note it.'

Alison went on probing for ten minutes, then steered things round to the Quinns. 'How well did you know my client?'

'I told you – just as a neighbour. But I've been here five years, so I'd say I knew him moderately well.'

'You told George you couldn't see him as a murderer? Why?'

'I told George, Miss Hope, that he *isn't* a murderer. I'm sure of it.'

'No one else seems to be, least of all the police.'

Alan Mar poured more malt. 'You just get feelings about people, don't you. He was a decent, level-headed sort of bloke. Cared for his wife and family – there was nothing *violent* about him. A very gentle sort of man. I suppose that's the key. I simply can't imagine him harming anyone.'

'Could it have been an accident – he pushed her, she fell and injured her neck, he panicked?'

'But why should he panic? He wasn't that kind of fellow. I can't even imagine him pushing her, let alone hitting her. But if he did and it went wrong, why not just call an ambulance and say it was an accident?'

'Yes, why not? When we go to trial, would you be prepared to give evidence of what you saw, and of Geoff's character?'

'Gladly. I'm sure he's innocent and I'll do anything I can to help. I wish I could do more.'

Again she felt wary: it came out too pat, but she managed to conceal her suspicion. 'Do you know you're the only person in the whole of Abbots Leigh who's said that, Mr Mar? No one else saw anything or admits to really knowing either of them. I find that strange.'

'Ah, well, they do keep themselves to themselves in Abbots Leigh, you know.' He smiled. 'Snobby lot, but it suits me – I see enough people in the rest of my life and this is a kind of retreat. What you say doesn't surprise me – but the indifference of the police does, you know. I told some bobby who appeared on the doorstep what I just told you, but no one ever came near me again. I haven't been asked to make any sort of statement. I'd been wondering what to do when your man George appeared. Are the police so sure Quinn's guilty, or is someone paying them?'

'I don't know yet, but I'm damn well going to find out. But, tell me, you said he cared for his family. I'm sure he did, but how well did he and Nikki get on?'

Mar did not reply at once, studying the rippling blue water of the pool. Alison wondered if it would be unprofessional to bring her swimsuit next time. 'How do you know what goes on in any marriage, Miss Hope, if you're on the outside? Seemed OK to me when I saw them together, but at the end of the day, I honestly wouldn't know.'

Later that evening George, too, was in Abbots Leigh, crouched by the wall of the churchyard, looking across the road at Rebecca Sayers's house. It was nearly eleven and dark; his watchers were sitting more comfortably in two parked cars, one a hundred yards past the house, the other close to the corner where it joined another road looking out across to the lights of the city. When he had bought the short-wave radios from an army surplus warehouse, he had also acquired three state-of-the-art individual weapon scopes – night sights for sniper rifles. He had one trained on the Sayers's windows, like an eighteen-inch telescope, and the light filters gave a green and black image that was remarkably clear. Mrs Sayers had been followed for forty-eight hours, during which she had gone shopping, visited other middle-aged ladies, called at the library and spent a lot of time in her garden weeding. Now she was going to bed, apparently in a separate room from her husband, for there were two bedroom lights burning. She was in the bathroom, where the curtains were only half drawn and he could see her drawing a quilted dressing-gown over sharp shoulder blades. When all the lights went out, he sighed and rubbed the cramp in his left leg. Perhaps Rebecca Sayers was a waste of time.

The surveillance would continue all night and on into the morning, with a change of shift at six. They knew what they were doing, so George left them to it; they would call him on his mobile if anything happened. He decided to use the time to try something else.

He had known Eli Friedmann for a long time and was always welcome in the neat workroom behind his shop in the city centre. It glittered with expensive jewellery and silver. Not bad for a fellow who had left Budapest as a student in 1956, fleeing Russian vengeance after the Hungarian Rising, and arrived in Whitechapel as a penniless refugee. But Hungarians were survivors, Hungarian Jews mega-survivors; and his work as a silversmith and fence had paid him well for more than thirty years.

They sat at the high velvet-covered table, sipping strong Turkish coffee. Friedmann was a short, stocky man with a prominent nose and tufts of white hair to each side of his bald head. 'How it goin', George, you OK?'

'Fine, thanks. Busy, you know how it is.'

'Yeah, I know. I got a lot on, too. That's why I work late tonight. This a social call, George, or you need somethin'?' He shifted on his stool, the impeccable dark suit and grey tie radiating an aura of respectability.

George grinned wryly. 'Is it so obvious? Yes, I do – you hear things I don't.'

'Sure, I got a few contacts.' It was an understatement; Friedmann knew every corner of the Bristol underworld but he was also a prominent Freemason and close to several senior police officers. Perhaps that was why he had never been in trouble with the law. He gave an expressive Mittel European shrug. 'So what else friends for?'

George took a risk and told him the whole story – the murder, Quinn, the Jevanjee killing eight years ago, Carswell, Rebecca Sayers. Friedmann listened in silence, his face thoughtful in the glow from a green shaded lamp on the worktop, the rest of the windowless room in darkness. He offered George a cigar, bit the end off another and lit it for himself. 'I don't know none of these people, George – except Jevanjee of course. He's bad news.'

'In what way?'

'The filth got their eye on him. Never any evidence, only rumour. They say he's into hard drugs – and maybe arms.'

'Tell me, Eli.'

'I don't know no detail, George.' Friedmann rubbed the side of his nose meaningfully with his right forefinger. 'Just don't smell right, know what I mean? They says he handles consignments of arms – from Cardoens in Chile, Switzerland, Sweden. Containers probably never touch the UK but end up in the Middle East. May even be legal, for all I know, but Special Branch don't seem to think so.' He pulled on his cigar. 'Maybe it's all just talk.'

'Maybe I need to know more about Jevanjee, Eli, can you ask around?'

'Sure, but the police ain't fools, George. If they can't pin nothin' on him, I don' reckon you do no better. How about that girl of yours, George? You want somethin' for her? I got some perfect black jade, small stone on gold chain make fine pendant, real touch of class.' He winked. 'Special price for my good friend.'

Alison and Forbes went to see Quinn again the following afternoon. With pleading eyes he asked about the children, as he always did. She told him that she had put a team of investigators on the case, but there was no news yet, then steered the discussion round to Alan Mar and Rebecca Sayers. Quinn agreed that he and Nikki had occasionally socialised with Mar, but said he knew very little about him. They knew Rebecca Sayers because she lived next door, but had never been invited into her house, nor had they asked the Sayers to theirs.

'Nikki may have known her a bit because she was there all day.'

'George thought he saw a photo of Nikki on Mrs Sayers's bureau.'

'Did he? How odd. Perhaps they sometimes got together when I was working, but I don't recall Nikki ever mentioning that.'

'George thought she might be concealing something?'

'I can't imagine what.'

She had picked up his feeling of hopelessness and depression by the time she left the prison. Back at the flat she poured herself a gin and tonic and sat looking out over the garden, stroking Hamish who had woken up long enough to jump up on her lap. He purred and stared up at her through yellow eyes, looking smug. 'Good cat,' she muttered. 'Loyal cat, don't know what I'd do without you, scumbag.' And it was true. Hamish was always there, calm and contented, uncomplicated, undemanding and reassuring. He needed her and she needed him. The rest was all so bloody hopeless. She felt like slitting her throat. When the phone rang she almost ignored it. It would be George and she was not ready for him yet, that part of her mind was still in turmoil.

But maybe it was the jail again, maybe Quinn really had topped himself this time. Maybe the police had found her car bomber. Maybe … She picked up the receiver. 'Alison Hope.'

The soft Scots voice was a shock. 'It's Alan Mar,

162

I'd like to talk to you again, I've been thinking.'

She recovered quickly. 'Of course, let's get together. How about tomorrow?'

He paused as if considering. 'Actually, I'm a wee bit tied up tomorrow, Alison, but could we mix business with pleasure? I know it's short notice, but are you doing anything for dinner tonight?'

She hesitated. She should not be seen with Mar if he was to be a witness, she could be accused of coaching him, but she also felt a surge of curiosity. Was he genuine or out to deceive her? Be careful of those ice-blue eyes, she told herself sharply, but there was only one way to find out – and at least it would save her cooking. 'No, I've only just got in. What do you suggest?'

'May I pick you up, say in half an hour?'

17

Alison groaned when the doorbell rang at eight next morning. It had been a good dinner, at a discreetly chosen restaurant well out of the city, and Mar had stayed, chatting over a bottle of malt, until two in the morning, leaving her with a feeling that maybe he was genuine after all. She groaned again when she saw who was on the step. 'Good God, George, d'you know what time it is?'

'Time you was at work, love. Can't I come in?'

Alison yawned. 'I suppose so, if you must.'

He followed her into the kitchen. 'You all right, Ally?'

'Fine, hope you are too.' Christ, that flat cap and anorak were irritating. 'Look, George, I had a late night and I've got to be in court at ten. What do you want?'

In among the whiskers of his great beard, he looked hurt. Inside, he felt angry. 'You asked me to work on the Quinn case, remember?'

'Yes, of course.' In fact, she had almost forgotten, despite the meticulous report he had left.

'I sent you a report, Ally. Now I've got something else.' He took an envelope from his pocket and spread a series of black and white photographs on the kitchen table, like a deck of cards. She picked up one of them and met his eyes, puzzled. It showed two women on a bed, naked, obviously making love. It had been taken from an awkward angle: one woman's face could be seen, pretty though not young, the other had her back to the camera, but she plainly had a good body, long curving back, even longer slim legs.

'Just who *are* these people, George?'

'The woman whose face you can see is Rebecca Sayers, one of Quinn's neighbours. She told me she had never met Quinn's dead wife, but I know she was lying so we've had her under surveillance. It's mostly in the report, but Dougal got these last night – almost broke his neck up a tree in the garden of a place out in Westbury. He'd followed her to some kind of party, got the shots by chance, bloody lucky: she just happened to be in a room with open curtains and he had his camera with a night filter.'

'George, I don't *believe* it – have you really woken me up at this time of the morning just to show me dirty pics of a couple of dykes on the job?' Immediately she knew she was being unfair. 'Sorry, I know you think she's concealing something, and you might be right. We've precious little else to go on, but I thought Nikki was a little raver, not a lesbian.'

'I don't trust Sayers. She knows a lot more than she's saying. If I confront her with this, maybe I can crack it.'

'Confront her? That's dangerous.' She poured boiling water into a coffee pot. 'Supposing you're wrong? You could bloody well get me disbarred.'

'Can I *do* it, Ally?'

'I don't know. You'd better talk to Alan Mar first.'

'Mar?'

'Yes, we had a chat yesterday. He knows quite a lot and a reporter on one of his papers has some material that might just fit with all this. I didn't trust him at first but his stuff's so useful that now I'm prepared to risk it. I think he's straight.'

George looked disapproving and seemed about to say something but stopped and shrugged. 'OK, love.' He hesitated. 'You doing anything tonight?'

She hesitated, too. 'Yes, George, I'm afraid I am.'

Mar's office was on a trading estate on the southern fringe of the city. It was a large, modern room in a three-storey block, overlooking two long buildings with flat roofs, running down to a canal. One was a warehouse for his chain of supermarkets, the other housed the reporters and presses of several local newspapers. Standing by the window in his shirt-sleeves and bright red braces, he waved George to an armchair. Mar's secretary, a motherly woman in her fifties, came in with a tray of coffee. 'You said there was something you wanted to discuss, George.'

George watched as Mar sat in the other armchair. With those arctic-blue eyes and the handsome, craggy face, he looked like what Alison said he was

166

– a hard but straight fellow with a considerable interest in money. George wasn't so sure about the straightness. He couldn't see Mar doing anything for nothing, and he looked used to getting what he wanted. George wouldn't want to cross him. 'Yes. I want to know more about Nikki Quinn, what she did for entertainment. Alison said you have something about exclusive raves, lots of drugs and sex; we thought maybe your neighbour Rebecca Sayers was involved.'

'Did you now?' With that soft accent he sounded like the best kind of old-style country doctor – and really phoney. 'I don't know about that, but the raves, yes. We have a damn good reporter on the Axbridge paper who stumbled across them quite by accident.' He switched on an intercom on his desk. 'Hey, Gina, it's Alan. Could you spare me a minute or two with the Hell Fire Club file?'

The woman who appeared shortly afterwards was black, her huge smile framed by twisting Rastafarian locks. Her body flowed sensuously under a loose white top and long, multi-coloured skirt. Mar stood up and waved her to a chair, behaving exactly as a newspaper proprietor would, but there was electricity between them that made George wonder if there was more to it than that. 'This is George Kristianssen.' No explanation of his presence was given or, it seemed, expected. 'He's interested in the club. As are we all.'

She opened the file on her knees. 'It's not really a club, of course, just a commercial arrangement, Mr

167

Kristianssen. I discovered it when following up a routine car accident, someone quite well known who was over the alcohol limit but not prosecuted.' She had a low, beautifully modulated voice, like an opera singer. 'It seems there are enough people in this city prepared to pay for super-sex, to make exclusive get-togethers in private houses a viable business for the organisers. They seem to be done in a very civilised way. You ask a discreet group to a nice house in the country, somewhere isolated, lay on drink and reception-style food. A bit like going to a posh wedding.'

'And they all pay?'

'Sure.'

'And in return get what, exactly?'

'Whatever they want. Seems to be mostly cocaine – crack is well-known to heighten sexual experience. But also ecstasy, speed, LSD – all the drugs that work on energy or sensation.' She looked at Mar, as if to ask whether she was doing it right. He nodded. 'Plenty of young women available – no old slags, some are students earning their way through university now that grants are so small, quite a few nurses. For middle-aged men, bored with their partners and probably wanting things they won't get so easily from dolly birds in the office. Anyway, doing it at the raves is less dangerous than doing it on your own doorstep.'

'So far it's just drugs and straight sex, right?'

'Yes, And a bit of S&M and other way-out stuff.'

'So, at the raves you get whatever's on offer

from prostitutes in Clifton or St Paul's. What's the attraction?'

'It's less furtive and sordid, less chance of getting mugged or your wallet nicked. Pleasanter and safer – very up-market. You also meet those with similar interests, which means it may become free and you can spend the cash on doing it in a civilised atmosphere with decent wine. That's quite a bonus.' She gave a slight smile. 'My research suggests that if you're into way-out sex, using contact magazines and phone services is *really* grim and risky – and damned expensive. Anyway, it's drugs that are the focus. That's what it's really about for most of them. Cocaine and super-sex.'

George remembered poor, naïve Hannah Braithwaite, dragged naked and mutilated from the mudflats at Pill. 'Hard drug suppliers are hard men – you've been taking risks.'

She nodded. 'I know.'

'So, it's the kind of thing most of them might not want broadcast, but how much is illegal?'

Mar took over. 'What goes in the paper is up to Gina and her editor. These days, none of this is *that* unusual; we've no wish to trespass on the privacy of folk harming no one else – and some of our readers might react negatively if we did. Others would love it, but I don't run that kind of paper. The drugs *are* illegal and there are some alarmingly prominent people involved. Very well-to-do media and business types, some local politicians, we believe one national political figure, but we don't know who yet.' Mar paused to fill his pipe, then lit it, tamping down the glowing tobacco with a scorched box of Swan Vestas. 'There's one more bit, and it's nasty. All this spills over, for just a few of them, into sex involving under-age girls – thirteen, fourteen ... and younger children of both sexes. We don't know if they are all aware of that, but it taints the whole thing.' He met George's eyes searchingly. 'The drugs and under-age sex are *very* illegal. That's where we're at. We've put nothing in the paper and told no one – and that includes the police.'

He nodded to Gina and she handed George a list of names, some without surnames, some with addresses and occupations. He whistled. 'A black-mailer could make a fortune with this.'

'Of course, but that's not our trade. Gina has spent months gathering the material, with great difficulty, and believes it should be made public. She's had quite a few threats, menacing phone calls, men following her home, all that. They're a dangerous bunch.'

George was staring out of the window. Two men in blue overalls were unloading rolls of newsprint from a truck. 'If these people are deeply involved they'd lose everything if it came out. Go to jail as well. There are great reputations and fortunes to be lost. Would they kill to keep it secret?'

'Who knows, George? I suppose *one* of them might, and that's all it would need.'

'Is a Dr Jevanjee involved?'

'I know who you mean,' said Gina. 'I've had

170

some hints that he may be supplying, may even be the main supplier. A lot of pseudonyms are used and I think he may be the one known as Selim.'

'But you don't know if Nikki was mixed up in all this?'

'No idea at all.'

'Or Rebecca Sayers?'

Gina shook her head.

'But if they were, that would explain the threats to Quinn, if the organisers believe he knows all about it. It might explain why someone tried to kill Alison. This is bloody dangerous stuff. Can I read the file?'

Alan Mar drew on his pipe and a ring of blue smoke spiralled up to the ceiling. 'As you say, George, it's dangerous stuff – and it could become a major story for us. But if it might help Geoff and Alison, of course you can. But read it here, I don't want it to leave the building. There's an empty office you can use down the corridor. If anything seems relevant to the case, we'll talk about how to handle it. Fair enough?'

18

The woman lay naked on a plastic sun-bed by the pool. But there was no sun: the rectangle of blue, highly chlorinated water was in the basement of a large house in Backwell, a commuter village just outside the city.

After much agonising, George had decided to put Mar's information to the test. He still did not quite trust the man, but he did trust Gina and her brilliant piece of investigation; and he was not going back to Alison with empty hands. She would be furious if he put the screws on Rebecca Sayers and it went wrong, so he would try one of the names on the list first. He had parked in a road that was half suburban, half rural, shaded by trees that formed a roof like a cathedral. The house was of no particular style, probably 1930s, with a tiled roof, more red tiles cladding the upper storey, ivy climbing the brick walls.

As he rang the bell, he noted that everything was neat and in good repair. The place must have been worth half a million. He wondered who Denise might be, to afford all this. The teenage boy who answered the door had a long, ethereal face and looked half stoned: lank yellow hair and a filthy sweatshirt, something between Jesus and a drop-out.

'Yeah?'

'Could I speak to Denise, please?'

'Yeah.' The boy gestured him to some stairs, plainly impatient to get back to the heavy metal thudding from his room. 'She's down there.'

The stone steps curved down through walls painted a cheerful yellow. At the bottom the floor changed to blue tiles and George stepped through a doorway framed in flowering creeper. He suddenly felt overdressed.

'Hi!' She smiled at him as if men in flat caps always walked in on her when she was naked. 'Do come and sit down.'

George had been about to apologise for the intrusion, but decided not to bother. Instead he took off his cap and settled on a plastic chair by the sun-bed. She stretched like a cat, giving him a calculated flash of dark pubic hair and neat breasts, then turned on her stomach to hide both. She must be in her early forties, a classically good but arrogant face, flawless skin, very tanned, crimson toenails. The long blonde hair was dyed; she swept it back from her face and smiled again. 'Sorry – are you shocked? My children are always letting people in like this. Can I help you? Would you like a drink or something?'

The heating was turned well up and he could feel himself sweating under the anorak. He pulled it off, rolling up his shirt-sleeves. 'No, thank you, not just at the moment. The young man who answered the door said I could find Denise down here?'

'That was Benedict, my son.' She gestured with an elegant tanned arm. 'There's no one else here, as you can see. I'm Denise.'

'Then I wonder if I might talk to you?' He produced his card. 'As you can see, I'm a private investigator.'

Her face showed no emotion, but her ears went slightly pink and he could see the muscles of her shoulders and neck tense. 'I'm not sure I understand – what do you want exactly?'

'I'm retained by the lawyers defending Dr Geoffrey Quinn on a charge of murder and I believe you may have met his wife, Nikki Quinn.'

'I don't think so.' She sat up, pulled on a long flowered robe and knotted its sash. She had stopped smiling.

'I think you may have met her socially, at a party out in the country possibly?'

He could tell at once that she was scared, but she was giving nothing away. She paused as if trying to recollect, then shook her head. 'No, I'm sorry but you must be mistaken. I've never heard of anyone called Quinn.'

'Are you quite sure, Mrs – ah?'

She hesitated, but plainly in a big house in a small village there was no point in dissembling. 'Lang.'

George did a quick double-take. Gina had a

different surname for her – plainly a false one – and the real one set alarm bells ringing. 'We are very discreet, Mrs Lang. I'm only concerned to piece together the last few months of Mrs Quinn's life. Are you quite sure you never met her?'

She nodded firmly, but there were the faintest traces of moisture on the smooth tanned forehead and her fingers were drumming unconsciously on the book she had been reading. 'Absolutely. I can't help you. Now, unless you have anything else to ask, I must go and fetch my younger child from school.'

George knew she was lying, but there was no point pressing her. He allowed her to walk him back upstairs and see him out of the front door, still charming, still smiling, still bloody scared.

Back in the van, he called his office on the mobile phone. 'Hi, Joan, it's George. Would you look somebody up in *Who's Who* for me?' Two minutes later he knew he had guessed correctly. The good book knew her as Lady Denise Lang, daughter of a Viscount, a Tory grandee, married twenty years ago to Charles Lang, now a long-standing Member of Parliament for a safe seat in Wiltshire. After faithful years as a whip he had become Minister of State for Defence Procurement. Responsible under his better-known Secretary of State for buying and selling arms. The target of increasing suspicion of dirty dealing until Blair's victory threw him out of office – and even more so now he'd joined the board of a weapons manufacturer to supplement his parliamentary salary. Lang was vulnerable, dead vulnerable.

As the rusty Transit joined the road back into Bristol, George felt like hanging himself. It was a cock-up. If Charles Lang's wife was misbehaving, he would not want it on the front pages. Come to think of it, maybe Lang was a member of the club too? George might have struck gold, but he should have put Gina's list under a microscope before blundering in. All he could do now was to press on fast, before they could react.

An hour later George parked near the church in Abbots Leigh and walked briskly up Mrs Sayers's drive. This was when it could all go even more disastrously wrong.

She answered the door herself. 'Yes?' She eyed him with distaste.

'May I come in, Mrs Sayers? There is something I'd like to discuss with you.'

She kept the door half closed, peering round it warily. 'Who are you? What can you have to discuss with me?'

'I am a private investigator, Mrs Sayers, as you know perfectly well from my previous visit – and what I have to say would best be said in private.'

She did not move to let him in. 'I'm very busy, you know, and I don't know who you are. I suggest you ring and make an appointment.'

George sighed, reached into his pocket and

pulled out a large black and white print, showing it to her in silence. He might have struck her a vicious blow across the face. Her eyes widened and she went white, swaying as if she might faint. She tried to speak but could not, struggling for breath. She stood back unsteadily and gestured him in.

In the drawing-room she swayed and flopped on to a sofa, closing her eyes. It reminded George of a scene from a bad television adaptation of Jane Austen – but only until she spat at him: 'Where did you get that obscene thing? You bastard! You utter *bastard*.' Her eyes were full of hatred, but also fear. 'For God's sake, what do you want of me?'

George looked at her firmly. He fanned out the set of photographs like a deck of cards. 'Don't you want to see them all?'

She was recovering, guile struggling to take over from naked fear. 'How much do you want for them?' She was panting breathlessly and could hardly speak. 'For the negatives?'

'They *are* genuine, then?'

Her hands were shaking in her lap. 'Does it matter to a poncy little blackmailer like you?'

'I'm not here to blackmail you, Mrs Sayers.'

'What do you want? What the hell do you *want*?' Rebecca Sayers shook her head wretchedly. 'Just tell me what you want for the negatives.'

'Ah, yes. The negatives.' George pulled out his notebook. 'I called here before, as I'm sure you remember. I am retained by the lawyers defending

Dr Quinn on a charge of murder. I asked you some questions and you did not tell me the truth. In particular you did not tell me that you knew the late Mrs Quinn, that you went to social gatherings together. That you knew each other very well.'

Her eyes were filling but she was angry, too. 'Does it bloody matter? She's dead, isn't she? And he killed her. I know nothing about it.'

'Perhaps not, but you do know a great deal about Nikki Quinn, Mrs Sayers, though I can understand the awkwardness of my asking you about activities that were secret from your husband and against this country's law.'

Now she was weeping freely. 'I never did anything illegal. You've no charge to lay against me.'

'Nothing but perverting the course of justice, perhaps, but I think you should tell me everything you know about Nikki, don't you?'

'How can I trust you?'

'You don't have much choice, do you? If you don't talk, these pictures go straight to the local press. Today.'

'But you *will* give me the negatives – and all the prints?'

'I will. You can rely on it, Mrs Sayers. I am working for a leading member of the Bar and both of us would be finished in our professions if we did not keep our word. Blackmail is a criminal offence.' George reached into his jacket to switch on the tape recorder concealed in the breast pocket.

The microphone was mounted as a pin in his tie. 'So, tell me, please. When did you first meet Nikki?'

Rebecca Sayers did not reply, as if still weighing up the odds. Eventually she spoke very quietly, staring out of the window as if George were not there. 'About three years ago, I suppose. We'd both been living here for some years, but I hadn't noticed her before. I was going through a bad patch with Arthur and feeling bored and frustrated. She was younger – and so pretty – but I had a feeling that she was facing the same kind of problems.'

At first Nikki Quinn thought Mrs Sayers obnoxious. She swept up and down the street, all rustic chic in her Laura Ashley headscarf and waxed Barbour, that ridiculous dog trotting at her heels. She glared at the children, shouting and quarrelling in Nikki's garden, as if they were dangerous vermin. She always sounded so dismissively upper class.

But Nikki also secretly envied her style and confidence. She was surprised but flattered when one day Rebecca Sayers stopped by the gate and smiled in an almost friendly way. Over the next few weeks she often stopped for a chat and eventually she went a little further. 'I'm having a few friends in for drinks before dinner on Friday. I wonder if you and your husband would like to come?'

Geoff was working late. He was always bloody working. But Nikki fixed a babysitter and went on her own.

After giving the children their tea, she lounged in a warm scented bath for half an hour, then put on a plain but expensive short black dress and long silver earrings. Her wavy, dark hair fell in a cascade on tanned shoulders and she knew she looked good. It might be only a few boring old farts swilling that old bitch's gin, but Nikki hadn't been out for ages and she was damn well going to enjoy it.

Which she did. Though only a few yards away from the chaos of her own kitchen, it was quite an elegant little party. She recognised well-known faces from the local papers: well-off businessmen, local politicians, an ex-Lord Mayor, a local television presenter. They spilled out from the pretty drawing-room, through French doors, on to the terrace behind the house.

Rebecca Sayers was an attentive hostess, flitting between the little groups introducing new friends to old, filling glasses, smiling a lot. Out of the perennial head-scarf and Barbour, Nikki was surprised how attractive she was. Arthur Sayers was much older, a grey-haired man, well over sixty, who disappeared from time to time, as if he were watching TV in another room. It was Rebecca's party, not his. She took Nikki's elbow and steered her into a corner of the garden. 'So sorry your husband couldn't make it. He must work long hours as a doctor.'

Nikki smiled. 'Yes, he does. Sometimes I get very fed up, left on my own with Jessica and Tom, though I know I shouldn't. People depend on him and I knew what I was marrying.'

'How long have you been married, Nikki?'

'Seven years. We've always lived here.' She wondered

why it had taken Rebecca seven years to get round to inviting her into her house. 'It's a good place to bring up children.'

'Yes, though mine are grown up now of course.' The older woman touched Nikki's arm again. It was a curiously sensuous feeling, and made her feel valued – she had been a wife and mother so long, she had forgotten what it was like to be touched by another woman. Rebecca was guiding her towards a pergola covered in roses; the scent was gorgeous. They were out of sight of the other guests. 'Mine used to love playing in Leigh Woods and swimming – do yours?'

'Oh, yes. But it would be nice to go with another adult sometimes – they don't really need me, except as a life-saver.'

'I go to the pool at the sports centre. It's marvellous exercise. I'd prefer to go with someone else, too. Why don't you come along with me, bring the children?'

They went two days later, after school. By then Nikki had realised that the only development that might have prompted Rebecca's invitation after seven years of ignoring her, was that she had seen Nikki playing with the kids in a very skimpy bikini during a hot spell; and that the trip to the pool was anything but spontaneous. But she did not care. Nikki was desperate for approval from someone, since she received none from Geoff, and there was something deeply flattering in the attention Rebecca was giving her.

The children laughed and shouted as they jumped up and down in artificial waves splashing against the sides of the modern pool. Then they played on the long, curving

181

slide, leaving the two women lying on towels shielded by a palm tree growing in thin sandy soil. Nikki looked down at her flat stomach and long legs, tan shown off by a white swimsuit, and knew that she looked good. For a woman who must have been over fifty Rebecca, too, had a remarkably young figure. She was thickening a bit around the waist, but still had firm breasts and beautiful legs. Nikki rolled on her side to check on the children, stiffening when she felt soft fingers caressing her back. Her first instinct was to recoil, but then she turned away to lie on her front, hiding her face in her arms, surprised but excited. Being touched by another woman was arousing in a way she would never have expected. She suddenly wished the hand would go lower, stroke her buttocks one by one and then her thighs, but the gentle fingers moved tantalisingly to her arms and shoulders.

'You're not happy, my dear, are you?'

Nikki stretched luxuriously like a cat and sighed. Was Rebecca a dyke or something? Strangely she didn't really care – she felt desired but not threatened, it was delicious. 'I do get very lonely with Geoff out all the time and the children drive me mad. I used to enjoy life before I married him.'

'You'll get through it, you know. I love my boys dearly, but I'm not sorry they've flown the nest. Arthur was always working too, and being a mother is isolating and lonely. It helps to have a few girlfriends, you know.'

Now her fingers were moving lower, running over the younger woman's thighs. Nikki wriggled and spread her legs slightly, raising her bottom a little, shamelessly inviting Rebecca to probe between them. She responded,

182

gently, momentarily, and Nikki was electrified by the sensation. The whole thing was crazy – the cut-glass accent, the bold approach, the sheer cheek of it. But Nikki didn't care – and Rebecca had known that she wouldn't. It was even more exciting that they were in a place full of other people, barely concealed by the haze of steam drifting over the warm water: like making love to Geoff, long ago, on the cliffs in Dorset.

Over the next few weeks they went to the pool several times; and shopping in the centre of Bristol. Once you got to know her, Rebecca was warm and kind; and she often had a sparkle in her eye that suggested she was not living a life of celibacy. It was early in September when she offered the next step. They were lunching in a Mexican restaurant off Park Street. 'What do you do at weekends, my dear?'

'Oh, just take the children clothes shopping, Jessica wants some new Doc Marten's this week, have their friends round, take them to see granny, take them to Sainsbury's.' She smiled wryly. 'Yes, what do I do at weekends?'

'Is Geoff often on duty?'

'He has a surgery every bloody Saturday morning. After that he's often on call – and he gets called out a lot, believe me. People expect service from their GP these days, you know – when I was a kid you wouldn't dare to phone unless you were dying.'

Rebecca paused thoughtfully. 'I'm going to a party organised by one of my girlfriends on Saturday. Would you like to get a babysitter and come?'

'Geoff couldn't.'

'No, not Geoff. Just you.'

Nikki half expected some kind of lesbian gathering and was quite nervous when the Sayers's Rover appeared at eight on Saturday evening. She had dressed to kill, in a new tube dress that showed off her figure to perfection. It stopped well above the knee, but she had spun and twisted in front of the mirror until she was certain her legs were good enough to take it. Rebecca smiled as she pushed open the passenger door. 'You look great, my dear.'

Nikki glowed. 'So do you, Rebecca. Where are we going?'

19

It was getting dark outside and Rebecca Sayers had not switched on any lights. She sat huddled into the corner of a sofa, her eyes bright: flickering and wary. She still looked like a child who was very, very scared. George seemed to tower over her, even though he was not standing up. His face was taut and unsmiling. 'That was the first time for Nikki, I take it? The first of many?'

She nodded miserably. After all the aggression and bravado, she had collapsed. 'It was the first time – I'm sorry, I'm sorry, I'm so sorry I didn't tell you before.' She wiped the tears from her face with the back of her hand and sniffed unattractively. 'I just never thought it was relevant – I mean, she's dead now and he killed her, whatever she may have done before …' Her voice trailed away. 'I'm sorry, but does it matter any more?'

George stood up and switched on the wall lights. 'Yes,' he said brutally. 'It does matter. It may matter very much.' He looked down at her, not moving, but his size alone was threatening. He felt sorry for the woman, but he could not let up now. He was certain he had found Nikki's great secret; and that in turn was going to lead him to her killer. 'Well, get on with it!' His voice was like a whiplash. 'Where exactly did you take her?'

They drove south out of the city, into the hills of Somerset, until Nikki was completely lost. It was dark when Rebecca turned the car into a driveway that ran down an avenue of trees. The house was out of sight of the road, either real Georgian or a modern imitation – Nikki could not tell in the dark – but she was definitely impressed. An octagonal lantern over the front door cast a pool of yellow light on a gravel circle packed with cars. Rebecca parked to one side of the house and they entered through the kitchen.

Nikki was surprised that she wasn't introduced to a host or hostess, but it was a very grand kind of party. The men were all in dinner jackets, the women dressed expensively. Waiters in white coats carried trays of drinks through two large rooms, one brightly lit by a crystal chandelier, the other only by candles, making it mysteriously dark. There were at least fifty people there and the noise was deafening.

Rebecca steered her through the crowd, introducing her to a man here, a woman there. She used only first names, which seemed a bit odd at such a formal occasion. Nikki recognised a few of the faces – a woman MP, a well-known radio presenter, some men and women prominent in local business, a rear admiral whose picture, visiting Bristol docks, she had seen in the newspapers. She felt a little out of place, but a woman called Judith put her at her ease. She was middle-aged, but very attractive, with kind eyes. Everything about her was understated and expensive –

her perfectly cut hair, haute couture dress, above all the pendant hanging on a thin gold chain round her neck, rising and falling between her breasts as she breathed. The diamonds and emeralds had to be real, the setting two hundred years old. She had a warm smile. 'Is it your first time?'

Nikki was puzzled. 'I haven't been here before. Rebecca brought me – to be honest, I don't even know whose house this is.'

'No?' Judith did not enlighten her. A little later Nikki wandered upstairs, looking for the loo. The corridor was painted white and the first oak door she tried was locked. She grinned at the unmistakable sounds from behind it: a man's voice caressing, a woman giving sharp cries of pleasure. Maybe this whole thing was more lively than she had expected. The next room was unlocked and empty, a sickly smell hanging in the air. Marijuana? Well, that was harmless enough.

Downstairs she found a room now in darkness, apart from disco lights flashing across the ceiling: red, blue, green, startling orange. A band was hammering out heavy metal and black shapes were dancing, twisting, shouting. A man who had shed his DJ seized her hand and pulled her towards him. He was still wearing his black bow-tie and white shirt, glowing in the flickering light like phosphorus in water. Nikki responded instinctively, thrusting her hips towards him, letting her hair fly out as he twisted her round. She couldn't see his face in the darkness, but she sensed the power in his body and responded to it. She felt great.

He was shouting to her over the noise. 'You're a terrific

dancer – do you enjoy it as much as it looks?'

Even to Nikki it was a naff chat-up line, but she responded instinctively. 'Oh yes – it makes me feel so alive. When I dance I can feel all of me, pulsing with life.' She blushed. 'Does that sound silly?'

'No. It sounds very perceptive to me.' Rebecca had vanished. Nikki was sure she was upstairs with a man – or, more likely, a woman. There was plainly a lot of sex available in this house and if Rebecca was getting her share, good luck to her. Nikki stopped dancing and allowed the man to bring her a drink, a long cool Pimm's with lots of strawberries floating on the surface. She still couldn't see his face in the candle-light and did not ask his name. She had picked up the rules of this club.

It must have been one in the morning. Those who weren't upstairs were milling in the biggest room, the one with the crystal chandelier. The band had stopped and they were drinking and mingling quietly. There was an expectant air. But then a youngish man stood on a chair and tapped a glass with a knife. 'I'm so sorry, but Andrea has just telephoned. She's been delayed by an accident in which she tore a ligament in her leg.' Someone in the corner sniggered. 'She won't be able to perform tonight.'

Another snigger and a whisper of 'I bet she bloody does' brought a gale of laughter.

Nikki looked questioningly at a woman beside her. 'Who's Andrea?'

The woman gave a tight little smile. 'She strips. It turns the men on, the women too, not that most of them need it. Kind of climax to this part of the evening.'

Nikki's mind raced. This part? She knew what came

*next. She was cheerfully, but not disablingly drunk;
suddenly she could see a way to instant fame in this weird
company. She remembered the line drawings in a half
humorous paperback she had once bought on a station
platform, coyly titled* How to Strip in Front of Your
Husband. *Bugger Geoff – it had never seemed worth
trying it on him.*

As the murmur continued, she pushed her way up to
the man on the chair. 'I'll have a go, if you don't mind
an amateur.' She was pleased she sounded so confident
and casual, but inside she was terrified.

He looked at her appraisingly and raised an eyebrow.
'Terrific, but are you sure?'

Nikki threw her shoulders back and wriggled so that
she felt every part of her body. 'I am at the moment.' She
laughed nervously. 'You'd better start before I change my
mind.'

'Great, brill … sorry, I don't know your name.'

'Nikki. Just Nikki.'

The man clapped for silence. 'Ladies and gentlemen,
this beautiful lady here, the fabulous, talented and sensuous Nikki, has kindly volunteered to take Andrea's
place.' Two men were pushing a long refectory table into
the centre of the room. The lights dimmed and the band
were settling in the corner. For a moment Nikki felt sick
and wanted to run away, but then she thought of Geoff
and knew how much she wanted to do something that
would hurt him. And Christ, this would really destroy
him if he ever found out. Or make him value her at last.
Something was bloody well going to change. Nikki wasn't
sure what, but she was glad.

She knelt awkwardly on the edge of the table, pulling herself up. She stood up straight to conceal her fear and stretched out her arms in welcome. The burst of applause was reassuring and suddenly she could see Rebecca in the crowd, looking anxious, but smiling encouragement.

The band started slowly and Nikki swayed along the table, trembling slightly, but twisting as slowly and sensuously as she could. The crowd fell silent, with some clapping and a murmur of appreciation, as Nikki started to inch the red dress over her head, then threw it among them. Fortunately she had put on stockings and a suspender belt, not tights. Bump and grind gave way to a saxophone singing along with her movements, everyone was clapping in time, Nikki spun and moved from leg to leg, twisting and high kicking, smiling at faces in the back row, exulting in the display of the most valuable possession she had, carried along by the powerful and expectant atmosphere. She knew almost none of them, but she felt among friends.

Now that her nerves were gone, she threw herself into the music. A chair appeared on the corner of the table and she raised one leg on it to peel off a stocking. The whole room was clapping rhythmically now, the atmosphere electric with lust and admiration. Nikki's spirit soared above them all, she felt like God, she felt like a tart, she felt complete, she felt bloody marvellous. She loved displaying her body and threw all the energy and femininity she had into it.

She kept going for twenty minutes, ending in the traditional way, arching down with her bottom towards them to kick off her flimsy knickers. As she slowly stood *upright, legs provocatively apart, and stretched out her arms so that her body was an elongated X, the sensation was almost orgasmic. They clapped harder and cheered. As she jumped naked from the table she was surrounded by people saying admiring things. Rebecca took her in her arms. 'You were brilliant, love, I'm so proud of you.' Nikki Quinn was a new woman.*

A little later, with the band and the waiters gone, the nice man she had danced with led her upstairs. He was called Charles. 'Rebecca's right – you were absolutely terrific.' His eyes shone in admiration and Nikki enjoyed undressing again in front of him. They knelt on the floor together naked; he produced the white powder and showed her how to draw a line. The effect was swift. Suddenly all the anxiety and anger of the past months were gone. Her body floated, her mind glowed; and when they made love it was like a volcano erupting.

20

Rebecca Sayers had collapsed in his arms and was weeping freely. George held her and stroked her hair. 'And it was always like that? A party that turned into a rave, sex and cocaine?' She nodded miserably. 'But *why*, Mrs Sayers? Why? Weren't you all taking a risk – a huge risk?'

'I suppose that was part of it. The danger made it more exciting. And then I didn't care. I thought it would serve Arthur right if I was caught – perhaps everyone there had someone like Arthur who'd let them down, I don't know.' For a second her voice rose and the anger came back. 'For God's sake, how the hell can *you* understand? For a start you're a man. I've been a good wife and mother for thirty years – thirty years of being taken for granted, everything for Arthur and the boys, their comfort, their careers, their fun. I've wasted my whole life on them – can you begin to imagine what that *feels* like? We shared nothing, nothing at all. Oh I know Arthur *kept* us all, but he was a lousy husband, we never talked, never had a credible sex life. Cold silence, schoolboy sex with a man who thought I was part of the furniture – can you imagine it? But most of all, nothing for me. Nothing for me.' Her face was twisted in bitterness, her whole body shaking with helpless fury. 'I wasn't a real person till I found the group. It was just a way of meeting other people who wanted to be *alive*. I learnt to laugh again, I felt valued, I found pride in my body, in my own sexuality, I felt *good*.'

'Did you make love with Nikki?'

She shook her head sadly. 'No, I didn't. She wasn't interested and I respected that. Now I wish I had. Does that shock you?'

'No, of course not. Did Nikki go on stripping?'

'Oh, yes, she got rather good at it. A real professional. She practised in my house – we have a huge mirror on the front of a built-in wardrobe – and I gave her tips. She started to get bookings from other people in the city. Several men's dining-clubs hired her to perform on the table. She loved it – it turned her on as much as them. She got two hundred pounds a time.' She had stopped crying and looked defensive. 'Well, it's no different from after-dinner speaking, is it?'

'And her husband didn't know? Never even *guessed*?'

'I don't think so. He was always working. In any case, she *wanted* him to know. She just wasn't going to tell him herself – she wanted him to be frustrated, angry, then find out and be really hurt.'

'But he *must* have wondered where she was going at night?'

'He was often out at night himself, on house calls. It's amazing how many visits to girlfriends from the polytechnic, meetings at the kids' school, trips to relatives in other parts of the country a preoccupied man will swallow. Don't forget, until recently there was an au pair to look after the children.'

'An au pair?'

'Yes – some Yugoslav girl called Vesna. She left a while ago to look for a better job in London, but I know Nikki was hoping she'd come back.'

George made a note. 'Going back to the raves. How much did all this cost?'

'We just paid fifty pounds and then for the drugs; I only ever tried cocaine.'

To get those titanic, Oscar-winning orgasms, thought George. 'What else was there? Crack? Ecstasy? Speed? LSD?'

'I don't know, but I suppose whatever anyone wanted.'

'And who organised it? Who did you pay?'

'We paid three people who came and supplied. Their first names were Selim, Judith and Tom. I never knew who arranged it all. That was all very secret. Selim or Judith had to agree before anyone was introduced … Once you'd been accepted you came along and were told when the next session would be. No phone calls, nothing on paper.'

'You really don't know who was organising it?'

'No. I knew that to try to find out would be dangerous, we all knew the drugs were illegal.'

'But not just the drugs?' He paused questioningly. 'There was something else, wasn't there? Something that you didn't like – and aren't telling me?'

She looked afraid. 'Yes. But at first we didn't know, we thought it was all harmless fun. A little Rabelasian, but straight.'

'Straight?'

She flushed. 'I'm sure you know what I mean. We simply didn't *know* there was also, well, a more seamy side. I swear we didn't know about any of that.'

'Any of *what*, Mrs Sayers?'

She could not meet his eye. 'Anything you know about that wasn't – well – straight.'

'"Straight" again, Mrs Sayers?' George sighed. 'I take it you mean anything that wasn't straightforward sex, hetero or homosexual, between adults who were of the relevant consenting age?'

Her eyes were fixed on the floor. 'Yes.' She was barely audible, still capable of shame, though she did not want him to see it. 'I suppose I do.' She met his eye with an expression of sheer terror. He had struck the vital nerve and could see the fear and torment in her mind. She knew exactly what she had got herself into; she'd been torn apart by it every hour since Nikki died. And the consequences if it went wrong. Inside she was screaming and suddenly he knew why. A scared middle-aged woman sent to prison, surrounded by an angry crowd who would take her apart as a child molester, turn on the rush of water in the showers so the screws wouldn't hear, shove broken bottles up her vagina and her anus, slash her face and breasts with Stanley knife blades, push needles into her eyes, leave her broken or dead on the filthy tiles when they had had their fun. By God, she knew.

'There were *children*, weren't there, Mrs Sayers?' He spoke very quietly. There was no need for any more pressure.

'Yes.' Again, an almost inaudible whisper. 'There were children, but I didn't know that for a long time, almost until the end – and I had nothing to do with them, I swear I had nothing to do with them.'

'Children forced to commit sexual acts, emotionally and physically abused? How *old* were they Mrs Sayers?'

'I don't know, I never even saw them. I swear I was never involved in any of … that.'

George bit back his disgust, sat down and spoke gently. 'Oh yes, but you were under the same roof.'

'No, never! I'm sure we weren't.' Then she saw the determination in his face and that he knew she was lying. She started to cry again.

'You were under the same roof. You did nothing to stop it. You did not report it to the police, even though you knew it was a serious crime. You could go to jail for some years. You wouldn't be treated well.'

She shuddered. 'I know, oh God, I know.'

'Then you're going to help me, Mrs Sayers, or I'll see you in a cell by tonight. And this is serious – don't think your husband will get you out on bail.' She was helpless, crushed in defeat, as she nodded again. She was weeping silently.

George's mind was racing, somewhere there was still a gap, an inconsistency. Dougal's photograph of Rebecca and the other woman had been in a modest suburban house, not the kind of place she was talking about. He reached out and took her hand; it was trembling and her eyes pleaded with him to help her. 'There's just a little more, isn't there? When did Nikki last actually go to the club?'

'About six months ago.'

'And you?'

'The same.'

'So, what happened? Why did you stop?'

There was an unwilling silence and for a long minute the room stood still. Eventually she spoke in a monotone. 'We realised what was going on.' She glanced up wryly. 'Oh, don't misunderstand. We loved the crack and the sex – but we discovered that a few of them had gone over the top and the children had become involved. We were both appalled, scared too.'

'What did you do?'

'Don't rush me, it was very complicated. By then Nikki was sleeping with one of the men on a regular basis, deep in an affair. He was called Charles, very glitzy wife, but I guess Nikki gave him a much better time – she was incredibly physical and sensuous, you know.'

'Charles who?'

'I don't know.'

'You don't *know*?'

'It was all very secret, we are all taking a risk, she was just keeping to the rules.' She hesitated. 'I think he was an MP. She was very happy at first, then she learnt about the children at the raves and challenged him about it.'

'And?'

'He was angry, told her to forget it. She said she couldn't, it was wicked, against the law, she had a damn good mind to go to the police.' Rebecca smiled slightly. 'This all happened when they were in bed together, at his cottage in Wiltshire. In the end she got so furious – Nikki was a gutsy lady, you know – that she walked out. Getting dressed would have lessened the effect, so she grabbed a handful of clothes and put them on in a field, just jeans and a shirt. Ended up walking six miles to Trowbridge in pouring rain. I drove out to pick her up.'

'The parting of the ways?'

She shook her head. 'Oh no, I wish to God it had been. Nikki had really blown it, become a loose cannon. They were afraid she would blow the whole thing open.'

'How did you know?'

'The very next day a stranger turned up at Nikki's house when she was alone. Told her to forget Charles, forget everything. He told her very plainly they had documents that would ruin her husband, send him to prison, lose her the house, lose all her friends, put her in a rented flat on income support. He told her she was a prostitute and they'd expose her as one. He told her that if she went near the police or the press, they'd kill her.'

'How did Nikki take this?'

'She was absolutely terrified. She knew it was for real.'

'And she told you all about it?'

'Yes.'

'But not her husband?'

'No, I'm sure not. She didn't know *what* to do, she was beside herself. She was still in shock when … they killed her.'

'*They* killed her?'

She nodded, hollow-eyed. 'Who else?'

'And you've just *sat* here, and watched her husband arraigned for her murder?'

'I thought they might kill me, too.'

George stood up. He still felt sorry for her but it was mixed up with deep waves of disgust. 'I want you to come with me to my office where we can continue for not more than an hour. I require a list of everyone you can remember who went to these sessions, with addresses where you know them.'

'I can't do that. They'll kill me.'

'I doubt it, Mrs Sayers.' He wished he believed it.

'But if you are charged and go to prison, even only on remand pending trial, you know what the other prisoners will do to you.' She nodded with eyes full of terror again. When he brought her coat she put it on and followed him out.

21

It was barely eight next morning when Alison met Bill Taylor in the empty reception area at the building society. 'Sorry it had to be so early.'

'No problem.' He smiled diffidently. 'I try to be in about this time most days. Gives me a quiet hour before the calls start.' When they emerged from the lift twelve floors up, he showed her the view across the steep slate roofs of central Bristol to the harbour and the start of the Avon Gorge. Taylor pointed out a long grey submarine tied up at a jetty, White Ensign hanging limp at her stern. 'Been there three or four days as an ad for the Navy – she'll be covered in coach-loads of schoolkids in an hour or two.'

'It's brilliant – you can see everything! Was the society always here?'

'Good lord, no. I persuaded the board to put up this tower about eight years ago; we were in dreary offices down behind Queen Square till then.' They certainly weren't now, she thought, as he sat her on a long, squashy leather sofa in the managing director's penthouse. A VDU was humming on his desk; all the furniture was light oak and elegant in design, probably Scandinavian.

'Have you been to see Geoff recently?'

'I went last night.' Taylor had taken off his jacket and, under the crisp white shirt, she could not help noticing the powerful muscles of his chest and shoulders. The insignificant front he put on was very deceptive. 'He's very down, isn't he?'

Alison nodded. 'Yes, but I think we're getting a defence together.' She took out her notebook and ran over their earlier interviews: every contact between Taylor and Quinn in the last three years, dates, places, times. She slipped Alan Mar into the conversation at the end. It would have been impossible to explain exactly why, but the evening out, the sudden offer of help, had all left her confused, still half suspicious. 'He's one of your non-executive directors, isn't he?' She tried to sound as casual as she could, finishing her coffee and returning the notebook to her handbag.

'He is.'

'Are his businesses sound? Any problems?'

For a second Taylor looked awkward. 'He's an account holder, too, you know. I really can't …' He met her eyes and smiled. 'But I'd say the businesses are sound enough.'

'The thing is, Bill, he'll be a witness when we go to court. I just need to be sure his credibility can't be attacked. Checking out people who are on your side is distasteful, but I have to do it …' She hesitated deliberately, but Taylor did not respond. 'I've heard nothing bad about Alan, except for some odd rumours about the death of his wife.'

Taylor still looked defensive. 'Yes, there was some gossip. It was a skiing accident, you know – she broke her back when they were on holiday in Austria. They were alone up a mountain and he said they both fell a long way into a crevasse, it took him hours to struggle back to the hotel and fetch help. She was dead when a helicopter got there to bring her out.'

'So?'

'I think it's just bitchy gossip, but some said she'd have been found alive if he'd moved faster, some even said he'd pushed her. I don't believe any of it, but I can see how they ...' He looked away from Alison, out of the huge window to the harbour. 'At that time his businesses certainly *were* in a bad way and with her death he inherited a packet. If she had all that dosh, one wonders why it hadn't come into the frame before? Had she refused to bale him out?' He shrugged. 'We'll never know, will we?'

'That was about a year ago?'

'About that.'

'Any connection between Mar and the Quinns?'

'They lived very close to each other, but Geoff never mentioned Alan Mar. I don't know if they ever met.'

'And you don't believe the rumours?'

'I want to help Geoff, Alison. But Alan Mar's a friend of mine and a director on my board. I really can't discuss him any more. I'm sure you understand.' As they shook hands and went back to the lift, she thought how ambivalent he'd been. Behind that polite correctness, was he trying to give her a hidden message?

She was back in her chambers, still puzzled, when George telephoned. His voice made her feel awkward and defensive. At the other end of the line, he understood why, but it still upset him. Trying to control his anger, he found himself sounding suddenly cold. 'Look, Alison, I don't know what game you're playing at the moment; or perhaps I do and I don't like it. But we're still working together, so exactly *when* are you finished in court?'

'About twelve.'

'Right, I'll be round then. Your chambers. Don't say anything now, just *be* there. OK?'

George found Alison looking distant, sitting in the window seat that looked out over the sunny little graveyard. She was wearing a powder-blue dress that made her look even more washed out than she did anyway. Her face was strained, the skin pale and taut on her cheekbones, eyes surrounded by dark hollows. George wanted to kiss her and sweep her up in his arms, but reluctantly kept his distance. He stretched back in one of the armchairs. 'What's that rozzer doin', walking up and down John Street with a bump in his tunic like a badly concealed four-inch Smith and Wesson?'

'They've been keeping an eye on me since the car bomb.' She sounded only half interested. 'He isn't there all the time and at night it just means a patrol car passes by the flat a few times, but they've given me a bleeper to summon help if I need it. Very decent, considering the number of times I've got off villains they've spent years trying to send down.'

'Someone tried to take you out, kid – they ought to be watching you twenty-four hours a day.'

She shrugged. 'They say they're too overworked to do more. I'm not complaining.'

He had arrived feeling buoyant after yesterday, but her despondency was catching. When he produced his trump card, the triumph he had felt outside was missing. 'Look, Ally, I think I've cracked it.'

'Have you, George? It still looks pretty hopeless to me.'

'Yesterday I had a rough session with Rebecca Sayers. She made a written statement, in the form of an affidavit. It's properly signed and witnessed.' He handed her two typewritten sheets. 'It changes everything – read it.'

They sat in silence while Alison quickly scanned the document. 'Is she telling the truth?'

Despite the love and concern bursting to get out, he nearly hit her. 'Jesus Christ – of course she is! Getting that lot out of her almost broke the woman.' He reached into his pocket, took out the rusty tin, made a thin roll-up, strands of tobacco drooping from both ends, and lit it. She wrinkled her nose, her eyes crinkled into a smile and for a second it felt almost like old times.

Alison's expression returned to sceptical. 'OK, so

one woman – who may later claim you intimidated her – has signed a piece of paper confirming what we believed already, that there were these up-market drug and sex sessions and Nikki was involved in them. That's good, a real help, but she's only one witness – and what happens when she denies it in court? Or if they get at her? If she refuses to testify? Can you see her coming to court?'

'Not willingly, but you can get a witness summons.'

'Yes, I could. God knows how she'd react under cross-examination ...'

George stubbed out the roll-up angrily. 'For Christ's sake, what more do you want? It's a credible explanation of Nikki's murder. It's the break-through we need. Well – *isn't* it?'

She met his eyes and half smiled. 'It's pretty damn good, George. It really is. Now we know for sure that Nikki *was* mixed up with these comedians. We don't know how it all fits together, but we do know a lot of people had good reason to silence her when she turned difficult. Lang has a hell of a lot to lose. In a different way, so does Jevanjee.'

'The one thing I don't get is the stuff about them trying to blackmail her with something against Quinn.'

'I think I know what that's about. But look, George, we're still only halfway. OK, we can connect Rebecca Sayers and Nikki to the raves – but we need to connect Jevanjee and/or Lang with Nikki's death. We need not just suspicion, but something hard to link one of them with killing her and disposing of the body.'

George nodded mournfully. 'Yeah, you're right. How long have we got?'

'The trial has been set for two weeks on Monday, the notice came this morning.'

Now George understood why she looked so down. 'Can you get it adjourned?'

'On the basis of a lot of stuff that looks like pure speculation and hearsay? I doubt it.'

Walking back to the van, George realised what had to be done. To tie it all together they needed some harder facts about what Gina called the Hell Fire Club. Rebecca Sayers had given a few more names, and places that she thought were no longer used. They needed to harden that up: *they had to penetrate the club*. Then they might find something, or someone, to tie it all together.

Gina was at the newspaper office in Bedminster and he took her to a pub round the corner, where she had a coffee and he felt guilty with his lunch-time pint. She said she still did not know where the gatherings took place, except that they were mostly in large houses outside the city, often deep in Somerset. 'I thought of trying to get in myself, you know.' She smiled and tossed her wild hair. With that long neck, enclosed by a gold band, and her upright back she looked like an African princess, though George knew she had been born in St Pauls. 'I couldn't hack it. You have to be invited by someone already involved – and frankly, you have to be white.'

'You have to be an upper-class twit and white to be a *guest* maybe – but they have waiters and kitchen staff, don't they?'

'Suppose they must – I never thought of trying that.'

George drained his pint and gestured towards the bar. 'Another?'

'When you're ready. Look – getting in as the hired help might be the answer, though I wouldn't want to get caught.' A troubled shadow passed across the striking face. 'They seem to have killed one woman already – and they tried to kill Alison.'

'It wouldn't be that simple. The catering must be provided by a contractor who's sworn to secrecy, maybe someone they have a hold over to guarantee silence. I don't suppose the actual waiters know where they are – it's an out-of-town job for which they get paid better than usual and they're gone before the real fun starts.'

'So, how do you find a discreet caterer in Bristol, George?'

He fished in the anorak for his tobacco tin and cigarette papers. 'Never needed one, wrong social class. Christ, there must be a hundred people into outside catering in a city this size.'

Gina stood up. 'Let me get you another beer while you think.' He made to protest but she waved him to silence. 'It's called liberation, man. You must have heard of it, with a barrister for your girlfriend.'

Now, how had she guessed that, he wondered, watching her walk gracefully to the bar, long willowy body flowing under the electric blue dress that brushed her ankles. She came back with a pint and another coffee.

He picked up the glass. 'Cheers.'

'Cheers, George. So, who else needs caterers who have to be discreet?'

He shook his head. 'You tell me, Gina.'

'The Freemasons for a start. Must be a lodge meeting most nights at the Temple in Park Street, always with a dinner afterwards. Still very secret, whatever they say about being more open these days. Know any Masons, George? There's at least a possibility of the caterer being the same.'

'As a matter of fact I do.' For the first time that day his whiskers parted, and his face broke into a huge grin and he kissed her affectionately. 'That's it, Gina, my lovely, I think you've cracked it!'

22

A phone call to Eli Friedmann was all it needed. 'See what I can find out, George.' He phoned back in two hours. ''Fraid it's quite a list, a lot more than I thought. I better fax it to you at the office.'

Armed with a phoney reference from Friedmann, typed on the letterheading of his lodge, George started to ring round offering his services as a casual waiter. The pay was lousy – usually less than four pounds an hour – and you were expected to provide your own working clothes, so it was not difficult to get taken on. Ten days dragged by while Alison fretted and George Dyer, as he had become, solemnly turned up to serve at a society wedding, a bar mitzvah in Clifton and an evening at the Masonic Temple. He was about to give up when Mr Sweet rang him at home. Sweet had catered for the wedding, a bald, sweaty man in a tight-fitting black suit; now he had another job to offer. 'Come round in the morning, George, this one's a bit special-like.'

Town & Country Catering (established 1932) worked from a yard behind some shops in Mont-pelier. The office was a Portakabin. Little Mr Sweet explained that they would be providing drinks and light refreshments at an exclusive private party. 'Important people, George, need to relax sometimes, we all do.' He winked, met George's eye and tapped his nose meaningfully. 'So be discretional, know what I mean?' Like many Bristolians he ended seemingly random words with 'al' or 'ial'.

George winked back. ''Course I do, guv.'

'Good man. Well, anyway, it's not an orgy or anything, just a drinks party, that's all. Forget it as soon as you leave, OK? You've worked at the Masonic Hall, haven't you? It's in your references.'

'Yes, often.'

'Well, it's the same. You don't talk about who you've seen there. I know you won't let me down, George.'

'Of course not, guv.'

'That's right. I'm short of two blokes, in fact, they prefer all men. Don't know anyone reliable, and discreet-like, do you?'

'I have a friend called Dougal, trained as a mess orderly in the parachute regiment. Think he'd meet the bill?'

'Send him round, George. Servicemen are usually very smart, very clean. Now, it's twenty-five quid for the evening, good money – they're paying for discretional.' He looked at him sharply. 'And if you *did* break my trust, George – of course, I know you won't – you'd never work again in this aerial. You understand?'

'I understand, sir.' If this was it, and it might not be, George wondered how Sweet had become involved. Perhaps it was managed so well he did not even know what was going on.

They were being driven out of the city, eight of them sitting facing each other in the back of a closed van, their catering gear in cardboard boxes between their legs. Separated from the driver by a steel bulkhead, they could not see where they were going, nor had they been told. Except that it was a forty-five-minute drive south-west of Bristol, afterwards they would have no idea where they had been. They had been told to confine themselves to the kitchen and the downstairs reception rooms; they must not on any account go upstairs, that was the host's private quarters. They would leave by eleven. George and Dougal, sitting at opposite ends of the van, knew what they were looking for. The others would see little or nothing that was unusual.

When the van stopped, there were footsteps outside and the rear door clanged open. They were in a yard, surrounded by high walls of mellow brick, at the back of a large house. Sandstone, oldish, maybe Georgian, hills in the distance. The air smelt fresh, salty, perhaps they were not far from the sea? George joined in unloading and carrying the boxes of glasses into a huge kitchen: a large refrigerator, modern gas hob and two chest freezers like white coffins, all grouped round a scrubbed oak table. The food had already been delivered in plastic cool-boxes. Sweet joined in, vibrating like Mr Blobby, bald head glistening with sweat.

212

By eight everything was ready, the team smart in black trousers, starched white shirts and black bows. Trays of canapés were warming in the ovens. Red and black caviar waited in silver bowls cradled in ice. The kitchen table was covered in trays of drinks, campari, gin and tonic, champagne, Pimm's. They had not seen the host: they did not even know his or her name.

The guests arrived in a rush. One minute the two long reception rooms, separated by an arched doorway, were empty, cool, scented by simple flower arrangements in the marble fireplaces. The next they were full of men in dinner jackets, women in expensive dresses, alcohol fumes and the bray of the English superior classes at play. George slid through the crowd balancing his tray of drinks, smiling fixedly at the customers as they seized them.

The rooms opened on a terrace with a white stone balustrade. There was a long, empty view of hills in the moonlight, a flash of sea in the distance. It was gone nine and there had not been a frisson of impropriety yet. George had recognised a few faces from the lists provided by Gina and Rebecca Sayers. Charles and Denise Lang slipped in about nine thirty, after which George busied himself in the kitchen to avoid being recognised by her. There was no sign of Jevanjee. There were certainly no children. By ten, things were easing up and they were already washing some of the glasses.

Perhaps the whole thing had been a waste of time. They would see. The delicate bit would come around ten thirty, when the van returned to Bristol. There were two vans, including the smaller one in which Sweet had brought the food and drink. The plan was to leave it to the last moment, then George would tell the others that he and Dougal were going back with Sweet, who was such a fussy little sod they were sure he would be the last to leave.

As the six other men climbed into the back of the van, the driver could not see what was happening at the rear. Dougal was already concealed in one of the outbuildings, the yard in darkness. 'OK, fellas.' George spoke just loud enough to be heard. 'Dougal and I gotta help that old bugger Sweet finish up. He'll bring us back. See you next time – have a nice flight!' He slammed the door firmly and banged twice on the roof of the van. The driver heard the signal and let in the clutch. George dived behind a row of black plastic dustbins so that he would not be seen in the van's cracked mirrors as its tail-lights vanished through the gate and down the drive. He joined Dougal in the disused wash-house and they pulled black sweaters over their shirts. George opened the shoulder bag that contained a camera, miniature cassette-recorder and a more bulky camcorder, as well as a small can of oil and a jemmy. He settled down to wait in the dark; they would leave it till midnight before going back into the house.

Earlier that evening a neighbour had called at a prim house in Abbots Leigh and, getting no answer at the front door, wandered round to the kitchen and the garage. She was surprised to hear the car engine running with the garage doors closed. Then she suddenly realised, panicked and wrenched them open. The hosepipe was taped neatly to the exhaust, snaking round to the crack at the top of the almost closed driver's window, the narrow gap blocked with an old jumper. Rebecca Sayers lolled inside, face scarlet from the carbon monoxide but still, deadly still among the swirling grey mist as the fumes condensed inside the car.

Just after eleven, Alison was leaving Harvey's fashionable restaurant in Denmark Street, on the arm of a tall man who smiled down at her. 'I love you when you laugh, Alison. And you laugh a lot.'

'That was terrific, John, best "working dinner" I've ever had, you old fraud.'

'I didn't stop noticing beautiful women just because I got divorced, you know. Anyway, it *was* work: we agreed we don't trust Alan Mar an inch – and that could be important.'

'Yes, it could.'

John Forbes was a gentleman, and more entertaining company than she had expected. His Daimler Sovereign was parked in a dark alley by the Lord Mayor's Chapel and he opened the door for her with a flourish. 'Shall we go back to my place for coffee?' The archway into the street was pointed like a church window, figures flitting past under an orange sodium lamp, beyond them the grey triangle of College Green, the floodlit cathedral and modern Council House. But here in the shadows, the soft leather cushions of the car felt protectively womb-like. She took the invitation at face value, then immediately started to regret it. 'Yes, John, that would be great. But I mustn't be too late, I've got to go to London tomorrow.'

She sensed he was smiling in the dark. 'Let's see how it goes.'

On the first floor of the large house in Somerset, the alchemy of crack and ecstasy was starting to work. It was an old building and most of the internal walls offered solid sound-proofing. The couples and threesomes who twisted naked on the beds and carpets, nerve-endings unnaturally but brilliantly alive as the drugs took over, were centred on their own pleasure and oblivious to their neighbours. In a book-lined room at the end of the corridor, the small Indian with the high bald forehead poured himself a lime juice and raised his eyebrows in mock disgust. 'Animals.' He flicked the switches of a TV screen divided into four to show three views of the outside, relayed from temporary security cameras, and one of the bedroom corridor. The black and white image of the yard at the side of the house was empty now except for a single car. The intruders he had been warned about were still in the wash-house.

The door opened and another man in a dinner suit came in, about forty-five with a boyish, unlined face. He had first come to the house as one of the 'animals' and could barely conceal his distaste for the Indian. He looked very agitated. 'Are they still outside, Anwar?'

'Yes, two of them. One is this man who has been nosing about, the PI working for the woman lawyer.' Jevanjee's face was in shadow, but a lamp on a low table caught the hardness in his eyes. 'He has miscalculated.'

'So what the hell are we going to *do*?'

'What do *you* suggest … Minister?' The small man's gaze mocked him. 'They already know far too much and if they enter this house tonight unhindered, they could obtain evidence that will stand up in court.'

Charles Lang looked horrified. 'You can't –'

'You have no balls, Charles, metaphorically or physically.' Jevanjee shook his head. 'The bearded one is dangerous and must be silenced. So must his companion.' Lang looked even more horrified. 'Go home, Charles. You're out of your class.'

The younger man flushed angrily. 'You can't do this. There must be another way. We all pay you handsomely to see that we can take our pleasure in private, not to be implicated in murder.'

The Indian sipped his lime. 'It is just a matter of degree. You have already broken the law on controlled drugs. Some of you have broken other laws that really matter.'

'Well, Denise and *I* certainly haven't.' His eyes were full of terror, but he remained bombastic. 'This really won't do, Anwar – if there is a problem, you'd better sort it yourself and close the whole shebang down. I'm going to find Denise and leave. I'm having nothing more to do with this. I was not here tonight and you will not be seeing us again.'

'The lovely Lady Denise appears to be engaged with your Iranian friend, Charles. No doubt she will feel hungover tomorrow and be walking like a duck for a week.' Jevanjee illustrated his point by doing a suggestive Max Wall walk across the room to refill his tumbler. He laughed derisively as the younger man bit back his fury. 'Just go home and forget it. Forget everything – except that you're in this as deeply as I am and if anything happens to me you're going down too. You'll lose your seat in the House, go to jail and be disgraced, an outcast for the rest of your life. Did they prepare you for all that at Charterhouse? Have you ever *been* in a prison, Charles? Now *I* have the benefit of three years in Amritsar jail – but I shall be lost in the Indian subcontinent long before they crucify you, little boy.'

'It's too risky – you're mad!'

'They came here as waiters and went back with the others, didn't they? Sweet will say whatever we tell him, otherwise his unpleasant criminal past comes to light and he goes out of business. Miss Hope may well guess what happened – and I hope it terrifies her – but there will be no bodies, no trace, no murder … It won't be the first time.'

Again, Lang looked frightened. 'What the hell do you mean?'

'You are my friend, Charles. Don't provoke me. You've had your fun for more than four years – just go, prepare your alibi for when the shit hits the fan. The group has been penetrated and all I can sell you now is a little time.'

In John Forbes' neat suburban drawing-room, Alison curled up on the sofa and sipped Armagnac. He had thrown his jacket in a corner and loosened his tie. 'I sometimes wish I'd gone to the Bar too, you know.' They were both slightly tipsy.

She laughed, gesturing at the antique bureau, the deep carpet, the Meissen in a glass cabinet. 'God knows why, John – you've done pretty well, I'd say.'

'Yes, but I miss being the advocate, the one at the sharp end. Anyway, *you* didn't become a solicitor.'

'No, but then I almost gave up before I'd started. Reading law was Dad's idea, not mine. He was a Presbyterian minister and we were very close, I suppose because I was his only daughter – I've got four brothers. At first, I wanted to be a minister too, can you imagine it?'

Forbes smiled gently. 'Is he still alive?'

'Oh yes, over seventy, living in a retirement flat and going strong. Mum died ten years ago.'

'I'm sorry.'

'She'd had a good life, I think. But I was closer to Dad and I guess I wanted to please him. The trouble was, when I got the place at Oxford, everything changed. All those clever, beautiful, pushy people. For a time I felt inferior, then I realised I was as good as most of them – could get laid, pass exams, make people laugh – and so I joined the club, wrote for student magazines, acted a bit in revues. By the end I was in a real mess, torn between trying something glamorous like journalism or politics, or dropping out and backpacking to Kathmandu. Didn't know who I really was any more.'

'So what happened?'

'Well, I *did* get a degree, a decent second, despite wasting so much time. After finals I drove down to Italy with a friend I haven't seen for ten years now, a nice bloke called Richard who had an old Triumph sports car and a tent … So far as I can remember he screwed me every night, but I was so preoccupied with all those doubts – including doubts about him – that it must have been horrible. The tent took hours to put up and we always seemed to be doing it in rain or mountain mist.' She giggled at the memory, the Armagnac getting to her. 'The whole thing was ludicrous, but it wasn't his fault. He was very good about it. One night we were camping by a lake and I couldn't sleep. Went out by myself and suddenly saw the blindingly obvious. That I wasn't cut out for the chattering classes, that I was close to taking a road where I'd just get bitter and disappointed.'

'And that was it?'

'Pretty much. I decided to give the Temple a try if they'd have me. The Scot in me said I had to earn my own living, so I got on with it. How about you?'

'Oh, I just took articles when I left school at sixteen. I had to get a job too and it was the only chance I had – my father was a railway porter. But I enjoy it – you don't change the world, but maybe nobody does. At least you touch people's lives at critical moments, when they need you.' He poured two more Armagnacs and put his arm round her. When he kissed her on the mouth it was a surprise and she responded, but pulled away gently, leaving his hand resting on her breast until he took it away and smiled questioningly. 'You're beautiful, Alison.' They both stood up and he kissed her again, almost shyly, one arm round her shoulders, and she stiffened as she felt his other hand low on her spine, pushing her into him.

It hadn't been much of a pass, but she felt awkward as she stepped back. 'Thank you, John. That was a lovely evening and it was kind of you to ask me. But I must go home now, I'll ring for a taxi.'

'Must you, Alison?' He met her eyes wistfully. 'I'd like you to stay, I'd like you to stay very much …'

'Yes, John, I must.'

In the taxi she was glad they seemed to have parted friends. John was no predator. He was a decent, warm-hearted man and it must have been so lonely, bringing up two daughters on your own. And she was grateful to him, for a single evening with another man had taught her a profound lesson. How very much she needed George – rough, kind George, a diamond masquerading as a lump of coal. She smiled to herself: she couldn't imagine clumsy old George as a waiter. She hoped to God he was all right out there in bandit country; but he would be. George could look after himself.

23

Shortly before midnight, George nodded to Dougal in the dim light of the wash-house. 'Time to go.' He spoke very softly.

The other man had been squatting in a corner, doing small, silent exercises to keep alert. 'OK. You want to prove Jevanjee is here, right? See what we can overhear from him or Lang? Evidence of drug supplying would be useful?'

'That's about it. We've already seen the Langs, so we can say they were here, but a photo of them – or Jevanjee – would help. I reckon you could get one from the bushes in front of the house, the porch is well-lit.'

'You take the fire escape first, see what you can hear from the rooms.' He grinned in the dark. 'Don't get carried away. I'll wait here till you've done a recce.' George nodded again. He paused by the door and Dougal whispered, 'Good luck, mate.' The door opened silently on the hinges they had oiled and warily George stepped outside.

He immediately knew that something was wrong. Peering into the gloom, he could see figures moving silently towards him under the arch, the glint of metal. He cursed silently, realising that the door was still open and Dougal beside him. The blaze of white flame blinded them. It was as if a search-light had been switched on. George reeled back, covering his eyes. 'Stay where you are!' roared a man's voice. 'Hands on your heads. You're covered from two directions, you cunts. Do exactly as I say or we'll waste you.' To emphasise the point, a single shot splintered the wood close to his head. They both froze. Peering into the glare, George saw that the light came from the headlamps of a large car.

Three shadows approached, stocky, in dark boiler suits, wearing Hallowe'en masks. George felt every muscle in his body tense. They were plainly not worried about the noise of shots, so they must be in a very isolated spot. 'Keep your hands on your head, both of you, and walk towards the lights, slowly.' The voice was quite cultivated for a thug. 'Slow, real slow. Try anything clever and we'll shoot you in the legs.' There was a low, threatening laugh. 'Then the stomach …'

George did as he was told, treading carefully on the slimy cobbles, in case he slipped and they thought he was trying to make a break for it. He peered forward to see how many other opponents were behind the car. The white glare from its headlamps still dazzled him, but he thought he could make out two more figures. Five of them altogether. Lousy odds, and Dougal, breathing heavily to his right, was giving off panicky vibes.

What a fucking mess.

It felt cold as a grave in the yard, eerie shadows playing on the walls as he moved. There was a little grey moonlight, enough for George to make out that the gates in the archway were open, ready for them all to drive off. He reached the car; it was a Mercedes. 'Stop there,' ordered the voice. 'Stand and face the car, feet together, then put your hands behind your back.' So they were going to tie his wrists.

Before George could respond he heard a shout and turned round sharply to see Dougal trying to make a break. He had already run six feet, got beyond the area lit by the headlamps, and was sprinting for the gate. He had taken them by surprise. The five figures stood transfixed, not moving, confused. It was like a still from a black and white film. Then they came to life and one threw himself at Dougal, who struck out with his fist, twisted and kicked upwards viciously. A scream of pain and the man was rolling on the ground, clutching his groin. Another moved to intercept him but slipped and fell.

Dougal darted to the left, towards the arch that led to safety, running footsteps echoing between the walls. As George reacted there were shouts everywhere and he saw four black figures closing on the shadow as it weaved from side to side. One paused, raised his arm and there was a flash of red, a loud report. The bullet ricocheted off the brickwork. George realised that the car was still standing there, empty, pointing at the gate. Suddenly he was no longer afraid. The adrenalin started to pump even faster. No one noticed as he dropped silently to his knees, opened the door and slid behind the driving wheel. The keys were in the ignition lock. He released the hand-brake, breathed in deeply and engaged first gear, keeping his foot firmly on the clutch.

At the exact moment he started the engine, there were four more spurts of flame outside, four more rapid shots. On automatic pilot he let the clutch in sharply; the engine roared and the car sprang towards the rectangle of grey light in the wall. Dougal had vanished. The four men running after him were side by side in the gateway. George gunned the Merc at them and heard cursing as they flung themselves out of the way. Something struck the side of the car with a thud and there was another scream. Then he was outside, wheels spinning on the gravel. He slowed to look for Dougal, but there was no sign of him, no sign of anyone, though there were still lights blazing in the house.

Another volley of shots hammered into the car, shattering the rear window. A bullet hit the dash-board and George felt a splinter cut his face. He had no choice: get away and fetch help. He accelerated down the drive, weaving in case they aimed at his tyres, skidding round a bend, past a long iron fence separating it from the fields, down a dark avenue of trees. A pair of granite pillars marked the junction with the road. He braked sharply, but there were no other vehicles. He didn't know where he was, or which way to go, but turned left.

Half a mile behind, Dougal raised his head cautiously from the ditch he had fallen into, just a short distance from the house. His pursuers seemed to have gone back into the yard. He stood up slowly, his left ankle painful where he had twisted it, and started to stumble towards the trees.

He heard shouts, a second car starting and white headlights swept across the lawn. When the beam hit him he panicked and ran despite the agony in his leg, lurching from side to side like a drunk. The first bullet drove into his shoulder like a red-hot poker, seconds before he heard the shot, followed by another gouging low in his back. He cried out at the blinding explosion of pain, swayed and lost consciousness.

George drove fast along the country road, trees flashing by in the moonlight, steering the powerful car like a racing driver. He hoped to God Dougal had found somewhere to hide. After ten minutes he realised that no one was following. The excitement was over. He was back in sleepy Somerset, following an empty lane at one in the morning. A fox appeared in the beam of his headlights and he slowed to let it amble between the hedges.

The small town surprised him. He reached it after half an hour. The dark fields and woodland turned into a row of council houses, followed by some large executive places set back from the road. Then he was in a street full of familiar signs: Spar, Boots, the Midland Bank. Modern sodium lights reflected on Mendip sandstone. A few cars were parked at the kerb, but there were no people about. The police station was in the small square. When he slowed outside, he saw that it was closed. A sign on the door invited him to use a phone behind a glass plate in the wall. To his surprise, when he picked it up, a woman answered immediately. A patrol car arrived fifteen minutes later.

A constable got out of the passenger door, putting on his cap in a leisurely fashion. 'What's the problem, sir?' His tone suggested there shouldn't be one; and if there was, it was George's fault.

George explained tersely, ending: 'We must go back at once and see what has happened to my partner. I think he may be in danger. He may even be dead.'

'Been drinking, have we, sir?' The policeman's boredom and contempt were transparent as he reached back into his car for a notebook. 'Had an accident? I see your car is damaged.'

'No, I have *not* been drinking and that window was smashed by bullets – this is serious, a matter of life and death, and we need to get back *urgently*!'

'Of course, sir. May I see your driving licence?'

'I don't have it on me.' He had carefully removed any document with his real name from his clothes. 'For God's sake, constable, did you hear what I said?'

'Insurance certificate?'

'I don't have that either. This isn't my car.'

'And who would the owner be, then, sir?'

'I don't know.'

'Stolen, is it?'

'Of course not – I'll explain on the way back. Look – I phoned for *help*, we can't go on like this all night!'

The policeman shone a flashlight on the Mercedes' licence plate. 'Too new to need an MOT.' He started to write laboriously on a pad and tore off a form. 'Produce your licence and insurance at this police station within seven days.' He reached into the police car again. 'Now, if you haven't been drinking you won't mind blowing into this device, will you, sir?' He held up a flat black box with a green light glowing, nodding at the plastic tube. 'In there.'

George stared at the breathalyser in disbelief, resisting an overpowering urge to hit this idiot somewhere very painful. But it would only waste even more time and get him arrested for assault. He clenched his fists in his pockets, sighed and blew into the tube. The constable studied the light, looking disappointed. 'That's not good, enough, I'm afraid. Can't you blow any harder? Try again.'

George blew into the tube a second time, as hard as he could. Again the man waited for a light to come on. After a full five minutes he gave up, looking furious. 'Very well, sir. I needn't detain you.' He turned to get back into his car.

'I came here to report an attempted murder.' George spoke quietly, but with a harsh edge that cracked through the cold air of the empty square. 'Have you forgotten?'

The constable did not apologise. 'You serious? I thought you was just making that up to divert attention from your inebriated state.'

George took a step towards the man, towering above him, shoulders shaking with rage. 'You thought *what*? Listen, you stupid little fart, I'm a licensed private investigator working on a case headed up by Chief Superintendent Manning in Bristol. If I was driving over the limit, do you *really* think I'd have phoned for you in the first place? There are some paid-up villains down the road. They've been dealing all night in hard drugs and child sex and God knows what else. A man may have been killed. I have been the victim of attempted murder. We are talking about serious crime. So will you now stop pissing about and start doing the job you're paid for? Do I make myself *clear*?' He was shouting and overhead a window banged open.

'For Christ's sake, we're trying to sleep up here,' bellowed an angry voice, male, elderly, traces of Alf Garnett.

'OK, OK,' snapped the constable. 'Watch your lip – no need to carry on like that. I can book you for disturbance and insulting behaviour, you know.' Jesus, thought George, he was going to kill this bastard. 'We'll go and take a look if you think it's so important. I just hope you're not wasting my time. That's an offence, too.'

'These men are armed. Don't you need some back-up?'

'We'll just have a look first, sir. I can radio for reinforcements.' The man plainly did not believe a thing George had told him.

He went with the two constables in the back of the police car, guiding them with some difficulty because he did not know the roads. At first he missed the turning that led to the gates of the big house, realising his mistake when they entered a village he had not passed through in his flight. 'Sorry, could you turn round and go back a mile or so?'

The policeman who was now his enemy hissed through his teeth. 'If we *must*. This is ridiculous.' The driver had not spoken, but did an abrupt U-turn through the empty car park in front of the village inn and accelerated back up the hill so fast that George felt his shoulders pressing hard into the back of the seat. This time he knew where to turn and in five minutes they reached the drive with its granite pillars. Before he could suggest they stop and approach on foot, the driver had turned in and accelerated up the drive, engine roaring and headlights full on. Had these two goons never encountered real crime? Did they *want* to be shot at?

But there was no need for caution. As they emerged from the avenue of trees, a shaft of moonlight showed the house in darkness. Black patches against its white façade made it look like a skull until George realised they were shutters closed over the windows. The gate to the yard was shut. When the police car stopped he climbed out with the obnoxious copper and pushed at the wood, but the gate had been secured with a large padlock. They walked along the terrace at the front of the house, slipping on the occasional patch of moss, then across the lawn at its side. The silence was eerie. At the back the policeman's flashlight showed a wooden door in a brick wall; when they pushed it open, they were in an enclosed kitchen garden which looked derelict so far as he could see in the dark.

They came back to the front of the house. 'There's no one here, sir. No sign of this orgy, if I may say so. No sign of your friend either, *if* he ever existed.'

George looked at his watch. It was still only two. 'They were here less than two hours ago.'

'So you say. I think we'd better go to the nearest open nick and get a report made, don't you?'

Ten miles to the west, two men were slithering on loose shale up the side of a disused quarry. Their Range Rover was parked precariously above them. They had wrapped Dougal's body in polythene sheets and concealed it in a shaft cut into the rock. As they reached the Range Rover, there was a loud coughing sound as the small charge they had left brought down the roof of the tunnel. Looking back, there was nothing to see but a dent in the slope of loose chippings and rubble. It would take an earthquake for anyone to find him.

24

Early next morning, Alison took the train from Temple Meads to Paddington. She had rung George before leaving, but his answering machine was on. He was probably asleep after getting back late from the rave.

She was in no hurry and took a number twenty-three bus from the station to Fleet Street, getting off outside the Temple. Quite like old times. Some weeks before she had put out as many enquiries as she could about Jevanjee: to old contacts at the Bar, journalists and helpful souls in the Immigration Service. One had come back positively, but he wanted paying before handing over his report.

She met him in the George, opposite the Law Courts in the Strand, a neatly dressed man in his thirties with prematurely greying hair. His tweed sports jacket looked out of place among the waist-coated solicitors and barristers shorn of wigs but still wearing their white bands. 'Miss Hope? May I get you a drink?'

She looked at the heaving crowd. 'Thank you, but could we possibly have one later? Find some-where a little quieter to talk?'

'Of course. I didn't expect it to be so packed. There must be some high profile case over the road today.' They crossed the Strand and walked through an alley, then along the back of the ugly Victorian pile that was the centre of British justice: inefficient, out-dated and inaccessible like the system itself. In Lincoln's Inn Fields he guided them to a bench, near the Tarmac square where office girls were playing netball at lunch-time. He turned and smiled at her. 'I have what you asked for.'

'Excellent!' But, without offending him, Alison wanted to hear a little more before handing over the envelope with his fee, in cash as requested. 'I'm amazed at the way you do it.'

He shrugged at the implied question. 'I've been at it a long time, you know. I use a whole network of local lawyers in the sub-continent, and I go out there pretty often myself.' He smiled. 'I also have my professional secrets.' JF Cunningham – if he had a first name, neither Alison nor anyone else had ever heard it used – was the immigration adviser with a large East End firm of solicitors. He wasn't a lawyer, but a graduate in Hindi and Urdu, paid to produce the evidence needed to convince the authorities of the background of asylum seekers and supposed husbands, wives or children from Pakistan, India, Bangladesh and Sri Lanka. It was a job the average man in the street did not know existed, but at the age of thirty it brought Cunningham over fifty thousand a year. In the last ten years, immigration from the poorer parts of the world had become a mega-industry.

'Was Jevanjee a difficult case?'

Cunningham was distracted as sparrows hopped from the grass to peck expectantly round his feet. 'Sorry, chaps, I forgot to bring any bread today. Difficult? No – not once I found his real origins. He's not from Pakistan and wasn't born in Lahore.'

'No? That's what he's told everyone in Bristol for years.'

'Maybe, but he's lying. He was born in the Punjab. He's a Sikh.'

'But he doesn't wear a turban or call himself Singh?'

'Well, not *every* Sikh sports the bangle and dagger, you know.' He reached into his jacket and produced a thick manila envelope. 'It's all in my report, but Jevanjee is interesting. He's not lapsed at all. He's a major supporter of the KLF.'

'KLF?'

'The Khalistan Liberation Front. It's the movement campaigning for a separate Sikh state in the Punjab, Khalistan – you must have heard of it?'

'Vaguely.'

Cunningham shook his head ruefully. 'I suppose I expect everyone to be clued up on the things that I meet every day. The north-west of India has been the most God-awful mess ever since partition. The frontier states of Jammu and Kashmir have always been disputed by India and Pakistan – there've been a couple of wars over it. At the same time, just to the south, the Sikhs have been campaigning to turn the Punjab into a separate country. The KLF is a serious political and terrorist movement, has popular support and can be violent. Do you remember the siege of the Golden Temple in Amritsar? Dreadful business, Indian troops shelling the holiest Sikh shrine and Sikh zealots dying in the ruins. Led to Mrs Gandhi's assassination. It's boiling up all the time and I think one day they may get their separate state, just as the Bangladeshis did.'

'Where on earth does Jevanjee fit in?'

'He provides money for arms and explosives. He supports the exiles over here, makes sure photographs of torture victims get to Amnesty and the press.'

'He does *what*? Are you sure? In Bristol he can only be described as a paid-up crook.'

'You should read my report, Miss Hope. Do you want it, or not?'

Alison nodded. 'Of course.' She handed over her envelope and he gave her his. 'And you say Jevanjee is on the side of the angels?'

'He is in Amritsar. He's one of the overseas heroes of the movement.'

'I just don't get it. He's a drug peddler, probably dealing in arms, the man's a bloody *criminal*.'

Cunningham gave a half smile. 'He can be a hero *too*, you know. A lot of people are both where I come from.' For the first time she noticed the traces of Ulster in his voice. 'He's found a way of making a great deal of money in Bristol, I'm sure he regards his clients with contempt and he keeps plenty of the profit for himself, but his commitment to Khalistan is real – that's where much of his money goes. He's a crook who also believes in something. If he deals in arms, I suspect that's just for his friends in India.'

'And what's his real name – his Sikh name?'

'He was baptised Gurjit Singh.'

'But he practises as Jevanjee? Must have studied under that name?'

'Miss Hope, this man has been involved with the KLF all his adult life.' His sharp sideways glance suggested that he did not like having to explain everything twice. 'As a young man he fought with a guerrilla group after partition – he was a leader of the movement. But he was captured and faced hanging by the authorities. He was rescued in a prison break-out, fled from Amritsar and studied medicine in Pakistan under a new name – that's where Jevanjee the non-Sikh comes from. He's lived abroad, mostly in England, ever since. But one day I'm sure he'll go back to Khalistan.'

Alison stared at the young women leaping about on the netball court. Some people had nice uncomplicated lives. 'Thank you, Mr Cunningham. I'm afraid you've rather thrown me. I thought I was dealing with a simple murder, then it got complicated, now I'm totally out of my depth.'

Cunningham stood up to go. 'I'm sorry, but I can only give you the facts.' He hesitated. 'Look – I'm sure I don't need to say it, but be careful. Jevanjee might be a hero in the Punjab, but he would be dangerous if cornered.'

Alison remembered sitting on the doorstep in Clifton, feeling the heat from the blazing car. 'Yes, I know.'

She phoned the remand centre from a call box in Aldwych. Time was short now before the trial. She had left her car parked at Temple Meads so, when she arrived back in Bristol, she drove straight out to see Quinn. She had to wait in the interview room for a quarter of an hour before they brought him. 'How's it going, Geoff?'

'How the hell do you think it's going? Like all the rest of you, I'm coming to believe Jess and Tom are dead. Nothing else seems to matter very much. The food's diabolical and I'm not mad about the company.'

'OK, Geoff. OK. I get the message. But you'll be in court in a few days and I'm still baffled about whole chunks of the story.' Alison sat down opposite him. 'So, may I run through them?' He shrugged vaguely. 'As we've discussed before, over the past year or two Nikki was going to gatherings with your neighbour, Mrs Sayers. These were events involving beautiful, or at least well-heeled people, sex and hard drugs.'

He nodded. 'You've told me before.'

She sighed wearily. 'Yes, Geoff. And you've told me you were unaware of it. Mrs Sayers was so aware of it that when we contacted her she committed suicide.' She looked up but he showed no reaction. 'OK, Geoff, so lots of your neighbours in dear old

239

Abbots Leigh commit suicide? Right? They do it all the time?' She shot him a hard look, raising her voice. 'Well? *Do* they?'

'Of course not.' It was a disinterested mumble. Quinn was falling apart again. 'But, the truth is, I barely knew this Sayers woman. I never knew where Nikki was going or what she was up to.'

'You didn't know she was having an affair with Charles Lang, MP and has-been minister?'

'I thought she must be having an affair, but I'd never heard of Charles Lang until you told me about him.'

'OK.' She sighed. 'I believe you. As to Lang and Sayers and Jevanjee, I guess you can't give evidence about what you don't know. It's pretty clear where the truth lies. Jevanjee was deeply into criminal sex and drugs, thought Nikki had become a threat and was trying to blackmail both of you. I can issue a witness summons and make the bastard answer questions in court. I can also summon Charles Lang and his ghastly wife, who I'm told goes like a rattle-snake even when she's not high.'

'Will they come?'

'It's not the best way of making a case, but actually they don't have any choice unless they're prepared to be jailed for contempt. What they will *say* is another matter, but that's my problem. I have to know all the answers before I ask the questions.'

Outside the prison, the phone was buzzing in her car. It was past seven in the evening and she desperately wanted to go home and put her feet up. She opened the door and reluctantly picked up the handset. 'Alison Hope.'

'It's George, love. Can you come and bail me out? I've been at the Central nick all day – I've been arrested for wasting police time.'

25

The workman on the demolition job was dressed traditionally. His T-shirt asked, *Fancy a Quickie?* and his jeans were a size too small. Every time he bent to swing his pickaxe, they slid down to reveal a good three inches of muscular buttock. The building he and his three mates were blitzing had been a petrol station, put up only eight years ago, now closed due to the owner's bankruptcy. It would be replaced by five houses built on spec; very likely the recession would send their builder to the wall, too. Maybe this tatty quarter-acre would stay barren to the end of time.

Nigel did not much care. He had been a stevedore at Avonmouth docks, just the other side of the road, until they laid him off. At six pounds an hour he was glad of the work. Everything above ground had been smashed, leaving two large heaps of bricks and splintered blocks. Now they were breaking up the concrete floor of the new car wash that he'd watched some other blokes in hard hats erect less than a year before. Even to Nige, who rarely read beyond page three, that really *did* seem barmy.

He ran his hand across his forehead, wiping away the sweat. It was stuffy with all the dust in the air. Then Terry did another burst with the Kango drill and the concrete cracked. A full-blooded swing with the pick and it started to splinter, chips leaping up to bounce off their plastic goggles. Nigel raised his pick again, but suddenly paused. The tan of his face paled. 'Blimey, Tel, what the fuck's that?' He was pointing into the newly opened cavity.

Terry knelt and started to stir the rubble with a crowbar. 'Christ.' He looked up nervously. 'It's a hand.' As he uncovered more, they could see that it was a left hand, well-preserved in the concrete, joined to a wrist and an arm fractured in several places when they poked it. The concrete was cracked for some ten feet and it was not difficult to prise up more pieces, enough to show that it concealed a whole body, of a tall man clad in the remains of a blue battle-dress top and trousers. When they got to the face, Nigel threw up and Terry went to find a phone.

George was being interviewed for the second time by Manning, not in his office but a bare interrogation room at Central. A woman inspector called Curzon was also present. The interview had been icily courteous, every word taped, but it was plain that Manning was hostile and sceptical. He leaned back in his chair, tapping a pencil on the table and eyeing George dismissively.

'Look here, Mr Kristianssen, you have a job to do and so do I. I'm sure you're doing your best for your client, but what do you expect me to believe? You say some kind of Roman orgy was taking place at Hammond House, but when my officers went back with you, it was deserted. It appears to be owned by a trust registered in the British Virgin Islands. It is partly furnished, and was let until three years ago, since when it has been unoccupied. It is for sale. I believe all that, because I've checked it out. Those are *facts*. You've made a whole string of allegations which I *don't* believe, because they're without a shred – I repeat, without a *shred* – of substantiation.'

'I wouldn't be making them unless I was certain.'

Manning lit a small cigar, blowing a stream of blue smoke towards the ceiling. 'You allege that a former Minister of the Crown and a prominent doctor in this city, to name but two, are trading Class A controlled drugs, and a venue to use them for enhanced sex, to a select group of wealthy people. That's it, in a nutshell?'

'Yes. I also believe that Jevanjee and Lang are involved in illegal arms trading. That they believed Nikki Quinn might blow the whistle on them and killed her, setting up her husband to take the rap.'

'Balls, absolute balls.' Manning's tone was contemptuous. 'Quinn killed her. That makes a damn sight more sense.' He looked up as the door opened and a policewoman came in to hand him a note.

Glancing at it, he stood up and left abruptly.

About fifteen minutes passed, during which George stared at the wall. Inspector Curzon faced him in silence and two constables came and stood in the corner with arms folded, as if they thought he might turn violent or try to escape. When Manning returned, he was half smiling, studying George's face thoughtfully before he spoke. 'OK, Kristianssen, your lady friend's come to rescue you. She's very persuasive – we could prosecute you for wasting police time, but I do not propose to do so. You may go.'

George stood up slowly. 'Thank you, Chief Superintendent.'

'Just *go*, before I change my mind.' As George reached the door, Manning called after him. 'By the way.' George stopped and turned round. 'Tell your Miss Hope that a body was discovered this afternoon by workmen demolishing a garage in Avonmouth. It was Simon Boniface. According to the pathologist he's been dead for six months, probably from within days of his escape from custody. He was still in the remains of his prison uniform.' George stared at him. 'That makes sense to me. He paid to be sprung, then they worked the bastard over until he gave enough details for them to access his overseas bank accounts, and took him out. No honour among thieves these days.'

George did a quick double-take. 'Thanks,' he said. 'I'll tell her.'

'Do that, squire. You can also tell her to forget her conspiracy theory. In my book, this means the trial judge had a lousy car mechanic, Mr Justice Carswell was a disgusting old pervert – and Dr Quinn will shortly be convicted, rightly, of murder. Now, piss off.'

26

Only two days to go. Alison was as ready for the trial as she ever would be. It was to be taken by Mr Justice Egan, a young and liberal High Court judge who would not give her as hard a time as some. He was only fifty-two, a leading QC until three years ago. The prosecution would be led by Rick Fennel QC, also young, but less civilised. Known in the trade as the Rottweiler, Fennel pursued his cases ferociously and usually came out on top.

Apart from Quinn himself, her main witnesses would be Mar, Gina, Taylor and George. The suicide of Rebecca Sayers, potentially the star turn, was more than a disaster

Alison had managed to retain her own forensic pathologist, who had examined what remained of Nikki Quinn, stored in a cardboard box at the city mortuary pending release by the coroner. Bones and ash did not need to be kept refrigerated. He would cast doubt on the claimed cause of death; and suggest that no one could know exactly when death had occurred, so it might have been when Quinn said he was hundreds of miles away. Trouble was, it could equally have been when he was in

Bristol; and the jury read the papers and would already have convicted him.

She had applied for her witness summonses: for Dr Jevanjee, Charles Lang and his wife, Lady Denise. The judge had granted them all, despite Lang sending down a Treasury solicitor to plead for Crown immunity. 'This case has nothing to do with Mr Lang's former ministerial duties,' he ruled firmly. 'I expect him to appear and will send the police to arrest him if he does not.' A few days later, Alison was surprised to return to her chambers and find a young woman sitting on the stairs. She was smartly dressed in a pinstripe suite. 'Miss Hope?'

'Yes.'

'I'm Elaine Maitland.' She produced an identity card in a plastic wallet. 'From the Ministry of Defence. Could we talk, please?'

Alison unlocked the door. 'It's hopelessly inconvenient, you know – do you always turn up without an appointment?'

'Always.' The girl had a beautiful smile and was not what Alison would have expected from MI5, which was plainly where she came from. 'We find it works better that way.' She took a chair without being asked and smiled again. 'What a lovely room.'

'Thanks. Have you come to persuade me not to force Charles Lang to appear in court?'

'Good lord, no. Go ahead, that's nothing to do with us. The fact is, my part of the Ministry—'

'You mean the Security Service, I take it?'

'Well, yes, perhaps I do. Anyway, we were just

interested in your reasons for summoning Mr Lang. Strictly off the record, of course.' She reached into her briefcase and put a small black box on the coffee-table. 'It's not a recorder, quite the opposite, in fact. The signals it emits will make it impossible for any bug or recorder within earshot to pick up anything except white noise. Clever, eh? So we can talk quite freely. You see, there have been rumours about Mr Lang being involved in activities that might endanger security.'

Alison was gobsmacked – not by what the woman said, but by the way she had launched straight in to accuse one of her ex-masters of – of what exactly? Breaching the Official Secrets Act? High treason? She tried to look unimpressed. '*Whose* security, exactly?'

'The security of the realm, Miss Hope – your security.'

'I feel secure enough.'

'It affects us all if a senior politician is open to blackmail. Or is involved in criminal activity concerning arms trading. Not that he necessarily is, of course. We thought you might have discovered facts that should properly be brought to our attention.' She was very chirpy, this girl, but Alison took in her firm-looking body, tough manner, the way she asked outrageous questions as if she had every right to do so. *I just want to run over your sex life, bank balance, secret fears and fantasies, how often do you masturbate? Of course you won't mind me asking …*

'Well, *have* you?'

'Have I what?'

'Discovered anything that you feel my service should know, in the interest of what might broadly be termed national security?'

Alison stared at her. She had met Security Service officers before and this girl was out of the same mould. Looked like a young ex-army officer: bright, charming, tough as old boots. 'Let me get this straight.'

'Of course.'

'You believe that I may have gathered, as a defending counsel, evidence of wrongdoing by an ex-Minister of the Crown, one Charles Lang? And you're asking me to hand it over to you *before* the trial of my client?'

'Exactly.'

'But why on earth should I? Even if your assumption is correct? How do I know you won't use it to conceal whatever Mr Lang's been up to? Are you willing to come to court as a witness and confirm that you approached me like this – which some might see as a serious indication that all is not well with Mr Lang's activities?'

'Certainly not.' The young woman stood up, skirt swinging from muscular hips, but she plainly had no intention of leaving. She walked to the window overlooking the old graveyard. 'Nice outlook, that patch of green right in the city centre.' She turned round abruptly. 'This meeting is entirely off the record, Miss Hope. The fact is that my masters have no intention of helping Lang – they are concerned that he may have been breaking the law. I'm an investigating officer and I can talk to you now when it might be difficult for Special Branch, with Quinn's trial imminent. That's why I'm here, not the police. All I can do is ask you to trust me and appeal to your sense of public duty.'

Alison resisted the urge to throw her out. 'What you're asking is absolutely outrageous, at least until the trial is over. I have a duty to my client, for God's sake, not to MI5.'

'And I haven't come to obstruct you, believe me. We really would be grateful, in absolute confidence, to know of anything significant about Lang that you may have turned up. In return, I have something with me that may assist your defence of Dr Quinn. Now I can't say fairer than that, can I?'

Alison burst out laughing. Outside, footsteps were hurrying down John Street. 'For cool cheek, you really take the biscuit, do you know that? But let's talk about it. Would you like some coffee?'

27

The morning of the trial was sunny. Alison had spent the whole weekend putting her notes in order and felt confident when she met Quinn in the cells. Upstairs in the robing-room, black-clad figures wandered about like a flock of ravens, the QCs in their plain-backed silk, the rest with coarser gowns incorporating a vestigial hood at the shoulder. A short man with a chestnut beard approached and held out his hand. 'Rick Fennel.'

She recognised him. 'Shall we both wish each other luck?'

He smiled like a man who expected to win. 'Why not? You should meet my junior, Susanna Cohen.' The young woman also shook hands, just as the Tannoy summoned them. 'Regina versus Quinn in court one, please.'

The jury box, the bench and the dock were empty, but the rest of the high, panelled, slightly dusty room was crowded. A cluster of young men and women at the press table, and the public gallery at the back was packed. One of the ushers, a middle-aged woman in a black gown, opened the door to let Alison and Fennel in. The long counsel's table in front of the bench was empty, but Forbes and the CPS solicitors were already ranged along the one behind it. Alison took the defender's traditional seat on the left, nearest the jury box.

The clerk, a weedy young man in wig and gown, slipped into place immediately in front of the judge's dais. Under the royal coat of arms, a door behind the bench was opened by another usher. 'Court rise!' Sir James Egan was in almost before they could stand, a stocky figure in scarlet, jowls wobbling under a discoloured wig, black scarf draped over his left shoulder. He smiled and bowed, first to Alison, then to Fennel. They bowed back and resumed their seats as the clerk gabbled the opening sentence: 'All persons having anything to do before my Lords the Queen's Justices, draw near and give your attention.' The court was in session.

Mr Justice Egan opened the thick bundle of papers on his sloping desk, an exact copy of the photocopied bundles lying before Alison and Fennel. The days of 'Put up the prisoner' had gone; he just nodded quietly at the screw standing at the top of the steps leading down from the dock, the screw beckoned and Quinn appeared, first his head, then the rest of him, neat in a clean white shirt, red tie and pressed suit. He stood erect between two prison officers as the clerk read the charge, the unlawful killing of Nicola Caroline Quinn on or about the sixth day of September ... 'How do you plead? Guilty or not guilty?'

'Not guilty, sir.' At least he sounded as if he meant it.

The judge glanced down at the two counsel. 'Any points of law, Miss Hope, Mr Fennel? Otherwise we should proceed to swear the jury.'

'We've had a word outside and are happy to proceed, m'lord,' said Fennel. Alison nodded agreement.

Another nod, this time to an usher. It was uncanny, like a ring bidding silently at an auction from which the public, though present, were excluded. Two dozen men and women shuffled through a door to the right of the judge and filed into the two long benches for the jury. Clutching women's magazines and copies of the *Sun*, they looked as if they had been hanging about for a case for days, bored and irritable like disgruntled holidaymakers waiting for a delayed charter flight. With one or two exceptions they all looked incredibly scruffy, as if they were unemployed and had been summoned from long days spent on sofas watching the box in gaffs rented on housing benefit, waiting for the next giro to arrive. One of them was clutching a Walkman, the headphones still covering his ears. Where were the literate middle classes, Alison wanted to scream? She knew where they were – they had been pricked off the electoral roll, too, but cunningly sent sick notes or pleas of foreign holidays to get out of it. Half of this shower would decide whether Geoffrey Quinn was guilty or not guilty of murder. Good grief.

The clerk seemed to choose twelve at random, six

men and six women. As he swore them one by one, Alison turned to give Quinn an encouraging smile. He stared back woodenly. There was a long pause while the judge seemed to go into a trance, thumbing vaguely through his thick file, then Rick Fennel was on his feet. 'If it please your lordship – ladies and gentlemen of the jury, I am Richard Fennel, prosecuting for the Crown, and my learned friend, Miss Alison Hope,' he gestured to his left, 'will be speaking in Dr Quinn's defence. I am assisted by Miss Susanna Cohen of counsel.' He paused and sipped a glass of water, waiting until he had the full attention of all twelve.

'Members of the jury, as I shall demonstrate, the evidence that Geoffrey Quinn murdered his wife Nicola, and attempted to destroy her body in a wood-burning furnace, is overwhelming. He has chosen to plead not guilty, as is his right, but when you have heard the evidence I have no doubt that you will feel no choice, no possible choice, but to convict him of murder.' He paused again and smiled, running his eyes along the two rows of faces, making eye contact.

Alison found it hard to concentrate. She tried to make notes as Fennel set out his case, but she knew John would be doing that behind her. All she had to do that day was stay awake and object to anything prejudicial. But Fennel's style meant there was unlikely to be anything over the top. He had an easy, blokeish manner, smiling at the jury frequently, using his strong Yorkshire accent. You had to give it to him: he came over just right, a plain man, a man to be trusted. Shit.

It took less than an hour. A short account of Quinn's life, leading up to the creaking marriage. Then the three critical days. Quinn vanishes, cannot account for his whereabouts for a whole twenty-four hours, the police are called, the remains of the body are found. Forensic evidence to identify them. The conclusion: 'It is plain, members of the jury, is it not? Dr Quinn and his wife were quarrelling, raised voices turned to threatening gestures, to a blow or blows. One way or another, Nikki Quinn was knocked down the cellar steps, breaking her neck and sustaining head injuries, as the forensic evidence will show. That fall killed her. It is always sad, more than sad, when a relationship breaks down like this – but nothing, members of the jury, can justify violence in a marriage. I suggest that Dr Quinn was angry, frustrated, furious. He *meant* to hurt his wife: to kill her or at least to do her very serious harm. That intention is enough to justify the charge. He struck her, she died, and he then went to *considerable* lengths to destroy her body. Dr Quinn is guilty of murder. That is all I have to say at present. I shall now proceed to call the Crown evidence.'

The evidence took hours. It always did. First the police constable called to Quinn's house, then Manning. That concluded the morning and Alison walked back to her chambers with John for a sandwich lunch. The comforting blue room was only five minutes from the court in Small Street. 'How do you feel?' he asked.

'I don't really feel anything much, a bit tense. I'm glad there isn't much for us to do today.'

'Fennel's doing a perfect job. Nothing to object to. Low key. Factual. Bugger, isn't it?'

After lunch, Fennel called the pathologist. He stepped into the witness box, neat in a dark suit, putting on a pair of gold half-moon spectacles to emphasise his learning. 'State your name and address.'

'Alexander William Baxter, Coombe Cottage, Penn, Somerset.'

'And your occupation?'

'I am a pathologist employed by the Home Office Forensic Science Laboratory.'

'What are your qualifications?'

'I am a Bachelor of Medicine and Surgery in the University of London, a Doctor of Medicine, a Licentiate of the Royal College of Physicians and a Fellow of the Royal College of Pathologists.'

'Were you called out by the police on the ninth of September?'

'Yes, I was. I was summoned to a house in Abbots Leigh, Bristol.'

'Who was the owner of this house?'

'Dr Quinn.' Alison listened intently, to pick up any leading questions or inconsistencies. Trouble was, everybody else in the court was listening intently too, particularly the jury. It would have been easier to face someone bombastic and bullying; Fennel was just too cunning, too clever – he had them in the palm of his hand.

'And what did you find there, Doctor?'

'A body had been burnt in the wood-burning furnace in the cellar, the source for the central heating.'

'The body was still in the furnace?'

For the first time the judge interrupted. 'Don't lead the witness, Mr Fennel. He has long experience and can speak for himself.'

'I'm sorry, my lord.' Then back to Baxter. 'Where was the body, Doctor?'

'It was in the combustion chamber of the furnace, a long steel cylinder. Apart from the bones, most of it had been destroyed: such tissue and ash as remained were still warm.'

'You say it had been destroyed, Doctor – would that have been easy to achieve?'

'Not too difficult, if the furnace was hot when the body went in and kept hot and burning for the three days it may have been there. It would help if the furnace was poked from time to time – to help the body break up. It would burn faster as it separated into smaller units.'

'Thank you, Doctor. So it would have burnt better if someone had tended the boiler at intervals? Could the body have been destroyed without that?'

'Yes, it could.'

'Who supervised the removal of the remains from the boiler?'

'I did. Everything removed was placed in

polythene containers, labelled and sealed under my supervision.'

'Was the body recognisable?'

'Not as such. The skeleton was no longer complete and the facial features had been destroyed by fire, only the skull and jawbones remained.'

'What steps did you take to identify the remains, Doctor?'

'Suspecting that the body might be one of the Quinn family, the next day I obtained their dental records from the family dentist. The teeth of the deceased were those of Mrs Quinn.'

The questioning droned on, turning to Baxter's conclusion that Nikki had 'fallen or been pushed down the cellar steps in the course of a violent argument. Her spinal cord was broken between the third and fourth cervical vertabrae, which I believe was the cause of death. There were injuries to the skull which suggested that she had not fallen voluntarily.' He went on to describe the bloodstains on the boiler door and his test to match them with a sample of Quinn's blood.

In the end Fennel sat down and Alison faced the witness. She swiftly established that the bloodstains could have been caused, as Quinn had stated, by a cut in the course of chopping kindling for the boiler, then turned to the bigger question. 'Dr Baxter, if I understand your evidence correctly, the remains you took from the furnace were mostly charred bone and ash?'

'That is correct.'

'So there was no face to identify, no distinctive scars or blemishes to see on the surface of the skin?'

'No.'

'How could you tell the sex of the deceased?'

'No organs survived to guide me on that, but the configuration of the pelvic bones were, in my view, those of a woman.'

'Apart from the dental evidence you mentioned, was there any other way of identifying the remains?'

'Not visually, no. DNA tests on the bones might help to confirm my conclusions.'

'Have you conducted such tests?'

'No, I haven't. I did not consider them necessary. Mrs Quinn's parents are both dead, her children were not available and her only surviving blood relative is a sister. I thought taking tissue for matching from her would cause unnecessary distress to someone who was already very upset. I had no doubt that the remains were Mrs Quinn's.'

'You felt matching the dental records was sufficient?'

'I did.'

'So you obtained her records from the dentist?'

'I did.'

'And where was his, or her, surgery?'

'It was a large group practice in Redland, close to the centre of town.'

'Did you obtain the records of the whole family?'

'Yes, I did.'

'How old were they? How far back did they go?'

'I should like to consult my notes, if I may?'

'Of course.'

He opened a green-backed binder. 'The children's went back to the age of two or three. Dr Quinn's records date from 1962.'

'And Mrs Quinn's?'

'They appear to go back to 1997, which was when she first visited the surgery.'

'Why would that be? Didn't she go to a dentist before that? Would you not expect a woman of thirty-three, brought up in this country, to have visited a dentist before?'

Fennel stood up. 'My lord, I hesitate to object, but …'

The judge shook his head. 'Then hesitate a little longer, Mr Fennel. It is a perfectly fair question for a man who is a physician by profession. Kindly answer, Doctor.'

'Yes, she had plainly been to other dentists in the past. The record showed a number of fillings carried out before her first visit to this practice.'

'So, where are the records?'

'I have no idea, but records *do* get lost, you know; or may not always get passed on as they should when a patient changes their dentist. Perhaps she had private treatment before joining this NHS practice and the private dental surgeon retained her records in case she came back?'

'But that is merely speculation, Doctor? You don't actually *know*?'

'No, I don't, but lost records are not that unusual.'

No, thought Alison, not looking at the man in the dock. 'So, what did Mrs Quinn's records since 1997 consist of?'

'A single card, giving the layout of her teeth, recording the location of a number of fillings and one extraction, replaced by a false tooth screwed into the bone. Also details of a routine check-up.'

'It did contain her name and address?'

'Of course.'

Alison paused for effect, then looked up sharply. 'So, let me get this right. All that actually identifies Mrs Quinn is a single piece of card?'

'Yes.'

She turned to the usher. 'Would you give the witness Exhibit G, please?' Baxter took the beige A5 card questioningly. 'Is that Mrs Quinn's dental record, Doctor?'

'It is.'

'Tell me, where do dentists get these cards from, before using them, I mean?'

'In packs of fifty from a medical stationers.'

'Can anyone buy them?'

'I suppose so, if they wish.'

'You don't have to be a dentist, or authorised by a dentist?'

'No. They are only blank cards.'

Alison fumbled among her papers and gave a similar beige card to the usher, who passed it to the witness. 'Is that a dental record, Doctor?'

'It appears so.'

'Would it surprise you if I told you that it had been filled in by me, with a little advice on style, copied from my own dental records?'

'That is perfectly possible.'

'Let me get this straight. If I wanted to dispose of a body – shall we call it Body A? – by burning it and giving it a false identity – say that of Body B – I could do so? By removing Body A's dental records from the surgery and substituting a new card with Body B's name and Body A's details?'

The judge intervened. 'I don't know about the jury, Miss Hope, but you are certainly losing *me*.' Everyone laughed politely.

'My lord, I was simply asking Dr Baxter how difficult it would be to falsify a dental record.'

'You would need to possess Body A's records,' replied the pathologist. 'And have access to the files in the dental surgery.'

'Those are my problems, Doctor. Would you just answer my question? If I can solve those problems, would it be possible?'

'Yes, I suppose it would.'

'Thank you. So, without a DNA test we cannot be sure that the body was Nicola Quinn at all?'

'From one very narrow point of view, perhaps not.' Baxter turned and appealed to the judge. 'But I honestly can't imagine who else it might be. Or why, if it wasn't Mrs Quinn, the body had been burnt in the Quinns' cellar.'

Fennel was on his feet as soon as Alison sat down. 'Just two questions, Doctor. First, how many murder victims have you examined after death?'

'About two hundred and seventy.'

'And are you professionally satisfied that the remains in the furnace on this occasion were those of Nicola Quinn?'

'I am perfectly satisfied.'

28

The second day was worse. Fennel produced one of Quinn's partners, who described his workaholic habits and the symptoms of a shaky marriage. She was a sharp-faced woman, to whom Alison took an instant dislike. She kept the cross-examination brief. 'Tell me, Doctor, how often did you actually meet Mrs Quinn?'

'Once, I think, but …'

'Once?' Alison interrupted sharply. '*Once*? Over what period?'

'What do you mean?'

'How long have you been one of Dr Quinn's partners?'

'Five years.'

'So, you met his wife once in five years?'

'I suppose so.'

'For how long did you meet her?'

'I suppose about ten minutes, she came into the surgery to pick him up, with the two children.'

'Ten minutes, over five years? An average of two minutes a year?' The witness did not respond. 'Do you really think that gives you the right to offer any comment at all on the state of his marriage?'

'I believe I know my colleagues pretty well.'

'How tall was she – Mrs Quinn, I mean?'

'I think about five foot six inches. I can't quite see …'

'No.' Again Alison interrupted sharply. 'She was five foot *eleven* inches, much taller than the average woman. And you didn't even notice? Tell me, Doctor, if you can't get something as basic as that right, how do you expect the jury to believe your surmises – and they are no more than that – on the condition of the Quinns' marriage?'

'My lord.' Fennel was on his feet. Alison sat down. He could object as much as he liked, the point had been made.

After a break, the judge took some time out to run through the likely timetable of the trial; and to deal with the written and photographic evidence. Fennel challenged the admissibility of Rebecca Sayers's affidavit. 'It is regrettable that this lady is dead – I trust Miss Hope's other key witnesses will survive the night.' A polite titter ran round the court. 'But Mrs Sayers's statements are worthless if they cannot be tested under cross-examination.'

Alison objected, the judge sent the jury out and the next hour was consumed by legal argument. The public, who were allowed to remain in the gallery, must have been bored out of their minds and, glancing over her shoulder, Alison saw that their numbers were rapidly thinning out. Eventually,

Egan agreed that she could do what she proposed; and then, of course, they adjourned for lunch. 'We will resume in exactly an hour, at two o'clock,' said the judge, known to be a quick sandwich and coffee man. He was clever and quite a decent fellow, thought Alison: a grammar-school boy from Portsmouth, unclubbable, a teetotaller. Didn't want his free three courses with claret at the Judges' Lodgings. God alone knew how he had ever made it to the High Court bench.

In the afternoon, there was Nikki's sister, with more bad news about the state of the marriage; though under cross-examination she did confirm, with some reluctance, that Quinn had arrived on her doorstep during the critical weekend, saying he was looking for Nikki and the children. The family dentist had retired and returned to Australia, but his successor confirmed the authenticity of Nikki's record card; and explained how his records were kept in locked cabinets that had not been tampered with. There were some other technical points and the whole courtroom started to doze off.

Fennel's conclusion of the prosecution case took them all by surprise. He stood up at ten to four, as ever smiling conspiratorially at the jury. The only man in the box wearing a suit, who looked like a retired bank clerk, stared at him woodenly; the only other juror over forty, a woman in pearls and a home-knitted cardigan, smiled back. The judge tapped on his desk gently with a pen. 'One moment, Mr Fennel: in view of the hour, would it not be preferable for us to adjourn until the morning?'

'I have no more witnesses to call, my lord, and there is no one I wish to re-examine. That is the evidence for the prosecution.'

'Very well. Then the defence will begin at ten tomorrow, Miss Hope.'

Alison was caught off-guard; she had been expecting Fennel's case to go on for at least another day and was still wrestling to structure her defence. She had been bounced. On her feet she leant heavily on the small wooden lectern that stood on the table. 'Yes, my lord. That's fine.'

But it was not fine, as she discovered an hour later. She was back in chambers working on her opening speech when John Forbes burst in. 'Alison, I'm sorry to bring bad news, but Jevanjee has skipped the country.'

'He's done *what*?'

'Buggered off. He hasn't been seen for some days, the surgery is closed, his house in Westbury is shut up. He's summoned to court tomorrow, but I can't believe he'll turn up.'

'Where do you think he's gone?'

'Where no one can find him. I suppose he's seen the writing on the wall and cleared off back to India. He's left nothing much behind, so far as I can tell – his property was all rented, and I bet his fortune was already stashed away in some tax haven.'

She stared out of the window. 'You're sure about this?'

'I'm sorry, yes. I guess the fact that he's fled the country can be used to prove *something*?' His tall figure folded elegantly into one of the leather armchairs. 'It's hardly evidence within the rules, but you can chuck it in somehow. As to *real* evidence – who've we got left? There's Quinn himself—'

'I may not be calling him.'

He looked up sharply. 'Why ever not?'

'I can tell his story better than he can. I think he'll go to pieces under cross-examination. You've seen what he's been like in prison, crushed and defeated right from the beginning.'

'It's dangerous, though – think what Fennel will make of it.'

'That's between him and the jury. I think he could do more harm by actually taking Quinn apart. It's what they did at the Jeremy Thorpe trial, remember? Didn't put three of the defendants in the box – and they were all acquitted.'

He shook his head. 'I don't like it. But we still have Mar, George, Gina, Taylor, your rival pathologist, the Langs.'

'The Langs *have* been properly summoned, haven't they?'

'If they don't appear, they'll be in contempt and Egan will send the police to arrest them.'

'They can't get out of appearing on a technicality?'

'Relax. I served the papers on them myself, made

them sign receipts on their own doorstep. Thought they might set the dogs on me!'

'You should've sent George.'

'I couldn't bloody *find* George.'

'He *has* been keeping his head down this week. I saw him last night – he'd been out to Hammond House to see if he could find any trace of what happened to Dougal.'

'No sign, I suppose?'

She shook her head. 'Well, we *do* need to map out tomorrow. I suggest you take evidence from Mar first, then Gina and George: that way you can use George to bring in anything the others missed. Explain about the club, go straight for the jugular?'

'Sounds right to me.' She grinned. 'You ever thought of becoming a barrister, John?'

He looked embarrassed. 'You know I have.'

'You'd be damn good.' She sighed and nodded through the window at the lights of the pub across the alley. 'Let's get a couple of pints to keep us going.'

Eli Friedmann lived in a thatched farmhouse built in the sixteenth century and set in an acre of garden along the coast from Portishead. Although not far outside the city, it always seemed remote. George left the lights of the suburbs and took the coast road, which rose and fell in corniche hairpins by the darkening sea. Twisting through woodland, it was a dangerous road if you were driving fast:

narrow, with many blind corners. As he negotiated the bends towards Clevedon, the weak winter sun finally vanished behind the coastal hills, its dying crimson glow making their jagged peaks look like bloodstained broken glass. Eli's home was round the next curve. He welcomed George warmly, scruffy at home in his leather slippers and frayed cardigan. 'Come in, come in, George. Esther is out at the WI, but you like a drink or some coffee?'

Walking in the darkened garden, he proudly showed George a floodlit corner where they had restored a Tudor well: a brick-lined shaft some four feet across, surrounded by low flint walls and falling deeply to a circle of still water. 'Pretty good, eh? A touch of olde England.'

'It's beautiful.' George was shivering with cold. 'You've done it perfectly – it could all have been there hundreds of years.'

'Most of it has. It take a bloody foreigner to appreciate your beautiful country.' Friedmann laughed, a cynical chuckle that would not have been out of place in the Budapest coffee house where with different luck he might have been. Thankfully, George was ushered into the warm study, a small room with dark-green leather arm-chairs and a beautiful inlaid Biedermeier desk. A bottle of Hungarian Bull's Blood was opened. 'How it goin', George?'

'Not too good. But thanks for helping me get into the club. Trouble was they sussed me – and I think they killed Dougal.'

'*Killed* him? You pull my leg?'

'Never been more serious, mate. He vanished after I got away and they cleared the place out before I got back with the police. The Bill have noted him missing and are making a few enquiries, but frankly they don't believe me. You can't blame them – whoever killed Nikki Quinn is darn good at covering up, I suppose because the stakes are so high.'

'Very high, George.'

'Wish I knew exactly what the stakes *are*. So does Alison. She's halfway through a murder trial and we still don't know the whole story.'

'Like you said before, it's drugs and arms, a lot of money.'

'But they seem to feel so secure, so certain they can get away with things. They tried to kill Alison. I think they *have* killed Dougal, and some poor bloody journalist who was on to them. Rebecca Sayers killed herself, at least I suppose she did. They thought Nikki was a danger so they took her out, leaving her husband to take the rap. They tried to kill *him* in prison, too, and if they'd succeeded they'd have closed the circuit. His apparent suicide would have been taken to show his guilt. No trial. End of story.'

'That's about it, friend. And I still don' reckon your girl will get him off. How's the trial going?'

'So, so. Rebecca Sayers was our star witness but she's dead. Jevanjee had been subpoenaed, but now *he's* skipped the country.'

'That's a real bugger. He was key to all that sleazy stuff and if your girl could prove that, maybe the jury would start to believe Quinn's story.'

'How come you know so much about him, Eli?'

'I got a few friends in the police, you know how it is. They keep me in touch.' He rubbed his nose with his right forefinger and smiled, showing the glint of a gold tooth. 'They wanted to nail Jevanjee for supplying. But he also been on fringe of arms and explosives deals, some say mixed up with exports to Iran and Iraq. They leave him free because they think he only foot soldier, will lead them to big fish.'

'Is Charles Lang a big fish?'

The old Jew poured more wine and shook his head. 'Word is Lang don' come into it. His terrible wife get him into this crack scene and Jevanjee is blackmailing him for protection.'

'Protection which he can't deliver?'

'No – but Jevanjee don' know that. If he found out, I guess Lang get balls cut off and end up in river like all the rest. Lang must be mighty relieved he's gone.' Friedmann gave a hard little chuckle. 'Killin' didn' seem no problem to Jevanjee – and your police were stupid enough to leave him free, so he got away with it.'

George lit a roll-up and puffed on it quietly. Eventually, he said, 'Know what I think, Eli?'

'You tell me, George.'

'I think Jevanjee's done some piddling little arms deals for his friends in the Punjab, but he's got nothing to do with Iran or Iraq – it's just not his league. We're talking about corrupt *governments*, why the hell do they need a small-town Bristol doctor? Jevanjee's created a legend to protect himself. His link to the KLF may be real, but it amounts to bugger all and he's used it, and no doubt Lang, to create a miasma of international crime that doesn't exist. The police are up a gum tree and meanwhile that bastard has been making a fortune on drugs and getting away with murder.'

'Could be, George.'

'Now he's finally lost his nerve and gone, leaving all this mayhem behind him. And Lang's just an idiot who can't keep his dick inside his trousers. A shit but not into dealing – drugs *or* arms.'

'I don' reckon so.'

George stubbed out his roll-up on a heavy glass ashtray. 'There's just one other thing that puzzles me.'

Friedmann looked up questioningly.

'How come Jevanjee always knows so much about my movements?'

George left the house at nine, the best part of a bottle of wine swilling about in an empty stomach. He cursed himself quietly. He felt OK to drive, but he knew that was an illusion and he was well over the limit if he was stopped. If he lost his licence, he'd be out of work for at least a year. He decided to follow the empty road towards Clevedon and find a lay-by to sleep it off for a few hours.

He drove carefully, keeping the Transit below forty, slowing and pulling to one side to allow a few cars to pass. He was also feeling edgy – just who *had* been betraying him? The last few days had convinced George that someone he trusted had been willing to warn Jevanjee about his infiltration of the club, in full knowledge that George was likely to be killed as a result. It was an uncomfortable feeling. A long oil tanker slid by on the other side, grinding slowly up a steep incline. Then he was on a stretch where trees met overhead and shut out the moon. The road twisted sharply from side to side and he put his feeble lights on full beam. It made little difference.

There were headlights behind him, coming up fast, and he cursed quietly, but his mirror showed a low, black shape that did not match any make of car known to the Avon and Somerset constabulary. He breathed a sigh of relief, but the twin points of light grew and were soon irritatingly close behind. He started to accelerate, as there was no way the car could pass. He decided they were joy-riders, probably a lot more pissed than George, and he didn't want them driving into his tail. An accident and the breathalyser were the last thing he needed.

They stayed close, hooting impatiently, and he went faster until he was doing sixty, clinging to the road on the bends, feeling his back wheels slide, but still in control. Damn them, bloody vandals, but there were only a few miles to go before Clevedon.

Then he could lose them. Now it was seventy, the worn-out engine screeching in pain, and he was sweating profusely, a mixture of fear, physical effort and alcohol. He steered through another corner, the wheels sliding really dangerously this time, past a lane leading down to the sea, gathered speed again and braked instinctively as the road tilted sharply downwards. Suddenly he was blinded by a blaze of white light. The headlamps behind were on full beam and a spotlight had been switched on. The glare reflected back from his mirrors and the windscreen, blinding him.

He saw the long articulated truck when it was only yards away, unlit and drawn right across the road, its cab on one verge, rear wheels on the other. A solid steel girder lashed to it was level with his chest and he was flying towards it like a comet spiralling out of control. In the last few seconds of sheer terror George knew who had betrayed him. How could he have been so bloody stupid? The little Hungarian shit. He cursed and twisted the wheel sharply; the van skidded, he felt all the wheels lose contact with the Tarmac and he was sliding, rocking wildly, tree branches outside swaying in slow motion in the glare. There was a white-faced figure by the verge.

Just before the crash he recovered enough to release his seat-belt and throw himself sideways. The impact jarred every bone in his body. The pain made his head swim, he heard a scream of tearing metal, broken glass flying everywhere, something struck his head and he was floating into darkness. He did not hear the explosion of the deadly plastic container of petrol, engulfing the wreckage in a burst of yellow flame.

29

It was John Forbes who brought the news, looking embarrassed on the doorstep at seven in the morning. 'George doesn't have any relatives, so the police rang me when they traced the owner of the van, or what was left of it … I suppose they knew he was working with us at the moment.' He hugged her. 'Oh, Alison, I'm so sorry.'

It didn't hurt at first; as with any really vicious blow, the pain could not be absorbed all at once. It grew like the mushroom cloud of an atom bomb and she did not feel the full blast until John had guided her back inside. She still could not believe it, but a terrible gnawing agony told her that George's death was at last going to teach her how much, how painfully much, she loved him. 'Oh no, *no*, please no, tell me it's not true.' She slumped at the kitchen table, *Today* crackling out of her transistor. 'Not George, not now, not when I need him so badly.' And then she wept, unable to stop, the tears stinging her eyes, feeling her face grow red and puffy, wishing she could die too. As John held her tightly, she could feel his shoulders moving with hers and when she looked up his eyes were full as well and she thought what a kind and giving man he was. 'I can't go on, John, not after this. I loved him so much. I just can't do it.'

'You will, love. I don't know how, but somehow we'll get through.'

'I can't, I'm sorry but …' And she was weeping again, this time uncontrollably, knowing what it meant to feel your heart was breaking.

Afterwards, she could not remember how the next two hours passed. John stayed with her, comforting, warm, not encroaching: a gentle father or elder brother. He produced coffee and toast, but she could not eat. Somehow she got dressed. Overwhelming grief mingled with the routine of getting to court by ten. She took a tranquilliser he offered, without asking what it was.

Sitting next to him in the Daimler, all her senses were acutely aware but she also felt anaesthetised. They did not go into the robing-room. John borrowed an office where she put on her gown, away from curious eyes, and Rick Fennel came to say how sorry he was. Then she was in court. It was as if she were listening to somebody else explain, in flat, formal tones that one of that day's witnesses, Mr Kristianssen, a private investigator, had been killed in a road traffic accident overnight. The judge nodded sympathetically, as if he knew a little more than that. 'Would an hour's adjournment suffice to let you regroup your forces, Miss Hope?'

'Thank you, my lord. I am most grateful.'

She and John walked back to her chambers in winter sun that was cruelly bright. Her eyes already ached and stung, but she started to weep again as they turned into John Street. They talked about George; and about how it had happened. What was he *doing* on that isolated road in the middle of the night? It was clearly no accident but who, from their long list of enemies, would have gone so far as to kill him?

But they both knew grief would have to wait. At eleven Alison went back to the court. As if in a trance, she took her seat, only half aware of the routine going on all round her: the usher calling everyone to their feet, the judge entering and bowing, the gabbled summons from the clerk. The tranquilliser had kicked in and made her feel distantly calm, but it also made her mouth dry and her vision slightly blurred. She was in no state to be defending a man on a murder rap, but somehow she was going to get through it. She would not let Quinn down.

She stood, took a sip of water and faced the jury, making eye contact with each one in the back row, smiling slightly. Damn it, she still had her notes and she could pull the same tricks as Fennel. 'Ladies and gentlemen of the jury, you have heard what appears to be a solid case from the prosecution. Why should you not accept it at face value?' The woman in the pearls and cardigan stared back at her, sceptical and hostile. *Yes*, she was saying to herself. *Why not, indeed? He's guilty as hell.*

'I intend to suggest – and then to prove – that there are two reasons why you should be wary of what you have heard so far. The first is the character of Dr Quinn. You are not dealing with a monster or an idiot. This man is a doctor who has chosen to work in one of the poorest districts of this city for many years. Plainly, a man who cares, a man of proven decency. Rocky marriage he may have had – as do many other NHS doctors, nurses and health professionals who spend too much of their lives working and neglect their spouses. But there is not the slightest evidence that he was a man of violence. Rather, he was trying to patch up his marriage, he was a loving father, a man concerned for his wife and children.

'And if, by chance, Nicola Quinn had died in an accidental fall, as my learned friend has conceded might be possible—'

Fennel was on his feet and she gave way to him. 'My lord, I must object. I conceded only that Dr Quinn may have struck his wife intending to harm, to hurt very much even, but not necessarily to kill. There was no reference to an accident.'

The judge nodded and spoke to the jury. 'I uphold Mr Fennel's objection, members of the jury. You will disregard Miss Hope's last point.'

Alison started again, feeling on edge and shaky. 'I stand corrected, my lord. I meant to say that in my submission Dr Quinn had no intention of killing his wife; in which case if she died in a fall, as has been suggested, he was informed and intelligent enough to know that he only had to dial 999 for an ambulance, report what had happened as an accident, and he would not be here today. So why *is* he here? I would submit, because he did not *know* of his wife's death – he simply wasn't aware that it had happened and therefore took none of the obvious courses of action that would have put him firmly on the right side of the law. He believed Nikki had left home with their two children, deserted him with a view to ending the marriage, and he was driving to various addresses as far apart as Dorset and North Yorkshire in an attempt to find them. He was not in Bristol and knew nothing of the murder.'

She paused to let that sink in, running her eyes firmly along the faces of the jury, then passed on. 'So, if you accept that, who *did* kill his wife? That is the second point which my learned friend has not mentioned, though I have given him notice of it. The truth of this matter is that Nikki Quinn was a woman bored in her marriage, who had sought entertainment elsewhere. In doing so, she had become the lover of a man who, with others, was engaged in criminal activity: at this stage I mention only the illegal sale and use of Class A controlled drugs, but there is a great deal more to it than that. He had a lot to lose if this became known.

'This gentleman and his accomplices are not on trial here. But I intend to show that he feared Nikki Quinn might reveal his activities to the police, leading to his prosecution, to the end of a glamorous career, to social ruin. He was threatening her, trying to make her keep quiet. She had spurned him as a lover and rejected his pleas. He or his accomplices decided to kill her – and did so. They – not Dr Quinn – destroyed the body, in a way that was intended to cast suspicion on Geoffrey Quinn and conceal the truth of the crime.'

Despite everything, she was on automatic pilot now. The adrenalin was running and she felt in command of herself, consciously acting and persuading, winning their attention, if not their sympathy. She knew she would feel like death later. 'This may sound like a thriller, members of the jury. But I have a duty to present the truth. Dr Quinn had no reason to kill his wife. Others did and I shall in due course name them. Truth can often be stranger than fiction.'

She sat down. The buzz in the court was less than she had hoped, but she had certainly surprised them. The judge rapped on his desk. 'Silence, please. Miss Hope, do you wish to call your first witness now?'

Alan Mar was called and sworn in, looking grave in a dark suit. He confirmed that he was the proprietor of a local newspaper, which had been investigating strange gatherings discovered by one of his reports, Georgina Manley. It took an hour to explain the existence of the club: how Gina had discovered it, what it did, where it met. The press table perked up enormously when Alison came to the drugs and sex. 'So these people were basically meeting for sex, sometimes way-out sex – even involving minors – often enhanced by hard drugs? Is that correct?'

'Yes, it is.' The Scots accent added to his calm credibility.

'Can you tell me any of their names?

'Some, yes.'

'Please do so.'

The judge intervened. 'Is this really necessary, Miss Hope? Whoever these people are, they are not on trial and will have no ready way of countering your witness's allegations, which do sound somewhat damaging.'

'I believe it to be necessary, m'lord.'

'Mr Fennel?'

'I can't see the relevance of any of this, my lord, it's all hearsay and fantasy, but as to the names, I am agog.' Laughter ran round the court. 'I have no objection.'

'Very well – Miss Hope, I shall not look favourably on your damaging third parties who are in no position to defend themselves, but go ahead. I hope your claim of relevance can be sustained.'

Alison, on her feet again, turned to Mar. 'Please go ahead. I should like the name of anyone in respect of whom you have hard evidence of involvement in these events.'

'Yes, I understand. I hold written statements and/or photographic evidence showing that the following were present at some time: Dr Anwar Jevanjee, the Right Honourable Charles and Lady

Denise Lang.' There were audible gasps, silenced by the judge, and Mar gave six more prominent names. The silence and shock were palpable.

Mr Justice Egan stopped taking notes and leaned forward. 'Mr Mar, you are suggesting that *all* these people were involved in activities that are against the law?'

Mar did not hesitate. 'I am, my lord.'

'Mr Lang was a Minister of the Crown, until the election, so these are particularly damaging and serious allegations – and you say that at least one of these people was prepared to kill to conceal their guilt?'

'I believe that to be true, my lord.'

'Hmm. Well, Miss Hope? I understand that Mrs Sayers has committed suicide and Dr Jevanjee has left the country, but you intend to call Miss Manley and the Langs?'

'I do, my lord.'

'Very well, please continue.'

Alison went over the facts of the club again, then turned to the rest of Mar's evidence, his friendship with Geoff and Nikki Quinn. Mar gave his account of Quinn as a caring father and said he was unaware of any strains in the marriage.

'If there had been any, can you envisage Dr Quinn resorting to violence?'

'No, I cannot.'

'Why?'

'He always seemed to me a reasonable, intelligent, gentle man. I can't imagine him being violent in any circumstances, even under great provocation.'

Fennel took over to cross-examine. 'Tell me, Mr Mar, what is the circulation of your newspaper?'

'About twenty-five thousand copies.'

'And what was it a year ago?'

'Somewhat higher, about twenty-eight thousand.'

'So, it's going down?'

'It has reduced in the recession, but I've no reason to believe it's going down any further.'

'Still, a good, sensational story would help, wouldn't it?'

'A good story always helps.'

'So, may I put it to you, that the story you have told today – and will no doubt be publishing shortly – is pure fabrication?'

'It certainly is not. We have extensive evidence.'

'I disagree, Mr Mar. You say you have a few photographs, some notes from a reporter called Georgina Manley, which *may*, and I put it no higher, show that some of these people you are slandering have met socially. You have produced not a shred of direct evidence that anything untoward went on between them. Nothing but hearsay from your reporter and a statement from a woman who is conveniently dead.' There was a long silence as Fennel appeared to be studying his notes. Suddenly he looked up. 'Tell me, Mr Mar – how many acts of drug-crazed sex between these people have you witnessed yourself?' The effect was electric.

'None. I was not present at these gatherings.'

'So, in fact you don't really *know* from your own

experience that anything you have told us is true?'

'I was not giving evidence from my experience, but of an investigation carried out by a responsible and professional journalist.'

'A *journalist*, Mr Mar, a journalist. I think that says it all. No further questions.'

The judge seemed to wake up. 'Do you wish to re-examine, Miss Hope?'

'No, my lord.'

Gina followed and gave her evidence quietly and convincingly, standing up to an hour's tough cross-examination from Fennel. When the judge adjourned for lunch, Alison sighed with relief. It had probably been the worst morning of her life and she just wanted to be alone to recover. In the corridor, she saw Egan beckoning from the door to his chambers: he had taken off his wig but was still in his scarlet gown. 'Miss Hope?'

'Yes, my lord?'

'I just wanted to say how sorry I was to hear about Mr Kristianssen.' He smiled gently. 'You're coping very well.' Then he was gone and John was approaching.

'I just wanted to say the same thing, Alison. It must have been hell, but you were terrific.' He hesitated. 'So, it's the Langs next.'

'I just hope they can't find a credible excuse to duck out.'

They did. After a quick chat with Quinn, picking at a cheese sandwich in the cells, she was back in court at five to two. The clerk brought her a copy of a private medical certificate saying that Charles Lang was too ill to attend court due to a recurrent back injury, arising from a riding accident two years ago. His wife begged leave to stay at home and look after him. As soon as the judge took his seat, Alison was on her feet in protest. 'M'lord, I do not wish to impugn Mr Lang's motives, but—'

'Why on earth not, Miss Hope? It seems to me that you are being more than reasonable. Dr Quinn is charged with murder, a serious felony, and the court has *ordered* these people to appear. If Lang is at home in Backwell, I see no reason why he should not attend court, in a wheelchair if necessary; and, believe me, I shall need some convincing that he can't. The absence of Lady Denise Lang is outrageous: she is only a twenty-minute drive away and I cannot see why he cannot survive for a few hours without her. Clerk?'

The clerk turned to face him. 'My lord?'

'Kindly arrange for delivery to Mr Charles and Lady Denise Lang of further summonses requiring them to attend this court at ten o'clock tomorrow. If they fail to appear, without some very good explanation, I shall send police officers to bring them here, by force if necessary; I shall also be minded to commit them to prison for three months for contempt of this court.'

'I shall do so, my lord.' He left the court and another clerk came in to take his place.

Egan looked at Alison. 'How would you like to

proceed, Miss Hope? I will grant a short adjournment if you wish to revise your plans?'

After a twenty-minute break, Alison called the defence pathologist, who had examined the remains and tried to cast doubt on Baxter's conviction that they were Nikki's, since there had been no DNA test. It was plain that the jury did not believe him. He was followed by Taylor and one of Quinn's partners as character witnesses. No one looked unduly interested in what they had to say, either.

It was dark when John drove her home. She only had to close her eyes to see George's face. She wanted to be alone, there were so many things she wished she had said to him. She felt drained, and so exhausted that she dozed in the warm car, waking up as they approached the Down. Ghostly images from the past mingled with the lights in shop windows. They always came back to haunt her at times of crisis. David's lifeless body swinging from the beam, the cold crematorium chapel. She was not going to let Quinn down. She would never let anyone down again.

Later, they had an awkward meal together, at a bistro near the suspension bridge, its shape outlined by a string of lights in the darkness. She tried to concentrate on what had to be done tomorrow, but she felt lost without George. He had been such a *good* man – beside that, his booming idiosyncrasies were nothing – and every time she thought of him she wanted to weep.

Gently, John brought her back to the case. 'I'm sorry, but we do have to make some decisions. Personally I'd still put Quinn in the box. Let him speak for himself.'

'We've been over all that. What's he going to say? "I never done it"? Then Fennel says "but you *did*" – and they'll believe Fennel. Quinn's too broken up to sound convincing. His claim to know nothing about the club, or Nikki's affair, is true but almost impossible to believe. I've given an impression of him as a decent man and a bystander who's been drawn into something over which he had no control, something that might happen to anyone. But if Fennel cross-examines him, he'll come over as on the edge, unstable – I don't believe it's safe.'

'It's your decision, Alison, I just hope it works.'

When they reached the flat, she took a sleeping pill. She needed a few hours of complete oblivion. She was vaguely conscious of John putting papers in order, unplugging the phone and helping her to bed.

30

He was still there in the morning, asleep on the sofa. Alison woke first, slightly hungover from the slug of Zimovane, and smiled at his long body huddled in a foetal position under the spare duvet. What a star: not many men who'd been rebuffed so firmly would have rallied round like that. She made a pot of coffee as if it were a normal day and the instructing solicitor always slept in her flat. He looked embarrassed when he woke. 'I'm so sorry, Alison, I meant to get up early and do that.'

'My turn, John. You were brilliant yesterday. Thanks. Thank you for saving my life.'

By five to ten, she was robed and in court. Arranging her notes on the small lectern, she turned to John at the table behind her. 'I suppose neither of the Langs has actually turned up yet?'

He shook his head, but smiled encouragingly. 'We go straight for an arrest warrant if they don't appear, OK?'

'D'you think Egan will really do it? Bang up a Member of Parliament?'

'Of course he will, they'll be in grave contempt.

Egan's tough – he'd positively enjoy doing it, he hates the establishment.'

Alison laughed for the first time in thirty-six hours. 'As a High Court judge, isn't he *part* of the establishment?'

'He wouldn't see it that way. Actually, it would be better if they *don't* come – if they have to be arrested to get them here, maybe the jury will start to believe our story.'

Alison nodded, reassured by his presence, still wishing the vibes did not make it quite so obvious he was attracted to her. He was such a *nice* man – tall and good-looking, as kind as George, a real gent. That was the trouble. No electricity, no excitement. She could never be intimate with John, but he had saved her career and her sanity, just by being there. He did not push, was immensely considerate, but sometimes the soulful look in his eyes when he thought she was not looking made her feel awkward and guilty. She turned as she sensed one of the ushers was hovering behind them. 'Yes, Norma?'

'Miss Hope, Mr Forbes, the clerk thought you should know that Mr Charles Lang is in the corridor, waiting to be called.'

John whistled quietly. 'My, my. A lightning recovery?'

'More like he's found an alibi.' But there was no time for speculation. The judge was wobbling in from behind the bench, the court was silent and she was on her feet. 'My lord, I wish to call Mr Charles Lang.'

Egan gave a satisfied smile and nodded to the ushers. 'Call Mr Lang, please.' While they waited, he opened a new notebook, like an old-fashioned school exercise book with a stiff cardboard cover. Alison wondered if he took a meticulous record all day or sometimes lapsed into doodling, limericks or sketches of naked women.

Lang came in slowly, an usher holding open the glass-panelled door, leaning rather obviously on a stick and climbed painfully into the box to be sworn. Alison turned to the judge. 'May the witness sit down, my lord?'

'Of course, Miss Hope. Mr Lang, I understand that you have back problems at the moment and this court is grateful to you for making the effort to attend.' The courtesy was elaborate, but Alison noticed the unsmiling eyes: James Egan might have grown up in a dockyard worker's back-to-back house in Portsmouth, but he was well capable of playing the part of the Queen's justice when necessary. Lang was not going to have an easy time. She turned to the witness box. Forbes had interviewed both of the Langs for a preliminary witness statement, but Alison had seen neither of them in the flesh before. Charles Lang was about forty, overweight, smooth and pink like a flash young estate agent. He was, however, wearing an Old Carthusian tie.

She smiled reassuringly and ran through his name, address and occupation. 'I am a Member of Parliament.'

Alison nodded respectfully. 'And you live in London in the week, but come home to Backwell at the weekends?'

'Usually, yes.'

'How do you spend the weekends, Mr Lang?'

'On Saturday morning I often hold a surgery in my constituency, which is in Wiltshire. There are other engagements in the constituency, usually on Saturday afternoon or evening – fêtes, Party dinner-dances, that kind of thing.'

'And I imagine it means a lot to your constituents to see you among them?'

He smiled in a way that was meant to be self-effacing, but she sensed the innate arrogance. 'I take my job seriously, Miss Hope.'

'And on Sundays?'

'I try to keep Sunday for my family. I have two teenage children.'

'And I suppose you sometimes have an evening away from work, just your wife and friends?'

'When we can, of course.'

'I have a photograph, here, Mr Lang.' She gave it to the usher who handed it up to the witness box. 'Would you describe its contents, please?'

'It seems to be a picture of my wife and I leaving our home in my car.'

'You are in a dinner jacket, your wife dressed for a party, right?'

'So it appears.'

'Mr Lang, can you tell me where you were on the evening of Saturday, eighth December?'

He was ready for it. 'My wife and I were in Belgium. We had been visiting senior NATO officers in Brussels and spent the weekend as the guests of Major General Richard Fell.'

'In Brussels?'

'No, General Fell has a small cottage in the Ardennes.'

'Who was in the party?'

'Just General Fell, who is single, my wife and myself.'

'Major General Fell is an old friend?'

'We were at university together.'

'Were you? But he must be a little older?'

'I went to Cambridge straight from school. Richard Fell was already a serving Army officer, sent to learn Russian as part of his training.'

Alison nodded. The trap had been baited: now leave it until she was ready. 'Now, Dr Quinn is on trial for the murder of his wife, Nikki.' Lang eyed her expectantly, looking uncomfortable. 'Did you ever meet Mrs Quinn, Mr Lang?'

'Not that I am aware of.'

'You're quite sure of that?'

'Perfectly.'

'Forgive me then, but may I put it to you – as, indeed, I believe I must – that this court has evidence to the contrary?' He faced her stonily, but said nothing. 'In the form of a sworn affidavit from Mrs Rebecca Sayers.' She gave a copy to the usher, who passed it to Lang.

'I have already seen a copy of this document,

Miss Hope.' She had to admire the way he was keeping his cool.

'Well, Mr Lang, Mrs Sayers describes at some length several encounters between yourself and Mrs Quinn at rather dubious social gatherings, a developing love affair, a powerful sexual relationship, and a painful parting.'

'This is all sheer fantasy.'

'Fantasy, Mr Lang? Are you sure?'

'Yes, *fantasy*, Miss Hope, and I am perfectly sure. It is totally untrue and I can only believe that the late Mrs Sayers was psychotic. I have no knowledge of her, nor of Nicola Quinn. People in public life are quite often troubled by lonely members of the public who fantasise about them, you know.' He sounded flat calm – he had not even blushed. 'It is very common and a great nuisance.'

'You never met Mrs Sayers, either?'

'No, I did not.'

'You did not have an affair with Nikki Quinn?'

'I never met her.'

'You did not go to these exclusive gatherings when hard drugs were in wide use?'

'Of course not. The suggestion is laughable.'

'And on the eighth of December you were in an isolated cottage in the Ardennes, with your old college friend?' He nodded. 'Is that a yes, Mr Lang?'

'Yes, we were in the Ardennes.'

'I showed you a photograph earlier. You still have it there?' He nodded unwillingly. 'You agree it shows you and your wife, in your car, with you driving?'

'Yes, it does.'

'Would it surprise you to know that it was taken by Mrs Joan Cook, who is a private investigator?'

'If you can obtain affidavits from a certifiable fantasist, nothing would surprise me, Miss Hope.' The ripple of laughter from the gallery said that Lang was doing too well: go for the jugular.

'It is only your contention that Mrs Sayers was unbalanced, Mr Lang – I believe that she was an intelligent, concerned but very frightened woman. Now Mrs *Cook*, who took this photograph, was formerly a petty officer in the Royal Navy, employed handling the most sensitive and secret Naval communications at Northwood. She is a person of proven integrity.' He said nothing: he was scared. 'The thing is, Mr Lang, Mrs Cook took this photograph at seven thirty on the evening of the eighth of December. She took it from the road outside your house. The date and time have been confirmed by Police Sergeant Anthony Smith and a constable accompanying him, both of the Avon and Somerset Constabulary, who were patrolling the area for reasons of your own security, Mr Lang. I gather it is normal procedure, but perhaps you were unaware of it?' And thank you Elaine Maitland of the Security Service, she thought, for that unbelievably disloyal tip-off. 'So, it seems you were *not* in Belgium after all?'

Lang looked really rattled. Every eye in the court was on him; but he struggled to keep going with an appearance of insouciance. 'I can only believe these people are mistaken, Miss Hope. General Fell is ready to confirm that my wife and I were with him and …' He dried up uncomfortably.

'The trouble is, Mr Lang, that as a lifelong friend he might not be seen as entirely, well, *objective*, whereas—'

Rick Fennel was on his feet. She was surprised it had taken him so long. 'M'lord, I really must object. Such comment is totally out of order at this point, when Major General Fell may be called as a witness himself.'

The judge nodded, though his manner suggested no sympathy for Lang's predicament. 'I uphold your objection, Mr Fennel. The jury will disregard the last point.'

Alison stood up again. 'Just to clarify, Mr Lang, quite frankly I do not believe you – and I intend to call Joan Cook, Sergeant Anthony Smith and his accompanying constable as witnesses to confirm this evidence.' Lang stared at her rigidly. 'I also intend to show that the strange gatherings described by Mrs Sayers certainly took place, and that one was happening on the evening of the eighth of December, at a mansion called Hammond House, outside this city, in Somerset. That's where you were going when the photograph was taken, wasn't it?'

'Certainly not.'

'I believe the jury will draw their own conclusions. Now, let us go back to Nikki Quinn.'

Alison pressed on for another half hour. Lang stonewalled, denying again and again that he had ever met Nikki or Rebecca Sayers. Fennel interrupted more often. The judge looked on with hard-faced disapproval – he had no sympathy with rich men who cheated on Parliament and their constituents. Lang had little alternative but to come when sub-poenaed, unless he was ready to leave the country for good like Jevanjee, but he was ill-prepared, over-confident. The arrogance and stupidity of that flimsy, transparent alibi … Then Alison was ready for the final kill. 'To recap, Mr Lang: you maintain that you have never heard of Mrs Quinn or Mrs Sayers?'

'No, I have not.'

'You never went to these strange gatherings?'

'No, I did not.'

'You never met Dr Jevanjee, who seems to have been the organiser?'

'No, I did not.'

Alison reached into an envelope on the table and gave another photograph to the usher. George had seen it tucked among papers on Rebecca Sayers's bureau on his first visit. On the second, he had taken it without asking. After he had broken her, she had reluctantly been forced to find the nega-tive. God, how she missed George … Copies were handed to the judge, to Fennel and to Lang, who turned a chalky-white. She slammed her advantage home as Forbes gave twelve more copies of the photograph to the usher for the jury. 'What do you see, Mr Lang?'

'This is a fake.' But he sounded scared, bloody scared.

'Will you kindly answer my question – what do you *see*, Mr Lang?'

He seemed to recover slightly. 'It is a photograph in which I appear, but—'

'And who else is in it, Mr Lang?'

Lang turned to the judge: 'My lord?'

Egan shook his head. 'Just answer counsel's question, please.' There was a long silence. The jury were riveted on Lang, as no doubt were the public, and Alison knew she had convinced them. The judge was getting exasperated. 'For heaven's sake, Mr Lang, you must be able to see – as can I and the jury – that this is a photograph of yourself and the late Mrs Quinn, at some kind of social gathering. There are other people in the background.'

'They include Dr Jevanjee and Rebecca Sayers, my lord,' said Alison.

'Thank you.' The judge turned back to Lang and there was another silence. 'Well? Do you agree?'

Eventually, Lang spoke. 'It appears so, my lord. I – I can only say that I have no recollection of this occasion, nor of a photograph being taken, perhaps it was at some constituency gathering …'

Alison returned to her examination. 'Mr Lang, as you well know, none of these people are, or were, your constituents. To suggest so is absurd. I put it to you that you have been lying on oath to this court. You *were* the lover of Nikki Quinn. You *did* know both her and Rebecca Sayers. Is that not true?'

The judge intervened again. 'A lot turns on the

authenticity of this photograph, Miss Hope. Do you have the negative?'

'Yes, my lord.'

It was passed up to him and he held the small rectangle of developed film up to the light and studied it. 'No doubt a forensic test should be carried out, but I'm bound to say it looks genuine enough to me.' He handed it back to an usher. 'Please show it to Mr Fennel.' Then he turned to the witness box. 'You must not be bullied, Mr Lang, but you really must tell the truth. I am bound to remind you that perjury is a criminal offence and punishable by imprisonment.'

Lang shook his head wretchedly. 'It is possible that I met these people, I suppose, I really don't know, I meet a lot of people in the course of my duties ...'

Alison twisted the knife. 'Possible, Mr Lang? *Possible*? You were Nikki's lover, weren't you? Let's have the truth for a change.'

The silence in the court was tangible, brittle. Lang seemed to stare into the panelling above the jury as if help might be found there. Eventually it was the judge who spoke. 'I should like you to answer the question, Mr Lang. If you don't we shall certainly assume that the answer is yes.'

Lang just shook his head miserably, muttering something inaudible, and Alison reined in. After all, she had no more hard evidence and she was certain the jury were convinced he had been lying from beginning to end. 'I think we have heard enough,

Mr Lang. No more questions, my lord.'

'Do you wish to cross-examine, Mr Fennel?'

Rick Fennel rose, clutching his gown about him, seemingly lost in thought. 'I do not wish to cause you further distress, Mr Lang, so I shall be brief. Mrs Quinn was murdered on or about the sixth of September. Where were you on that date?'

Lang still looked shaky. 'I was abroad, so was my wife. We were on a Parliamentary delegation to Australia and New Zealand from the twenty-seventh of August to the fourteenth of September. We returned via Singapore where we stayed with the High Commissioner until the twentieth of September.'

'I take it an appropriate official of the House – say the Clerk? – can confirm this by affidavit?'

Lang appealed to the judge. 'My lord, I am a Privy Councillor – I hardly think such confirmation necessary!'

The judge waved a hand dismissively. 'If you can't see why it is necessary, Mr Lang, I really don't propose to explain. Miss Hope and her instructing solicitor will arrange it. I expect a document to be here tomorrow. We can then decide whether it is necessary to call witnesses for further confirmation.'

31

The rest of the morning passed swiftly. Denise Lang stonewalled loyally in the box after her husband, but no one believed a word. Joan Cook confirmed the date and time of her photograph. The two policemen confirmed seeing her take it and seeing the Langs leave their house on the evening of the eighth of December. Suddenly it was nearly one and Alison realised that her case was complete. 'I have no further witnesses to call, my lord.'

Egan looked at her questioningly. 'No further witnesses, Miss Hope?'

She knew he was referring to Quinn. 'No, my lord.'

'Very well, then we shall adjourn until two.' He left the court. The two black-uniformed screws guarding Quinn stood up and followed him down the steps to the cells. Alison joined him a few minutes later.

'Hope you're feeling better about it, Geoff. I'm sure they all believe now that Nikki was involved with Lang, just as Rebecca Sayers said. I hope it's only a short step from that to them accepting that someone from that crew killed her.'

He nodded. 'I never met your George … but that was really rough and I'm so sorry. I don't know how you've coped these last two days. I thought you were brilliant in there.'

'Thanks.'

He hesitated. 'But it's still dicey, isn't it? That bloke Fennel's good, too. I wish it wasn't quite so knife-edge. What happens now?'

'Fennel and I make our closing speeches, the judge sums up and the jury retire. Keep the faith, Geoff, it's nearly over.'

After lunch, the judge had to hold things up for an hour while he heard an application on a completely different matter, and Fennel did not start his closing speech until three. But the jury were wide awake, having been locked up and bored witless for two hours, eager for something to stimulate them. Fennel ran his gaze along the two rows slowly, making eye contact with each one, giving that knowing smile.

'Ladies and gentlemen of the jury.' Alison squirmed as he laid on the trusty Yorkshire accent: good old Rick, the plain man, the man you had to believe. 'This is a court of law, not a court of morals. And we are in England, not the deep south of the United States. I am not here to demand that Dr Quinn goes to a gas chamber or an electric chair. We are here, on behalf of society, to clear up a nasty, unpleasant event. To decide what happened, to reach a verdict on Dr Quinn's guilt or innocence.

'Now, you have heard a great deal of evidence, or supposed evidence, that – however fascinating – seems to have little to do with reality. It has been suggested to you by a newspaper proprietor that people in this city are engaged in meeting for mutual stimulation by sex and hard drugs. That may or may not be true – I must add that I should find such an allegation more credible if it came from a police officer rather than someone whose liveli-hood depends on finding good stories to sell news-papers. But it is neither here nor there. Miss Hope has not succeeded in demonstrating any connec-tion between these jolly goings-on and the death of Mrs Quinn. And, I would note, that if any of the people allegedly involved in these activities per-ceived Dr Quinn and his wife as dangerous, they would surely have killed *both* of them – which they did not. So, I conclude that you should forget all of that because it is wholly irrelevant.

'Did Mrs Quinn have a relationship with Mr Charles Lang? Now that *may* be relevant. Let's not beat about the bush, members of the jury, Charles Lang may be a Member of Parliament and lately a minister, but he had to be threatened with prison to make him appear in this court. I don't know about you, but I wouldn't trust him an inch.' God, thought Alison, this man is *brilliant*. I produce someone to wreck his case and he turns them into a plank of it; and I can't even object. 'I should not be at all surprised if Charles Lang met Nikki Quinn at some party or other and had an affair with her. You have seen Mr Lang's wife, and they are plainly a glamorous couple and still together, so I doubt if the alleged affair was more than brief. But I concede that it may have happened.' He paused for effect, giving that damned blokeish smile, running his eyes along their faces. They were drinking up every sensible, logical, plain man's word.

'But so what, members of the jury? So what? When Nikki Quinn died, the Langs were on the other side of the world and we have heard evidence that can leave no doubt about that. Charles Lang was on a well-publicised visit to Australia, as the Clerk of the House will confirm. So *he* certainly didn't kill her. He may, however, have been part of the cause of her death.

'Look at it this way. Nikki Quinn was being unfaithful to her neglectful husband, perhaps grossly and repeatedly unfaithful. Yes – she is dead and I have no wish to speak ill of her, but my first concern has to be the truth. May I put it to you that Mr Lang's involvement only increases the likelihood that Dr Quinn killed her?'

Alison was on her feet. 'My lord, I must object. Counsel is wilfully misleading the jury. If Mr Lang had no connection with anyone else who might have an interest in Nikki Quinn's death, Mr Fennel's statement might be true, but there has been ample evidence of Mr Lang's involvement with others whom I believe conspired to take away her life.'

The judge nodded slowly. 'I am minded to accept that, Miss Hope, although your learned friend is entitled to state his case in any way that also recognises his duty to the court. Mr Fennel, I think the jury had better disregard your last point, although you may wish to rephrase it and try again.'

Fennel turned to the jury and raised his eyebrows. Yes, they knew what he had to contend with, they were with him. 'Thank you, my lord. I will press on. Members of the jury: one way or the other, I am in no doubt that Dr Quinn had reason to resent and even hate his wife. No doubt Mr Lang – with or without others – contributed. I say no more than that. But what we know – and I repeat *know* – from the police and forensic evidence is very clear. On the evening of sixth September, Nikki Quinn was knocked, or even thrown, down the cellar steps in her own house, sustaining a fracture in her spinal cord that killed her. A broken neck. And why? I maintain, because she was quarrelling with her husband, members of the jury, about his neglect and her unfaithfulness.

'As I said right at the beginning, maybe he did not mean to kill her, just to hurt, injure, frighten, punish, cause pain – but that intention is enough to justify a verdict of murder. She *died*, members of the jury: her life was cut short at the age of thirty-three. Don't forget that. Dr Quinn felt sufficient guilt to partly dismember her body – a task for which he was professionally trained – and tried to destroy it in the central heating furnace. Their children are not the subject of this trial, but I venture to mention that they have not been seen since and invite you to draw your own conclusions—'

Alison did not need to object, for the judge intervened from the bench. 'Please sit down, Mr Fennel. Members of the jury, I must emphasise that the children are not the subject of this trial. Sadly, I do not know what may have happened to them, and nor do you. We have no evidence as to whether they are alive or dead and, although it may seem a little artificial, you must shut them from your minds. The unproven possibility that they may be dead too, is not something that Mr Fennel is entitled to use to colour your attitude to the defendant. You must forget the point he has just made.'

Fennel was back on his feet. 'We must accept his lordship's ruling, members of the jury.' But they all knew he did not mean it. 'The evidence of Nikki Quinn's death is plain enough. Geoffrey Quinn has not given evidence in his own defence. Why not, I ask? Because, I submit, he has no satisfactory answers to the questions I should have asked.'

Alison objected. 'My lord, it is Dr Quinn's absolute right to remain silent. It does not prove his guilt. I have argued that he had no involvement whatever in the events that bring him here, and therefore no obligation to expose himself to even more innuendo and false accusations.'

The judge agreed, but without enthusiasm. 'That is correct, members of the jury. I shall comment on it later when I sum up: it is not for Mr Fennel to do so now.'

Fennel bowed slightly. 'His lordship is right, ladies and gentlemen: you must draw your own conclusions – and I am sure you will. But I submit,' he was suddenly speaking with great firmness and deliberation, 'I submit that Geoffrey Quinn is the only person with the motive and opportunity to have killed his wife. Why did he burn the body? Why did he flee? I believe the answers are obvious and I invite you to find him guilty of murder.'

The silence when Fennel sat down spoke for itself. Alison sensed that, at that moment, the jury had convicted Quinn. Whatever she did, she was not likely to change their minds. She had probably ruined Charles Lang, but that shot had misfired. Fennel had used every dirty trick in the book. As the judge adjourned until ten in the morning, she knew she had lost.

32

Alison went down the steep concrete steps and tried to buoy up Quinn before he was taken back to prison. He was alone in a small holding-cell, slumped in the corner on a scuffed wooden bench; the usual forty-watt bulb, concealed behind thick glass in the wall, had burnt out and the only light came from the barred rectangle in the door. The cells were underground and would have passed for quite a convincing medieval dungeon. Peering through the gloom, Quinn's face was as harrowed as when she had first met him. The optimism of three hours ago had gone. 'We've lost, haven't we? Thanks for trying so hard, but it's obvious. How long is life? Twenty years? Banged up till I'm past sixty? And Tom and Jess are dead. I'd be better off that way too ...'

She thought he was going to break down, but he just went on staring at the wall. Alison sat down and put her arm round his shoulders. 'I'll make my closing address in the morning, Geoff, and pull out all the stops. I promise. I'll do the best job I can for you.'

But she felt despondent as she walked back to

her rooms. There was a lot of material and she would put it in order straight away, go out for something to eat at the Watershed, then do her speaking notes. She must also be sure to get some sleep, or she'd be useless tomorrow. She needed George, but he wouldn't be there to share the long night. She pushed away a burst of self-pity and fury. This whole ghastly case had cost too much, far too much. The narrow chasm of John Street was empty and felt cold, her footsteps echoing on the cobbles; her shadow, under the cast-iron lamps, looked hunched, old and defeated.

By midnight, she knew what she had to do in the morning. When you drew the evidence together, the story she had to tell the jury was painfully thin. The prosecution case was clear-cut. Quinn had killed his wife in the course of a row that developed into physical violence, then panicked and tried to cover his traces.

Alison, on the other hand, was claiming that Nikki Quinn had become mixed up with a fast set into hard drugs and exploitive sex, both criminal and embarrassing if exposed. Someone among Nikki's new found friends – she would say Lang and Jevanjee – had decided she was a danger, black-mailed her and, when that failed, decided to kill her. To have a chance of convincing the jury she would have to accuse them outright. Well, why not? Jevanjee had vanished and could not defend him-self; even if Quinn walked free, she knew Lang would never be charged. But none of that mattered if she could plant enough doubt in the minds of the jury to last as long as they took to reach a verdict.

The next step in the argument was dodgy, because Fennel, damn him, was right – it *would* make more sense if they had killed both Nikki and her husband. That would have taken *all* the danger away, wouldn't it? With all those threats around, wouldn't a reasonable juror expect Nikki to confide in her husband? The fact that she had not, while true, was simply unbelievable. She could argue that they had decided to be more subtle: dispose of Nikki, then lead Quinn to be arrested as the only likely suspect for the murder. Silence her, discredit him. But the fact was that killing them both made a hell of a sight more sense. She could suggest that they *had* intended to kill them both, but the plan had gone wrong, so they had a second go and tried to kill him in prison. She had no hard proof of any of it; so why should the jury believe her?

Alison sighed and poured herself a small glass of malt. She was alone in her room looking out over the moonlit graveyard; when she opened the window and leaned out, she noticed a white cat prowling between two square tombs and thought of loyal Hamish. He would be curled up on the kitchen table by the radiator at home, too old and grand these days to go hunting at night. The city outside was silent, the buildings all around in darkness. Beyond them she could see the faint orange glow of street lamps in the centre. Somewhere up towards Clifton an ambulance siren was wailing.

She returned to her desk, eyes sore and wanting to sleep, but went on methodically making her speaking notes, neatly numbered, page by page. She did not hear the phone at first. It was ringing in the outer office and was not switched through to her. Probably a wrong number. No one phoned here at this time of night. But it kept on, becoming irritating, and wearily she stood up and wrenched the door open. The church clock was striking one as she picked up the receiver. 'Hello. Can I help you?'

The line crackled with interference. 'Alison Hope. Can I help you?' The echoing silence mocked her. It was either a wrong number or some shit of a hoax caller. She hung up angrily.

Suddenly she felt gutted. She wanted to curl up in a corner and weep. It was all happening again. Why her – it was so bloody unjust. She'd done nothing to deserve this. She'd given her skill and given herself, just as she had before, until it was all blown apart. At least that time it had been partly her own fault, but she'd paid for it in pain and stress and humiliation – *and* faced up to it and rebuilt a life. No one deserved to go through that twice. And this time Quinn was just a case, taking her where she didn't want to go, putting her where powerful people were determined to destroy her, not because she was Alison Hope, just because she was *there*, in the way. And why was she always left to face these blows so utterly alone?

She walked back to the open window, conscious

that she could not stop her hands shaking. The moonlight shone on the gravestones, no longer comforting, but harsh and bleak: how easy it was to forget that she worked next to a place of death. Death was real, failure was real, suffering was real. She tried clenching her fists, still wrestling with the waves of despair. Damn it, hope was real too. The crisis had peaked. She still felt shattered and tearful, but a remote, only half-perceived corner of her mind knew that some instinctive strength was fighting back, confronting her despair, cauterising fear, dredging up the shaft of steel that would sustain her. She was not going to admit defeat. Deep inside Alison Hope was an intense determination to survive.

She drove home to the flat shortly after two in the morning. She was ready for the last day in court, on paper at least, neat notes on A5 sheets held together in red-tagged bundles and safe in her case on the back seat. The streets were shiny after a shower of rain, empty except for the occasional police car and huddled figures covered by cardboard in shop doorways. She felt exhausted and despondent. Threatening images of George and David and Quinn whirled around in her head, when all she wanted was to be calm and sleep.

In the flat, she lay in bed with her mind racing. In the end she took a pill. Gradually she became drowsy; the last thing she remembered was George's figure, far away, waving through mist, as if he were trying to shout to her but she could not hear.

*

When he came to in a burst of panic, the pain was intense. He shut his eyes against a blaze of yellow flame, burning brighter than the sun. He was choking and started to cough agonisingly, uncontrollably, his whole body convulsing and jerking to expel the petrol fumes filling his throat and every cavity in his skull. His lungs felt scorched as he gasped to breathe. God, every nerve was electrified with acute pain: was this what burning at the stake was like? The crashing roar of the fire was terrifying, a rushing hurricane of heat swirling all around him, battering his eardrums so hard that he cried out and instinctively raised his hands to shield them.

As he moved his arms there was another spasm of pain, in his back; his eyes flew open and he gave a sharp cry. He forced his eyelids to stay apart, despite the blinding light. Damn it, he was conscious, he was not trapped, he could still escape. But as his vision focused he realised that he was not in the fire at all. The burning vehicles were about ten feet away.

He must have been thrown clear by the impact and rolled down the camber. Suddenly he felt that his clothes were wet. He was in a ditch full of muddy water, but burning debris was flying overhead, the heat was taking the skin off his face. Painfully, he pulled his body up the bank and crawled a few yards into the trees away from the inferno. He collapsed and lay there, panting from the effort.

His head was throbbing and the fumes swirling round it made everything swim; his eyes were watering so much his sight had gone again. When he coughed he started to retch until he vomited violently. But, still flat on the mud, he felt sensation begin to return to his arms and legs – he was able to scrape his feet on the ground, clench his fists, move his head, though that was crucifyingly painful. He must have whiplash injuries to his neck and the top of his spine, not surprising after that bang, but no bones seemed to be actually broken. There were burns and cuts on the backs of his hands and his forehead. Every part of his body sensed some degree of pain, but it had never felt so good to be alive. He pulled himself a few more yards before he passed out.

When his eyes opened, it was close to dawn. George had crawled further than he realised and could no longer see the road. Somewhere in the distance, blue lights flashed through the trees and there was the hiss of water. In the still air he could hear commands shouted: 'Get those fucking chains on, I want this heap off the road!'

'OK, guv. What about the stiff?' Stiff? What stiff?

'Put the remains in a body-bag.'

'What bleedin' remains?' There was a guffaw of derisive laughter. ''E's just charred bones and fatty gunge and a few burnt rags; we didn't even see the poor bastard till we hammered the wrecks apart. Skeleton's all in bits, after the heat and that bloody explosion … fuck all left. Come and look.'

'Bung what there is in the bag and the ambulance can take it away—' The rest was lost in the roaring of an engine and the screech of tormented metal. They must be dragging the wreckage off the road.

George was kneeling, supporting himself on a tree trunk. He only had to get over there and they would look after him, get him to hospital. Hospital? Hell, in a few hours Alison needed him to give evidence in *court*. He struggled up and tried to walk. The pain returned and his head swam. He swayed a few more paces, until his foot caught in a tree root. He put out his hands to break his fall, but before he hit the ground the blackness closed in again.

Afterwards, George had no idea how long he lay there, but it must have been over twelve hours. When he came to, his watch had stopped, it was dark and he had never felt so cold: he must be close to hypothermia. His limbs were shaking as he forced himself to stand, then to walk. After a few yards he had to stop and lean against a tree. There was no moonlight, but he could hear a car in the distance: that must be the road. As he hobbled towards it, he felt icy but was sweating. His back was agony, so were his lungs, but he knew he would make it.

God knows whose body had been in the wreckage. Probably some luckless wino reeling down the road just at the wrong moment. Hadn't he seen a face outside, just before the crash? It didn't matter – there was a body, so badly burnt as to be unidentifiable. By now Alison would have been in court all day thinking he had been killed. Shit! He had to find a phone. Eventually he hit the road and swayed back towards Portishead. It was very late, for no vehicles passed him in the half hour it took to reach a call box in a lay-by. He had a few coins in his pocket and tried Alison's numbers, but there was no reply from her flat or chambers. George was puzzled, she ought to be at one or the other.

He leant against the side of the box, breathing heavily. He needed help. He needed someone totally trustworthy. He was confused and angry at Friedmann's betrayal, but the longer Eli and whoever was paying him thought George was dead, the more likely he was to stay alive … He tried Alison again, then dialled another number.

She answered at once. 'Hi.' No number, no name.

'Gina?'

'Who is this?'

'Gina?' But he knew her voice.

'Yeah. Who wants her?'

'You sittin' down? It's me, George.'

A shriek. A long pause. 'Jesus, you're supposed to be dead. A car crash.' She sniffed, was she crying? No, now she was laughing. 'God, I was so pissed off. I *needed* you, I couldn't think who else to turn to – and you were bloody dead, you arsehole. I've been trying to ring Alison all evening but she's not answering either of her numbers. I was about to go round to her flat. Oh, George, where the hell *are* you?'

'I got a lot to tell you, sister. Can you come and pick me up?'

33

It was two in the morning when he finally stretched out on the double bed in her flat. Gina washed his cuts, applying ointment and sticking plaster, her face smiling down at him, striking as a carved ebony sculpture. She was wearing a simple pendant of a piece of jade on a gold chain, like the one he had bought for Alison. 'It's not as bad as I thought, George, but you do look dreadful. You ought to be in hospital.'

'Got a lot to sort out first, darlin'.' He groaned as she cleaned a scratch on his forehead. 'I feel like I've been run over by a steamroller and then fried.' He jumped as she dabbed a particularly tender spot. 'Bugger!'

'Sorry.'

By the time she found him, he had been slumped inside the phone box, his body icy to her touch. He was only half-conscious and so confused it frightened her. During the drive across the sleeping city, he mumbled as he dozed and woke several times with a shriek of terror. Now, comforted by her hands and the soft duvet, his exhausted brain was struggling to make sense of it. He groaned again.

'What day is it, Gina?'

'It's the early hours of Thursday morning. When did all this happen?'

'Sometime late Tuesday night. Some bastard tried to kill me.'

'Looks like they almost succeeded.'

'They put a bloody great artic across the road, then came up behind with lights blazing so I didn't see till it was too late. It was one hell of a smash.'

'Do you know who did it?'

He screwed up his eyes to look at her – his head was throbbing and his vision had gone crinkly – and gave a hard little smile. 'No, but I know a man who does.' Suddenly his head jerked up and his eyes opened wide. 'Christ, I knew I'd forgotten the one thing that really mattered – the trial!' He made to get out of bed, but fell back with a cry of pain.

Gina caught his shoulders and rested them back on the pillow. 'Just you stay where you are, buster. You aren't going anywhere yet. Yes, the trial went on today. I mean yesterday.'

'But what happened? For God's sake, I was supposed to be giving evidence!'

'Try to keep calm, George. The news of the crash came through early on Wednesday, so everyone knew when the court sat. They were all very upset, even the judge – you really have got some fans out there. Did you know that?' She smiled down at him again as she poured a brandy. 'This may kill you, but try it.' He took a sip and coughed. 'Alison was really broken up, but she got through it. The trial just went on – Mr Mar gave evidence, so did I and Mr Taylor. The Langs tried to get out of coming, but the judge said he'd send the police to arrest them if they don't turn up this morning.'

George tried to sit up again. 'But if Alison thinks I'm dead she'll be desperate. I ought to go round there right now!'

'You flatter yourself, George.' She gave that low, contralto laugh, like warm chocolate. 'Yes, she loves you and she was really, really upset. But just now it's three in the morning. I've been trying to phone her at the flat and her chambers all evening *and* since I got back with you. There's no reply. John Forbes took her home after court—'

The bearded face darkened. 'Slimeball?'

She laughed again. 'I do believe you're jealous, George. Yes, slimeball. Alison looked really dreadful, pale and haggard, and I'd guess that right now she's dead to the world, knocked out with a strong sedative, and the phone's been unplugged. We can go round first thing in the morning. *You* need some sleep too – you've had a hell of a shock and you got seriously cold. You must have been lying in those woods for hours and it *is* December.'

He nodded painfully and closed his eyes. 'Maybe you're right. We'll have to go to my place too. I need some clothes to wear in court.'

'OK, though there's some stuff of my little brother's here – he's about as big as you.'

He turned on his side and closed his eyes, but as he settled into the pillow some distant part of his brain suddenly remembered the call from the phone box. 'You said you was trying to get hold of me, Gina … before the crash.'

'It can wait till morning.'

He opened his eyes again. 'We're in the middle of a murder trial, kid. I'll sleep better if I know.'

She hesitated and lit a cigarette. 'OK. Remember you told me to keep an eye on Mr Mar?'

'Sure.'

'Well, I thought you were up the creek; and it seemed kind of disloyal, spying on him, he gave me some good breaks.' She shrugged. 'Now I'm not so sure – the last few days, he's been acting oddly, as if he's hiding something.'

George yawned. 'How do you mean?'

'Hard to put a finger on it – breaking the normal routine, vanishing when we expected him in the office, he's usually in constant touch with his mobile and we know where to find him.' She hesitated.

'Go on, darlin', I need some kip.'

'Then tonight something really weird happened.' She stubbed out the cigarette and lit another. 'We were both at court to give evidence, then I went back to the office. The editor had some urgent figures for the boss, so I said I'd take them round to him. I felt all upset after court … and about you and every-thing … I really needed to talk, I thought maybe Mr Mar would too … I don't know …' She trailed off.

George looked at her questioningly.

'It was dark when I got to Abbots Leigh, but there were a few lights in his house. I was just going to deliver my package like a good little messenger, when the front door slammed and a man hurried out.'

'A man? Mar?'

'That's the point – I couldn't see. He was wearing a hat and a raincoat, so it was hard to tell. You couldn't see his face in the street lamps.'

'And then?'

'He got into a car and drove off.'

'Alan's car?'

'No, it wasn't his Volvo, just a small hatchback – the sort you might hire if … if you didn't want to be seen in your own? Anyway, I followed it.'

'Where did he go?'

'Drove up to the main road, parked near Leigh Woods and walked off into the trees. I stopped further down and had a sniff round the car. It was a Ford Fiesta and I couldn't see anything except a briefcase on the back seat. I got the registration and it *was* hired, the company's number was on a sticker in the rear window, but their name had flaked off. Then I heard him coming back and had to hide. I *thought* he was carrying a package and I *thought* I saw moonlight glinting on a trowel, as if he'd been digging it up.'

'Sounds like the *Pink Panther*, kid. Maybe he was just going for a pee?'

'Maybe I was mistaken.'

'And then?'

'Then he drove off and by the time I followed, I'd lost him.'

'But it was Alan? You're sure?'

'No, I'm not sure at all, but he *did* come out of Alan's house – and when I rang there from a box ten minutes later, the housekeeper said he wasn't there. It's a very odd way to behave ...'

George nodded. 'You got the rental company number?' She nodded and he pulled himself up awkwardly on one elbow. 'Probably Hertz or Avis. Did I say something about kip? Can I have the phone?' She balanced it on the bed beside him. 'If I ring them now, in the middle of the night, I reckon I'll get some national switchboard; if I can still manage my police voice, maybe some prat will tell me something he shouldn't. Ah –' Plainly the call was being answered. 'Ah yes, Avon and Somerset Constabulary here. Detective Constable Jordan. Are you the owners of a Ford Fiesta registration number ...'

Gina watched mesmerised as he was transferred to a supervisor and told the story of a minor crash in which one driver had left the scene without exchanging insurance details. 'No, no one was hurt, but it *is* an offence and we need to contact him. The other car was badly damaged and there is an insurance claim to be pursued, possibly a charge of careless driving ...'

When he put the receiver down he gave a cry of triumph. 'They say the hirer was Dr Andrew Reinhardt, a Swiss national, using an international driving licence. The rental ends at Cardiff airport this morning, when he is catching a seven o'clock flight.'

'But an international driving licence must be child's play to forge or to buy? There must be stocks at every AA office!'

'Need a credit card, too, but that's no problem. I suppose it *could* have been your boss.'

'But what's he up to?'

'You tell *me*, darlin'. Scarpering with the petty cash in the middle of the night? Maybe there really *is* an Andrew Reinhardt? Some kind of legitimate business contact? A consultant advising Mar that he hasn't told you *hoi polloi* about? It's still very odd. I don't trust him, never have, shifty beggar, but I didn't have him down as a kosher villain.'

Her eyes flashed. 'Maybe you were wrong. It *matters*, George, I don't know how, but it matters.'

He shifted uncomfortably. 'You mind if I lie down again, darlin'? My back's bloody killing me.'

'What are we going to *do*, George?'

He groaned. 'You *might* just be right – it could be the break Alison needs, the last piece in the jigsaw. Only one way to find out – you and me is going to get a couple of hours kip, then you're driving us to Cardiff airport by six in the morning. Then we'll know who this Reinhardt is, won't we?'

'You up to that, George?'

'No, I'm damn near dead, but I'll cope. We can phone Alison when we get there. Wake her up with the good news before she goes to court. And I can be back by ten to give evidence.' He turned on his side again and was asleep.

*

They left wearily at four thirty. George had tried Alison's numbers again, but there was still no response. He left the burnt rags of his clothes in Gina's rubbish bin and wore an ill-fitting jacket and trousers of her brother's. At first it was freezing in her sports car, the hood flapping in icy wind, but the air blasting from the heater warmed them up as she drove across the new Severn Bridge and along the empty motorway into Wales. They met nothing but a few oil tankers and articulated trucks bound for Sainsbury's and Tesco's as her headlights flashed over the signs in Welsh and English. Newport, Cardiff, Barry, finally Rhoose airport.

The terminal was bigger than Gina expected. George left her outside in the dark. 'If it *is* Mar, you're just a fraction obvious, darlin'. I'll come back when I've had a recce. You stay here in the shadow and see if anyone else we know comes along.'

The concourse was unexpectedly crowded, with charter flights going to Tenerife and Alicante. None of the figures looked familiar and most were plainly holidaymakers, apart from a few men and women with briefcases and business clothes. George had slept for less than two hours, but he was starting to feel human again. The only scheduled flight seemed to be to Paris, so he went up to the check-in, keeping his back to the crowd. The girl looked as if she had been up all night, but forced a smile. 'Good morning, sir.' She had a pretty Welsh accent.

'I'm travelling with a friend, but I can't see him –

has Dr Reinhardt checked in?'

She tapped on her computer terminal. 'Yes, sir, but the seat next to him is taken.' She looked round the long hall helpfully. 'I do remember Dr Reinhardt, come to think of it, he's the rabbi, isn't he? Isn't that him over there, sir, by the bookstall?'

'Oh, yes, of course.' The only man by the bookstall was in the distinctive dress of a Hassidic Jew. Flat black hat, long twisting locks of hair half covering his face, shabby black suit. And he was going to Paris. George fumbled in his pocket. 'Damn, left my ticket in the car. Be back.'

Outside he found Gina and they crept back to the corner of the concourse, peering through the leaves of a large potted plant. 'Is that him, Gina?'

She shook her head. 'Good clobber – there's always a Hassidic and a nun on scheduled flights, you kind of expect it. But isn't Alan *taller* than that?'

'Then who the hell is it, darlin'?'

They stepped back into the corridor, out of sight. 'Only one way to find out.'

'You mean go with him? All the way to bloody Paris?'

'You said *I* was too obvious, buster.' She tossed her head. 'Anyway, I just *know* this is the key, George. Have you got a passport, credit cards?'

'Yeah, you never know when you're going to need them in this game and they weren't damaged in the crash. But what if we're wrong? Ally's got to be in court before I'd get back. I'm supposed to be a witness. She *needs* me.'

Just *go*, George. I'll tell her what's happened and you can be back by this evening. You can give evidence tomorrow. You might actually have something useful to say by then. You'll win the case for her!' She looked at her watch. 'It's just gone six and I'll phone her as soon as you take off. I *promise*.'

'I'm not sure—'

'Just *go*, sweetheart. This is what we've all been waiting for. I'd do it myself, but you're right – he'd spot me a mile off. Now *you* look different in that dark jacket. Shave off the beard and—'

He looked appalled. 'You must be joking, kid, I've had it thirty years.'

'It'll grow again.' She give him a huge hug. 'Might fancy you without it. Go *on*, George, just do it.'

It took twenty minutes for him to buy a ticket, then a razor and some foam. They went back to the car and she clipped off the beard with nail scissors and shaved him carefully. He found a cardphone and tried both Alison's numbers again, but there was still no answer. 'Shit. Look, Gina, you *will* go straight back and tell her what's happened, won't you?'

'Trust me, George.'

'You'll try her again as soon as I've gone?'

'Don't worry – she'll know in an hour or two, I promise.'

'OK. And I'll call you both from Paris.'

A swift good luck kiss and he was back inside, checking in. He felt naked without his beard. 'Any baggage, sir?'

'No, thanks.' Fortunately, the only seats left were at the back of the aircraft. He went through the departure lounge, following the phoney Hassidic into the bus to the plane. His quarry went up the front steps, so George went to the others, leading up under the tail. As he strapped himself in, at least his back was less painful. He noticed that the man was about ten rows ahead, still wearing his black hat.

Gina parked outside her flat in Brislington an hour later. She had stood in a cold wind by a stretch of chain-link fence until the aircraft took off, then driven back relatively slowly, for she was worn out and this was not the moment to have an accident. When she backed into the space between two other vehicles it was only just getting light. On the pavement, she fumbled to fit her key into the lock on the car door. She was still fiddling with it when she heard another car door slam and sensed footfalls approaching fast.

Before she could turn round a hand grabbed her and she felt a sickening blow on the back of her head. Thick hair protected her, but she staggered forwards. Then there was another, cracking against her skull, blinding her with an explosion of pain. She gave a small groan before everything went black.

34

They were flying in darkness over a long, narrow city. Mile after mile of lights, the neon of shopping centres contrasting with the flickering fires of shanty towns until they bounced on hot Tarmac again. In the sweaty baggage hall, George was overpowered by the crowds, the heat and the smell of burnt petrol flooding in from outside. The noise of shouting and traffic was deafening. The figure he was following collected his two suitcases from a carousel and put them on a trolley. George watched cautiously, but there were so many people it was not difficult to remain concealed. Once through immigration, steel bollards stopped the trolleys being taken further and his quarry hired a porter. The porter was an Indian and short, but George could still see the flat black hat bobbing through the crowd, following the signs for domestic flights. Wasn't this God-awful journey over yet? How long was it since they left Cardiff? George's back was killing him and he realised he'd been travelling for nearly seventeen hours.

The long concourse was even more crowded than the arrival area. Cripples and Indian women clutching babies crouched by the wall, holding out their hands for money. Everyone else seemed to be using a mobile phone; the noise was deafening. Eventually they reached the domestic area and black hat checked in again: a flight for Puerto Vallarta, wherever that might be. George watched him vanish through the gate, then looked for a ticket counter.

At Paris Charles de Gaulle, George had followed black hat, strap-hanging on a crowded bus, to another terminal. When he saw the nervous, shifty figure check in again, it had been a real body-blow. Flight AF036 to Mexico City. Damn. Damn. *Damn*! He should have guessed that Paris would only be a staging post. By now Gina would have told Alison, of course, but she needed him in court and he ought to be *there*, not poncing about hundreds of miles away. On the other hand, the key to her whole case might be vanishing through a departure gate just yards away. There was no time to think. The only way to nail the bastard, the only way to save Quinn, was to stay with it. George hurriedly found a shop where he bought a holdall, a couple of shirts, socks and underwear. He could not find a payphone for international calls that did not have a crowd waiting to use it. He swore quietly and was still fuming in a queue, when the final call came.

They took off smoothly at 11.10, with the rabbi by a window in Club Class and George hidden away in steerage, close to the back of the plane again. It would be a thirteen-hour flight, so he asked for a blanket and pillow, curled up as best he could in the narrow seat, and went to sleep.

He woke up about seven hours later. The plane was a large Airbus, with only one deck unlike a 747, so a walk to the toilet confirmed that black hat was still in the same place, tucking into a chicken dinner and watching a TV screen fitted into the back of the seat in front of him. Through the window, there were no clouds below the aircraft. They were flying in a clear sky with bright sunshine and he could see they were over a long lake. From a display on the bulkhead George saw that it was Lake Michigan. Soon they would cross Chicago, then the great plains around the Mississippi and Missouri rivers, down to Texas where they would stop for an hour at Houston. George felt light-headed: the whole situation was surreal. The fourth day of the trial would be over, Alison had no idea where he was. She'd be going potty; but there was no phone and no way to get off without a parachute.

But he watched the ground with fascination, for he had been to many American ports but never inland. There didn't seem to be much of the prairies left: just two thousand miles of huge fields, neat suburban housing, the high rectangular shapes of grain stores, some forest broken up by the broad, insistent, silver meanders of the two great rivers, until they joined at the next city he passed over, St Louis.

For the last two hours the flightpath was down

the coast of the Gulf of Mexico, at the head of the Caribbean. They were on the same latitude as Florida and Cuba, but there was no azure sea or tropical forest below, just a flat, brown coastline. Texas merged into Mexico, a hazy landscape of mudflats and swampy lagoons: empty, no people, no boats. A weak sun was setting on a horizon lost in mist. He had been disappointed that the Spanish Main looked so dull.

The flight north-west took an hour and a half. George again found a seat at the back, about fifteen rows behind his quarry. It was dark outside but he could see they were plainly crossing an empty area, which he worked out must be the mountains of the Sierra Madre. Occasionally there were the dim, twinkling lights of a village, but mostly endless black emptiness pierced by moonlight glinting on rocky peaks. Whatever his friend was up to, he had chosen the best place in the world to vanish. He hadn't needed a visa to get in and the chaos at Mexico City airport reflected a country with no immigration records. George had filled in a scrappy customs declaration on the plane from Paris, but he was sure the harassed girl who took it had dropped it straight in the garbage. This was a country you could get lost in, just as some of the Great Train Robbers had, until they hankered after fish and chips and made the mistake of going home. If you had money, you could disappear here for ever.

At Puerto Vallarta, the terminal had air-conditioning that worked. George left his target waiting by a carousel for his luggage. It would take time to arrive – everything took a long time here – so he hurried out to find a car-hire desk. Avis was there and his credit card was enough to rent a compact Chevrolet – he was getting quite cavalier about it by now, soon he would owe them thousands. The clerk did not even ask for his driving licence.

When George went outside, the heat and humidity hit him. They were on the tropical Pacific coast and his shirt was wringing with sweat in minutes. He sat uncomfortably in the rented car, started the engine and watched the front of the terminal with its rank of red-and-white taxis. Beyond them, palm trees were silhouetted against the night sky and an orange sodium glow in the distance. A figure walked past the car, eyeing George curiously: a middle-aged man with a pock-marked face, he looked like the head of the local Mafia.

After another ten minutes his quarry appeared with the two suitcases on a porter's trolley. He had finally taken off his hat and wig to reveal his face. The porter put the luggage in the trunk of a taxi and George followed as it moved off, keeping about a hundred yards behind. At first they drove through dark, open country, then suddenly they were in a busy street, passing brightly-lit hotels. There was a salty tang through the open window, so they were close to the sea. The hotels seemed to go on for several miles. They crossed a river and passed a harbour with floodlights shining on a large white liner moored by a pier. The road was twisting into hills by the sea and the streetlights came to an end. He was following the taxi's tail-lamps and had to brake when it stopped abruptly to avoid two cows wandering across the road.

Twenty minutes on, the taxi turned off through a gateway in a high wall. George drove past, stopped on the verge in the shadow of some trees and walked back in the darkness. Peering round the gateposts he saw a villa, white in the moonlight with a grey expanse of sea beyond. The man he had followed from Cardiff stood in the light under a porch, paying off his driver. 'Gotcha,' breathed George, pressing himself back against the wall as the taxi emerged and turned back towards the town.

When he was able to look at the villa again, the man was being embraced by a younger woman. He stumbled back along the verge, wishing he had a torch for it was dark under the trees. At the corner, the white wall ran down to the sea and George followed it, stepping on tufts of grass to silence his footfalls. There was a strip of sandy beach with a jetty running out to a motor cruiser. The wall gave way to concrete posts and chain link fencing stretching out into the water. They were standing there on the balcony, looking out across the Pacific, entwined together. Soon they would be in bed, so he had at least until morning.

35

It was midnight in Puerto Vallarta, six in the morning in Bristol, and oblivion was setting in. Back in town he looked for a large hotel. He needed phone connections that worked, local knowledge, somewhere to snatch a few hours kip. His back was getting really painful.

In the centre, the river flowed to each side of a long island crossed by two bridges. The streets were still busy, tourists with American accents drinking at tables outside cafés. A matchstick figure stood videoing a line of Japanese posing outside a bar. On a patch of waste ground, ragged street children huddled round a blazing fire. There were beggars just as in Mexico City, but also travel-stained cowhands with ten-gallon hats, boots and chaps, straight out of an old Hollywood movie.

The Hotel Bellavista was just south of the island. It looked clean and not over-expensive, so he turned into its short drive and parked under a row of national flags hanging limp on white poles. At reception he once again left an imprint of his credit card – at this rate the only way to avoid personal bankruptcy was to settle the case or stay abroad for ever – and rented a room. Stretched on a double bed with the window open to a balcony, he fought off sleep. He had tried to phone Alison from an international kiosk at Mexico City, but there had been interference on the line and she had hung up. The instructions on the phone by his bed said he could dial Britain direct, so he keyed in the number of her flat in Clifton.

Alison slept restlessly and woke at five thirty. She rarely felt nervous before a case these days, but this one had got right under her skin. Despite yesterday's emotional turmoil, and a short night, she did not feel so bad. On Black Wednesday after George's death, she and John had gone round to his flat and taken in Wedgie. The dog was awake in his basket, so she took him with her for a brisk walk across the Down. She would have a bath and dress for court when she got back.

Striding under the trees, she focused on the day ahead. She was going to get through it like a professional who expected to make a QC. Afterwards, God knows. Quinn would go down for life. George was gone. The police had found Gina's body on the rocks below the suspension bridge, but they were certain she'd been dead before she fell. Now the fast set would close in. She had done them a great deal of damage and they would not forget. They'd make sure Alison was so tainted by this case she'd never see another client; they'd leak sleazy material to the tabloids, question her honesty, end her career and ruin her. Looking back as the pink of sunrise glowed around the Victorian terrace where she lived, neat with its black doors and shutters like a row of dolls' houses, she pushed the thought away. The next twelve hours would take everything she had.

The phone was ringing as she opened the front door. Shooing Wedgie back into his basket, she picked it up reluctantly. It could only be another hoax call or some ghastly news; maybe Quinn had topped himself successfully this time.

'Alison Hope.'

There was a hollow crackling. 'Ally?'

'Yes, who the hell *is* this?'

The voice was distorted. 'Listen carefully, love, it's me, George.'

It was like a blow in the chest, stopping her heart so that a cold numbness flashed through her whole body. 'George is dead. Whoever you are, you bastard, get off the line and leave me alone!'

'No, Al.' The voice sounded desperate – and very like George. 'It really *is* me. I'm in Mexico. For God's sake, didn't Gina tell you?'

Alison sat down at the kitchen table, clutching the handset of the portable phone. She felt icy all over, covered in clammy sweat, and her hands were shaking. 'Gina's dead.' Her voice was hollow and she felt as if she were going mad. '*You're* dead – aren't you?'

'No, darlin', matter of fact, I'm not. Sorry about that. I'll tell you all about it when I get back. Look –

you got some paper and a pen?'

She fumbled among the newspapers, her mind in a maelstrom of confusion; but she was a barrister and suddenly a test occurred to her. 'If you're George, have you got a tattoo on your body?'

He paused. 'Not much time now, darlin', but you know I have.'

'What's it of?'

'You *know* what it is, Al – the Lamb and Flag.' The line was whistling and echoing painfully.

'Where?'

'Where?'

'Where on your bloody body?'

'Oh, I see, on my left, er, hip.'

'OK, brother, I'm starting to believe you. So what the hell are you doing in Mexico?' But then tears overwhelmed her and her voice broke. 'Oh, George, I'm so confused – are you *really* alive, I can't, I *can't* go through all that again.'

''Course I'm alive, darlin'. Never felt better.'

She wiped away the tears with the back of her hand. 'Christ, I've been so bloody miserable. Oh, George, I *do* love you.'

'Yeah, good, I love you too, Al.' He sounded confused. 'Honest, but look, I got a lot to tell you. It's complicated, so will you just concentrate? I know what it's all about now, so pin back those shell-likes and bloody *listen*. See, I followed your old friend Bill Taylor here—'

'Bill Taylor!' Alison almost choked with surprise.

'Yeah, Taylor. He must have managed to disappear

without anyone noticing, and left from Cardiff airport with a false passport. Alan Mar's mixed up with him somehow – you've got the whole story wrong, by the way. Whatever Jevanjee and the others are up to – drugs, sex, arms, world domination – it's *nothing* to do with Nikki and Quinn. Someone should check out the building society's bank accounts. I bet a huge amount has been mysteriously siphoned off.'

'What the hell are you talking about, George? Is all this *true*? You really are in Mexico? Where are you speaking from? Got a phone number? Fax?'

'Yeah, of course, but just *listen*, I'm not finished yet. I'm in a place called Puerto Vallarta on the Pacific coast of Mexico. Taylor's got a rented villa along the coast. Nikki Quinn and the children were waiting for him there.'

Alison was unable to speak; her heart was racing painfully in her chest, her breath would not come. Eventually she panted the words out. 'Nikki – Quinn's – not – dead?'

'No, darlin', that's what I been trying to tell you.'

'I don't understand – don't – do – this – to – me.' She was choking like an asthmatic and struggled to snatch a deeper breath. 'For God's sake, I'm giving my closing speech in a case for her murder in four hours' time.'

'Reckon you'll get 'im off dead easy now, flower. If she ain't dead, he can't have murdered her, can he?' Alison started to laugh hysterically. 'Not that

340

funny, darlin', it's almost bleedin' killed me to get this far.'

She pulled herself together. 'Sorry, George. Give me your phone and fax numbers.' He did so and she wrote them down. 'And where are you?'

'Hotel Bellavista, Puerto Vallarta, Mexico. What do you want me to do?'

'Get photos of them as soon as you can – Taylor, Nikki and if possible the children. Find someone official, not a Mexican, I'm sure they're all corrupt. The British consul, if there is one. Otherwise the American would do. Explain everything and make him go with you to the villa to see them there – without revealing yourselves, if you can. Then get him to witness a statement signed by you like a affidavit, confirming that Nikki is alive, and fax it to my chambers. Xerox the photos and include them – put in the statement when and where they were taken. Send hard copies by Fedex or some other overnight courier.'

'Do I go to the local police?'

'No, I don't think so, not yet. I'll see what Manning has to say for himself, see if he wants to extradite them. If you get the local police involved it will only warn them and they'll get away.'

'OK, Al, see what I can do.'

'I'm so glad you're alive, George.'

'Yeah, I'm pretty chuffed too.' He hesitated. 'Did you say Gina is *dead*, darlin'?'

'Yes. They found her yesterday. Under the suspension bridge with multiple injuries, but the police are certain she was murdered.'

'Oh shit. I never thought … if I hadn't …'

'Hadn't *what*, George.'

'It don't matter just now. I'll get on with the other stuff. Good luck in court, darlin'.'

There was no British consul in Puerto Vallarta. Thumbing through the local telephone directory, George found the United States had a consulate, as did Canada. When he rang them, both had answering machines saying they were open Monday to Friday, nine to one. But the Canadian message also gave the consul's private number 'for use strictly in emergencies'. When he dialled it, a woman's voice answered drowsily. 'McKenzie: can I help you?'

'I'm sorry to call you at home, and so late, but I need to speak to the consul urgently.'

'For God's sake, it's the middle of the night, the office is open at nine, can't it wait till then?'

'No, this really is an emergency.'

She yawned sleepily. 'Well, I'm Jo McKenzie, the Canadian consul, so go ahead, surprise me.' When George explained, she listened patiently, eventually interrupting him. 'OK, if what you say is true I'll try to help. I do look after British interests here. What do you want me to do?'

'The first thing is to get something official faxed to England for the lawyers employing me. Then I guess it's up to the police and our Crown Prosecution Service to seek extradition.'

'In this country – you gotta be kidding!' She

paused as if making a note. 'You'd better meet me at the consulate: can you find Hidalgo 226, it's north of the river, two blocks back from the sea?'

'I'll be there. Say in half an hour?'

'Ok, you've wrecked my beauty sleep anyway. In half an hour.'

Jo McKenzie was about thirty, short and dark-haired in a blue track-suit. She arrived in a white Volkswagen Beetle at the same time as George and led him briskly up a flight of stairs to her office, switching on the lights. He had fallen on his feet. She helped him type out a statement and faced him in a businesslike way, fumbling in her desk for a small black book. 'I've no way of knowing if any of this is for real, but you don't seem like a nut. I know nothing of your legal system, but we'd better make it as formal as possible. Take this New Testament in your right hand. Now do you affirm to the best of your knowledge and belief that the contents of this document are true?'

'I do.'

She rolled the single sheet higher in the type-writer and added 'Sworn before me, Josephine McKenzie, Consul of Canada, Puerto Vallarta in the United States of Mexico'. She lay the paper on her desk and signed and dated it. 'There's supposed to be a fee of ten dollars.' George felt in his pocket. 'Don't worry, it can keep. I'll make a couple of photocopies and then the fax is over there. Be my guest.'

'Thank you. Then will you come with me to the villa? Early tomorrow I want to get some photographs of them if I can and I could do with an independent witness.'

She nodded. 'OK, I'll do that. At least it makes a change from Toronto drunks run in by the local police.' She met his eyes sharply. 'But I'll be reporting this to Ottawa, so you'd better be on the level, Mr Kristianssen, or you'll be in real deep trouble.'

36

Alison reached her chambers at eight, just before Forbes whom she had phoned before leaving the flat. He kissed her on the cheek, and gave her a fatherly hug. 'Brilliant, isn't it!'

She unlocked the front door and he followed her upstairs. 'It's OK so far, but Nikki is still half a world away and the evidence is thin until we get her back here; it's going to be a difficult day.' She put coffee in the cafetière and plugged in the electric kettle. 'I rang Manning as well.'

'I thought his home number was a well-guarded secret?'

'It is. I phoned the nick and they patched me through to him in bed – he was furious. But when I told him what had happened he said he'd be here at eight thirty.'

'Not his office?'

'He chose to come to me. It could just be that even Manning is capable of a *frisson* of embarrassment when the murder victim at the centre of his prosecution is found alive. And Quinn's already been in jail three months, his life has been ruined, eight years ago he was a folk hero – I'd say

345

Manning has some problems ahead, wouldn't you?'

They did not pursue it, because there was the sound of feet climbing the stairs and a knock on her office door. Manning's neat silver hair peered round it. 'May I come in?'

For the next fifteen minutes he sat in one of the old leather armchairs, taking notes. He listened without moving a muscle, except when he sipped at his mug of increasingly tepid coffee, and accepted the faxed documents with a curt nod. 'So you contend that Mrs Quinn is alive and hiding in Mexico with Mr Taylor?'

He was so matter of fact that Alison wanted to jump up and down and scream at him. Didn't he care even a *little* that he'd been prosecuting an innocent man for murder? 'We don't *contend* it – we are certain it is true. We assume that Mrs Quinn and Taylor struck up an affair some time ago and decided to start a new life together. Up to a point it makes sense – he was a widower and she a grass widow. What doesn't make sense is doing it this way: murder, deception, crucifying Quinn instead of just divorcing him. Did she hate him that much?'

Manning stood up, stretching his back as if he had lumbago. It was easy to forget that he'd once been a copper on the beat in an age when they still rode old-fashioned upright bicycles, shielded from Bristol rain only by rubber capes. He walked over to the window and sat down again in the window seat. When he met their eyes he looked older, and tired. 'Very well. I should like to speak to you both in the strictest confidence – not about Quinn's case, but about how we can help each other. Will you give me your word that you will not repeat anything said from now on outside this room? Miss Hope?'

'I'm really not sure what you're suggesting, Mr Manning. I have my duty to my client – and to the court. We can have an off-the-record talk if you want, but I may have to terminate it if you start to mention things I can't possibly keep to myself.'

'I'll take that as a yes,' he snapped brusquely. 'Mr Forbes?'

'Fine, go ahead.'

'Right. First, Miss Hope, I want you to ask the judge for an adjournment today, for twenty-four hours.'

'Wrong, Chief Superintendent. I plan to be on my feet in court shortly after ten, pleading that Quinn has no case to answer.'

He looked threatened and even older. 'Yes, I can't stop you, but let me explain *why* I want twenty-four hours. First, I am prepared to ask the Mexican police to detain Nikki Quinn and Bill Taylor, then to seek their extradition. That will help you by proving beyond any doubt that she is alive.'

'You do accept that, then?'

'As a working hypothesis. I don't believe you made it up and I know Kristianssen is in Mexico – I spoke to this Canadian consul before I came to see you.'

'You did *what*?

347

Manning glared at her. 'I hold the office of constable, Miss Hope, I can talk to whom I choose. Your friend George may have found Taylor and Quinn, but I'm taking this over. It might have been better if you'd left it to the professionals all along.' Alison was stupefied by his outrageous cheek, but kept her trap shut. 'My office is checking on the exact procedure to get them arrested and initiate extradition. There are charges of murder to be answered – and major fraud.'

'Fraud?' queried Forbes. 'I'm not sure we follow.'

'Yes, fraud – or rather theft. Dr Quinn's case is not the only one I've been handling in the last few months, you know. It comes as no surprise that Taylor has fled abroad, although I'm furious we did not prevent it.' There was silence in the room as the two lawyers looked at him expectantly. 'This is where I must speak to you in total confidence. OK?' This time they both nodded agreement.

'Right. Well, Bill Taylor looks like a decent, honest bloke with a classic small-town rags to riches story. Office boy to MD of a modestly sized building society. But it's not all it seems.'

'I had thought he was about the only straight person in this whole saga,' said Alison.

'I believe he was straight once, but he seems to have changed after his wife died. Plainly felt discontented, poorly rewarded after working night and day for the society for thirty years, even perhaps exploited.'

'He *was* its managing director,' objected Forbes. 'He was hardly starving.'

'He was on sixty grand a year, not half a million like some. We shan't know the motivation until we can interrogate him, but I sense that he blamed the society for his wife's death, for ending what seems to have been a dull but contented kind of life. Then there started to be doubts, made known to my fraud squad, by the two non-executive directors of the society, about his drawings. He seems to have incurred some heavy and dodgy expenses, given himself interest-free loans. He had his hand in the till in a big way. He was questioned and, unfortunately, put on his guard, but no action was taken for lack of evidence. But the inquiry continued and now there is plenty of evidence. The board was closing in and so was I. This autumn I think he sensed that he'd come to the end of the road, that he would be sacked in a month or two and then arrested. Riches back to rags and a long jail sentence. He was desperate.'

Alison nodded thoughtfully. 'I'd never have guessed. He even turned up this week to give evidence for Quinn, cool as you like, when he was on the point of running. What about Nikki?'

'Believe me, I had *no* idea at all that he had taken up with her. If I had, the Quinn investigation would have been conducted quite differently. But I'm afraid I just didn't know until you phoned me an hour ago. I'm sorry.'

'So he fled to Mexico?'

'A little more than that, Miss Hope. He had plainly been studying the computer systems that controlled the society's bank accounts. He set up a very complicated plan – and seems to have executed it almost perfectly. He knew all the codes and had access to any terminal he chose in any society office. Yesterday, when you say he flew to Paris, thirty-two million pounds were moved from the society's accounts by direct computer transfer to accounts in Switzerland. He left about two-thirds of the society's funds in place so alarm bells wouldn't ring too soon, giving him a few days to vanish completely. Anyway, thirty mil would be enough for most of us, wouldn't it? We know the funds have already been moved on to Liechtenstein. After that, we've lost track for the moment, but I've no doubt they are heading for somewhere he expects them to be untraceable, in Mexico or the United States.'

Alison whistled quietly. 'So it was just an ordinary old scam? I've been threatening half the Bristol *nomenklatura* with exposure for no reason at all?'

'I'm afraid so, Miss Hope.'

'And you just let it *happen*? Let Jevanjee and his buddies try to kill me, then try to kill George? They *did* kill Gina and that other journalist. They killed my car mechanic, our postman and one of George's investigators. Have you *any* idea what these past three months have been like for us?'

'Don't be absurd, Miss Hope. Until very recently I had no idea you were tangling with that bunch of comedians – I didn't connect them with Quinn and his wife at that stage – but they're damned dangerous and, if I'd known, I'd have warned you off. There are certainly charges to be laid there when we are ready, and serious ones, but they have nothing to do with Quinn.'

Alison was boiling with anger, but held back: she still had a case to win. 'From what George told me, Alan Mar may be involved, too?'

'I don't think so, Miss Hope. Mr Mar is one of the non-executive directors of the building society who put us on to Taylor in the first place.'

Alison sighed. How easily Taylor had taken her in. 'I'm gob-smacked, Chief Superintendent. I always felt there was something shifty about Alan Mar.'

Manning shook his head. 'Leave it to the professionals, Miss Hope. On Wednesday evening, Taylor contacted his fellow directors to say he'd be away a couple of days for a family funeral – buying time. He called at Mar's house and, since Mar wasn't there, the housekeeper – who knew Taylor, of course – let him in to leave Mar a note. Then he drove into Wales and vanished for a few hours until he caught his plane with a phoney Swiss passport in the name of Reinhardt.'

Suddenly Mar's shiftiness was starting to make sense to Alison. 'Thank you for telling us all this, Chief Superintendent, but I think you'd better speak to the judge yourself – by phone if you don't want to be seen visiting him in chambers. I'll ask for an adjournment to present late evidence, but he won't give it to me at this stage unless you help.'

'Yes, I'll do that. May I phone from here?'

On the Pacific coast, a few miles south of Puerto Vallarta, George was fretting. Jo McKenzie had lent him a mobile phone, so he could stay in touch while keeping an eye on the villa. After a few hours' sleep at the hotel, he had spent all morning there, his car parked in a nearby wood, sheltering from blazing sun and watching the building from a rough hide he had constructed with branches and leaves. With some bread and goats' cheese, and a bottle of water, he was comfortable enough – but what on earth was Alison *doing*?

To be fair, there was no sign of Taylor and Nikki Quinn moving on immediately. So far they had spent the time drifting between the verandah and their strip of white sand by the sea. She had been here so long she had acquired a deep tan, shown off by a white bikini, as had the two children. Taylor's body was lily-white, but it looked as if he intended staying long enough to put that right. When George crept stealthily through the pine wood to the left of the property, he could hear them talking to each other.

'The children love it here, Bill – why can't we stay?'

'I just want to get right away from big towns for a year. Out of sight, establish our new identities. We've plenty of money, we can rent somewhere further down the coast where it's empty, or up in the Sierra Madre.'

'Are you afraid they'll come after us?'

'No, they can't trace us, we could be anywhere in the world.' But there was the slightest hint of doubt in his voice. 'I wish to God you'd done as I asked and helped me put that gypsy girl in the cellar. We only needed a few hours – it wasn't necessary to kill her.'

'I didn't *mean* to kill her and you bloody well know it!' It was plainly an argument they'd had before. George stood transfixed: stunned, as suddenly he understood. He was struggling to hear every word above the waves breaking a few yards away. Nikki sounded angry, shrill and dismissive, not a hint of regret or remorse. 'It was just sod's law, bloody Vesna coming back on the scrounge when we were packing up to go – I never thought we'd see her again, nor that she'd guess what we were up to. All she wanted was another hand-out to tide her over after losing her job in London. Fucking free-loader, it was pure blackmail. She fell down the steps when I tried to stop her leaving. It was an accident that she broke her neck and died. It was a bloody accident – it wasn't *my* fault.'

'I know, love, I know. Anyway, the police think the body was yours and that Geoff killed you.'

Taylor sounded guilty and upset; Nikki was laughing. 'So we should be safe enough, shouldn't we?' Taylor did not reply. George heard the splash of liquid being poured; he caught a whiff of coffee. It didn't explain everything, but at least he saw what had happened: he had been puzzling towards it ever since he, too, had escaped from the fire. It was not just Gina, but a half formed feeling – if he had survived a fire could Nikki have, too? – that had decided him to pursue the man who turned out to be Taylor.

One of the children was speaking, the little boy. 'When's Daddy coming, Mummy? Why hasn't he come with Uncle Bill?'

There was the crash of a wave and George could not hear her reply; he wished he could see the poor little beggar's face. His mind was racing. He imagined them back in Abbots Leigh, packing for the great escape when the ex-au pair turned up on the door-step. What shitty timing. A struggle when they tried to lock her in the strong-room down the cellar stairs and give themselves time to clear the country. An accident. Panic. Did they dismember the body together? Were the children upstairs asleep? One of them must have kept their nerve to go through with all that cutting up and loading the furnace. He bet that had been Nikki – Taylor still sounded shaken by it. The atmosphere of fear and tension must have been unbearable, as they sweated through the night in that cellar. What happened then? Maybe he took her across to Cherbourg or St Malo in the yacht, put her on a train to Paris, went back to Bristol to cover the traces? Must have been a real bonus when Quinn was arrested – that certainly hadn't been in the script. Taylor had pretty cast-iron nerves, too, to keep up the front in Bristol for three months, but now he was jumpy, dead jumpy … They would move on, and pretty soon. Back in his hide, George wondered just how long he had got.

In Bristol, Alison was driving out to the remand centre. She wanted to buoy up Quinn until the hearing tomorrow, when he ought to be released. She wanted to tell him that both Nikki and the children were alive, but that would break her word to Manning. On the other hand it would be ironic if he hanged himself in the cell when he was on the verge of being free – and he was so depressed that had to be a possibility. She wrestled with the problem as she drove through the suburbs.

East of the city, a police Jaguar was doing a ton on the M4 towards Heathrow airport. There were two passengers in the back, Manning and a female detective sergeant. The small Mexican embassy in Mayfair's Hertford Street had been remarkably helpful, as had the McKenzie woman, but both had urged Manning to get on the spot himself as soon as he could. Looking out of the car window, streaming with rain, his bones feeling arthritis and the cold more with every passing year, a trip to the tropics looked highly inviting.

37

It was the first time she had seen Quinn really smile. They were in a different interview room that offered no privacy: two walls were of glass so the screw outside could see everything, although he was not supposed to be able to hear what passed between lawyers and their clients. But the surroundings did not matter. 'You mean they're all alive? Jess and Tom too? They went off with Bill Taylor? I don't believe it.'

'That's how it looks, Geoff. Nikki and the children are *certainly* alive and I'll be able to prove that in court at ten tomorrow morning. The judge has another big trial on Monday, so he's agreed to sit for an hour on Saturday morning to let me present my "new evidence". Then he's expecting to decide whether we have to extend the whole thing to let Fennel cross-examine and so on, in which case we'd go on next Monday and a different red judge would be found to take the other case. He doesn't know the truth yet, but when he does I reckon you'll be free by lunch-time tomorrow.'

Quinn looked dazed. 'It's the best moment of my life, I thought it was all over, I'd lost everything ... I still can't believe it. What will happen to Nikki?'

'I hope she'll return with your children.'

'Hope? Won't she *have* to?'

'It's not quite as simple as that. Mexico has an extradition treaty with Britain, going back to 1886, but it doesn't work very well. That's why you don't mention what I've told you to anyone.'

'Who do you think I'll be seeing? They don't let me go down the pub at night, you know.'

'Not even to a friendly screw or the chaplain if he comes to see you. Not to anybody.'

'OK.' he hesitated. 'Alison?'

'Yes?'

'Do you honestly mean I might be free? *Tomorrow?*'

'I hope so, Geoff, I really hope so.'

And George was alive. He'd be home over the weekend. As she drove back into the city, she had never felt so elated. It was the best moment of *her* life, too.

In Puerto Vallarta it was midnight. George was waiting by the phone in his hotel. 'It's Jo McKenzie. If you want to be in on the last act, be downstairs in fifteen minutes.'

'What's happened?'

'A lot. I'll tell you in the car.'

Jo picked him up in the white Beetle and drove fast through busy streets, the small engine whirring like a sewing machine. 'Your barrister friend has really stirred it up in England. There's some senior police guy on his way here.'

'Manning?'

'Yeah, Chief Superintendent Manning. He's asked the local police to detain Taylor and the girl. Then your Crown Prosecution Service will seek extradition.'

'Still at the villa, are they? Haven't buggered off to Guatemala?'

She smiled. 'No, George. The local police were alerted today and surrounded the villa shortly after you and I left. Taylor and his girlfriend are still there. You'd better check my camera has some film in it. It's on the back seat.'

'Why d'you want a camera?'

'*I* don't. I thought *you* might – you said you wanted some pics of them being arrested to send back to Bristol? Some *evidence*?'

'Oh, yeah.' He sighed with exhaustion. 'I forgot.'

'Christ, you're supposed to be a PI. Haven't you read any Raymond Chandler?' They had passed the harbour, where the liner was still moored, and were switchbacking up and down along the coast road in the darkness.

'Do the police know I'm coming?'

'Good lord, no. You have no official status. They don't even know *I'm* turning up, but I've seen all the telegrams so I thought, what the hell.'

'And will they arrest them? Just like that?'

'No, not "just like that". It's not *quite* the Wild West here, you know, even though it may look like it. The wires have been humming between London and Mexico City. Your prosecution service has made a request to the Mexican ambassador in London, who passed it on to the Ministry of Justice; and they've authorised the local police to act on it. Our dashing Captain Menendez will arrest Quinn and Taylor and hold them for seven days. Then it'll be up to your people to get into court with a proper case for extradition or they'll be released. That's how it works here.'

A quarter of a mile before the villa, the road was blocked by a police car: a black-and-white American sedan with two blue lamps flashing on the roof. A policeman carrying a carbine waved them to the side of the road. Jo jumped out and started to talk firmly in Spanish, pushing her diplomatic identity card under his nose. He opened the door of his car to get to his radio and a dim light came on. After a few minutes he waved them on. 'We've got to leave the car,' said Jo. 'But he says we can witness the operation.'

They walked on the grass to make as little noise as possible. To the west, the sky was dark and the sea grey and empty beyond the trees. When they came to another car, a policeman in a visored helmet flashed a torch into their faces and spoke in a whisper to Jo.

'What's he saying, darlin'?'

'He says there are ten armed police ringing the villa, which is just a hundred yards away. We can go to the corner and watch, so long as we lie on the ground and shelter behind trees. He doesn't expect any shooting, but can't be sure.'

'*Shooting*? There are two children in there, for God's sake. Doesn't he know that?'

'Yeah – I'll check.' Jo asked a question in Spanish, keeping her voice low. The officer replied and Jo translated. 'It's OK. Captain Menendez knows. He also thinks Nikki and Taylor are in bed. Armed officers will go in to arrest them and he'll be following himself, with a woman officer, to make sure the kids are not hurt. Don't worry, George.'

'When are they goin' in?'

They had reached the end of the trees and could see the villa. Jo threw herself flat on the pine needles. 'In about five minutes.'

In the villa, their bedroom looked out over the sea. Shutters had been drawn over the glass doors leading to the balcony. Bill Taylor woke with a start and sat up, sensing that something was wrong. He could hear waves breaking on the sand, but had he also heard the creak of a door opening? Or an intruder outside? He smiled at Nikki, lying on her side in the darkness, fast asleep, long sensuous body covered only by a rumpled cotton sheet. Pulling on a pair of boxer shorts, he hurried across to the shutters.

He had half opened them, and was stepping out on the balcony, when the terrific crash made him freeze in terror. The lights went on. The gleaming head of an axe was still splintering the door as it fell from its hinges and four figures in black uniforms and helmets ran in. Nikki sat up and screamed. 'Freeze!' yelled a voice in heavily accented English. 'You is surrounded and we shoot if you try escape.'

Somewhere in the back of the house a child was howling. Nikki leapt naked from the bed and ran towards Taylor, but two of the men seized her arms and dragged her back, kicking out like a can-can dancer. 'Let me go, you arseholes. For Christ's sake, Bill, help me!'

Seeing her there, only yards away, twisting and spitting, nostrils flared, a tigress at bay, Taylor came to. Last night they had decided to go to sea, out of sight for a few days. The cruiser that came with the villa was provisioned, quite a lot of money was stowed in lockers under the bunks. He could do nothing here. He yelled 'I'll get you out, Nikki,' at the woman he had thought he wanted for the rest of his life, vaulted over the parapet of the balcony and vanished.

Nikki's face contorted and she gave an animal scream of rage and terror. 'Don't leave me, you bastard!'

When two police ran onto the verandah after him, they could see his shadow sprinting in the darkness. He was already halfway along the wooden jetty, running awkwardly as if he had hurt an ankle when landing. They shouted and fired a burst of bullets above his head. A man with a lot of silver on his uniform was roaring through a bullhorn: 'Stand still, mister, or we shoot to kill!' A second automatic burst raked the jetty,

361

splinters flying into the air, one bullet ricocheting off the steel mast of the boat with a whine. Then four more police appeared below, charging across the beach in pursuit, making it impossible to fire again. Taylor was in the cockpit at the stern of the white cruiser, swaying as if a bullet had winged him, but the engine spluttered into life. He was hurling the mooring ropes into the sea, letting in the throttle and spinning the wheel as the screw bit and the exhaust roared like a heavy motorcycle.

Now the four police were spread untidily along the beach, firing at random with revolvers and two machine pistols. But the cruiser was already roaring out to sea, a huge bow wave foaming grey on the dark water. When George and Jo McKenzie arrived, panting from the run, the children were both shrieking in terror, in a bedroom near the front porch, surrounded by two men and a woman in uniform. Jo rushed in and cuddled the little girl, her eyes like saucers, staring in horror. 'It's all right, Jess. Your mommy's all right.'

'Go away!' screamed the child. 'I hate you!'

George ran on down the corridor to the front of the villa, where Nikki Quinn was no longer struggling with the police. The room was full of men in gleaming black riot helmets. They had handcuffed her wrists behind her and taped her ankles and knees together; there were livid red and black marks on her arms and shoulders. She was still naked, huddled on the edge of the bed, staring in disbelief. 'The bastard,' she sobbed. 'The fucking *bastard*. He *left* me. He left the children. I hope they fucking kill him. He said he loved me. I must have been mad to trust him.'

'Outside, George turned to Jo. 'What happens now?'

'The police will take her to the local station and I'll have to look after her children.'

'And then?'

'Extradition could take for ever. If she gets a local lawyer, there could be endless delay, appeals, the law is very slow here.'

'That's bad news.'

Jo shrugged. 'Your authorities can ask for her to be kept in custody until there's a decision. Quite frankly the best thing is for her to return voluntarily. I'll try to persuade her. Whatever she's done under English law, the penalty is likely to be better than spending months, even years, in a hot concrete cell full of mosquitoes with a stinking hole in the corner for a lavatory – and your kids parked in a home where the nuns only speak Spanish.'

Nikki was being brought out, jeans pulled over her legs, a coat flung round her shoulders, her wrists obviously still manacled behind her back. In the light above the porch, they could see she was still struggling, surrounded by four uniformed men. Her legs had been freed to let her walk, but her ankles were in fetters joined by a chain. A policewoman followed, each of her hands holding a child's. Jessica was stony-faced with shock, Tom was crying. Feeling like a voyeur, George took half a dozen flash photographs and Nikki spat abuse at him.

38

Alison arrived at court soon after nine and went straight to the clerk's office. 'I need to see Mr Justice Egan in chambers before we start today. Would you arrange that, please?'

'Certainly, Miss Hope. I'll tell Sir James's marshal. Any particular reason?'

'I'd sooner explain that myself. But it's important, really important.' She left him, sighing to herself, to put on her gown in the robing-room. There should be nothing to go wrong now, but she still felt nervous. She was crossing the lobby when the well-polished Daimler flying the Union flag drew up outside, led by two police on motorcycles: the last vestige of the pomp that had characterised the assizes right from the Middle Ages. If Alison ever made it to the High Court bench she was determined to arrive on a bike, but reflected ruefully that she'd probably be too fat to ride one by then. An usher opened the car door and the judge stepped out, already robed in scarlet, black sash across his chest. He walked up the steps, nodding courteously to the saluting police.

Alison hung back as he vanished through the

door to his chambers, then returned to the robing-room to await his summons. It never came and she rang the clerk impatiently. 'I did pass on your message to Sir James's marshal, Miss Hope, and we ought to be in court in five minutes. Would you like me to try again?'

'Don't bother. That toffee-nosed little git doesn't listen to the likes of us.'

'Quite, Miss Hope.'

'So, I'll do what I have to do in open court. Then Egan will hang the little bugger by his balls.'

She walked slowly down the corridor. George had been on the phone again only an hour before. 'She'll probably deny it all when she gets back, but she confessed to the consul.'

'Admitted she was in cahoots with Taylor, knew exactly what he was doing?'

'She knew, Ally, but there was no plan to kill anyone. She was just going to leave for the continent and then fly to Mexico on the phoney passport he'd bought for her. He was going to follow a few weeks later. She left the house with the children at Friday lunch-time, which is why it was empty when Quinn came home from work. But she and Taylor went back in the evening to fetch some more clothes she wanted. It was sheer bad luck the old au pair, the Bosnian girl, turned up. She knew Nikki's little ways and guessed at once what Taylor was doing there – they knew Vesna could blow them and they panicked. There was a struggle when she tried to get out of the house, she fell down the cellar steps, broke her neck and died instantly. Nikki says it was an accident, but she still helped him put the body in the furnace and cleaned up afterwards.'

'But wasn't the body bound to be found later – by Quinn, if no one else?'

'Quinn was supposed to be in his surgery on Saturday morning and on call after that. Taylor intended to go back to the house after Nikki had gone, poke the furnace, and empty the ash while Quinn was at work on Monday. He could have buried the bones that survived and covered everything up, but Nikki was in a hell of a state – they both were – so in the end he drove to West Bay and took her across the channel in the yacht. He was afraid she'd draw attention to herself on a plane or ferry.'

'And by the time he got back it was too late. Someone had called the police.'

'And Quinn had dropped himself right in the frame.'

'And everything fell apart ... but she's the only one in custody?'

'Yeah, he's gone. She's on her own, facing a murder charge.'

'Which just leaves the dental records, George. Did they falsify them?'

'Nikki says she don't know nothin' about that nor – till Taylor got here – that everyone thought the remains were hers.' He hesitated. 'You know what I think, Ally?'

'No, tell me.'

'Reckon it was a mega cock-up by the police and the pathologist. Maybe Nikki had some posh private dentist, going back years, and sent the au pair to the same one as the kids when she needed her teeth done? Vesna hadn't got an NHS number, so she just said she was Mrs Quinn. Who was to know? And the police was too tight-fisted to do a DNA test.'

Alison whistled quietly through her teeth. 'You could just be right, George. You mean it wasn't *planned* at all? That does make a sort of mad sense – would explain the record card being only a year old. And they were so certain it had to be Nikki, they didn't bother to look any further. With the girl being here illegally, they nearly got away with it, too. There was no one to miss her – and no one did.'

The court room was unusually crowded, as if they all knew something dramatic was going to happen. John Forbes and the Crown solicitors were already at their table. Alison took her place at the long table in front of the bench. Rick Fennel smiled at her from the other end. He did not look concerned at the threat of last minute evidence that might blow his case out of the water. Very laid-back, our Rick, it would take a nuclear explosion to faze him. Maybe, although so tenacious, he was more distanced from the job than she had thought.

The gallery was full and there was a buzz of expectancy as the jury filed in. She felt a thrill of anticipation as the usher called, 'All stand, please!' The doors behind the bench opened and the judge came in, followed by the supercilious young barrister he had chosen as his marshal for this circuit. Mr Justice Egan bowed to Alison and then to Rick Fennel; they inclined their heads gravely and everyone sat down. Alison smiled. Odd way of dispensing justice in the twentieth century. Another nod from the judge and Quinn appeared from the stairs under the dock and stood there with his two prison officers, looking decidedly apprehensive. The room fell silent and she looked up at the judge. He responded courteously. 'Miss Hope?'

'May it please the court.' She paused deliberately, until the silence turned into expectation. 'My lord, I wish to make a submission that my client has no case to answer.'

He looked puzzled. 'Do you, indeed, Miss Hope?' He turned to the jury, who would have to leave while she was heard. 'Members of the jury, I don't think we need detain you while counsel make legal submissions to me. I suggest you all have a break and a cup of coffee.' They clattered out. Alison remained on her feet, conscious of many pairs of eyes focused on her back: one of the oddities of this kind of theatre was that you looked at jury and judge, rarely at the bigger audience behind you.

She straightened her shoulders and took a deep breath. This was it. 'My lord, my client, Dr Quinn, is arraigned on an indictment of murdering his wife,

Mrs Nicola Quinn, on or about the date indicated in the charge.'

The judge smiled. 'That much we all know, Miss Hope.'

'My lord, I submit that he has no case to answer. No case, because his wife is still alive.' There was a buzz all around the court.

'Still alive, Miss Hope?'

'Still alive, my lord. I have documentary evidence that Mrs Quinn was alive up to yesterday, living in hiding with her two children at a rented villa near the town of Puerto Vallarta in Mexico.'

There was a long silence. 'In *Mexico* you say? What kind of evidence, Miss Hope?'

'An affidavit from a private investigator, witnessed by the Canadian consul, who handles British affairs in that part of Mexico. There is also a supporting statement from the consul herself and I shall be producing photographic evidence.'

'Photographs seem to figure large in this case, Miss Hope. Please go on.'

'I further understand that Mrs Quinn was joined in Mexico by Mr William Taylor, managing director of a building society in this city. I believe a warrant has been issued for both their arrests, the Mexican police detained Mrs Quinn last night and extradition is sought. In these circumstances I submit that there is no case to answer, my lord.'

She sat down abruptly, murmurs of astonishment and muffled conversation all around her. The judge rapped on his desk. 'Silence please, silence or

I shall clear the court!' He waited for quiet and was obviously furious that she had not warned him of her intention. Well, there was a damn good reason for that: she had tried and there was nothing in the rules to say you had to kick down the door of his room if that prat of a marshal didn't do his job. 'May I see this evidence, Miss Hope?'

Alison handed the photocopied sheets to the usher, who passed them up to the judge, at the same time giving copies to Fennel. The judge scanned them quickly. 'I shall need to see original documents, you know, this is all very unsatisfactory. But I have no wish to permit a miscarriage of justice.' John Forbes was suddenly at her elbow, thrusting a note into her hands. She glanced down.

'My lord, I am further instructed that Mrs Quinn has agreed voluntarily to return to this country, and will be leaving Mexico City by air today. She will be escorted by an officer of the Avon and Somerset Constabulary and my investigator will be on the same plane, with the original documents you require.' She sat down again. The noise from the gallery was approaching uproar and the press reporters were already making for the door.

Finally, the judge was able to speak. 'And Mr Taylor, though he of course is not on trial here?'

'I am advised that Mr Taylor was not detained, my lord. He escaped.'

'Very well. The court is adjourned until ten on Monday. Take the defendant down again. And I wish to see both counsel immediately in chambers.'

*

They landed at seven the following morning, coming in from the west over the ghostly shadows of Windsor Castle. On the ground, the aircraft drew up at a flexible gangway by one of the terminals, but the centre door was opened and steps pushed up to it. Over the Tannoy, a steward asked everyone to remain seated. Two uniformed policewomen and a man in plain clothes appeared. Nikki was handcuffed and hustled down the steps. Each child was picked up by a policewoman who followed swiftly. They did not start to scream until they reached the ground. By the time George was at the door, they were all in two cars and being driven away.

'Sorry, sir. You'll have to go with the other passengers.' The stewardess pulled the door to and locked it again.

When he emerged from customs, Alison was waiting. He had felt exhausted on the flight, but that was forgotten as he hugged her and she threw her arms round his neck with a huge kiss. 'Oh, George.' Her eyes were startlingly bright and he had never seen her look so happy. 'I'm so glad.'

'That we won?'

'That you're *alive*, you halfwit.' There were tears in her eyes. He remembered that she had not seen him since she thought him killed in the crash. 'Sorry it's been so long, Ally, but worked out OK, didn't it?'

'Yes, George. *Everything's* turned out OK, for us anyway.' She hesitated, shyly, almost nervously. 'It has, hasn't it? Let's go home.'

POSTSCRIPT

It was a week later. After Nikki's return, the court hearing on Monday had lasted only ten minutes. The police confirmed that Nicola Quinn was back, the judge directed the jury to return a verdict of not guilty and Quinn walked from the dock a free man. Clearing up took a few days, then Alison took a week off. She and George drove down to Cornwall and stayed at a pub on the Roseland peninsula.

The second day they walked by the Tresillian river, past St Clement, where she had come so close to giving up. She had hated George, hated the law, hated Quinn, above all hated herself. Even though now she was trotting along by his reassuring bulk, that black night still seemed very real. She looked up at the kind face, the beard growing again, that awful flat cap. He put out an arm and tucked her under his shoulder protectively. 'Beautiful in winter, isn't it, darlin'?' He nodded towards the twisting outlines of trees, a cormorant diving in the still water. 'What will Quinn do now?'

'He's back in that gruesome house, trying to be a father to his two poor kids. He went back to the practice in Avonmouth, too – which must have taken more guts than I thought he had – and they're all going to see Nikki in the slammer this weekend. It's quite ghastly.'

'And Manning's thrown the book at her? Charged her with murder, not being an accessory?'

'You bet he has. Now she's trying to claim it was Taylor who killed Vesna but damn it, George, I believe her first story.'

'And Nikki will have to carry the can alone – they'll never find him, not over there, not now. Will they?'

'Probably not. Strange, isn't it? Taylor never occurred to me. I always had a hunch that Alan Mar would turn out to be bad, but we all got him wrong. As for all those coke-snorting toffs – Manning's launched a mega-investigation and I've been tipped off there'll be a dawn round-up soon. Got all that wrong, too, didn't we?' There was a splash as the cormorant dived again. 'Manning's an awkward bastard and he won't be intimidated, you know – he'll enjoy banging up an MP, half a dozen aristos and a few media stars.'

'And that bastard Friedmann.'

They walked on in companionable silence. For the first time she was certain. She really wanted him to stay there, to exorcise David and all the ghosts from the past – though she would have to do that part for herself – she still had to know why ... But that could wait. It wasn't critical any more. It was George who mattered and just now he felt very precious. Through hell and high water … and he was still there. A blissful evening stretched ahead. A few drinks by the blazing log fire, dinner under the low beams of the forge bar, lying with him in the huge four-poster bed, feeling loved and respected, protected and desired, for all the right reasons; and wanting him so much in return. It could take a lifetime to work all that out; and she was glad they had a lifetime to do so. She was smiling in the darkness.

Back in the car she cuddled him and he kissed her, very gently at first, then fiercely. 'Love you, Ally.'

'Love you, too, George.'

As he started the engine, the copy of the *Western Morning News* they had bought in the morning fell from the dashboard onto her lap and she switched on the interior light to pick it up. Glancing down, she noticed an item occupying a few inches at the bottom of the front page: 'Good Lord.' George turned to her questioningly. 'They've found him. They've *found* Taylor – washed up on some islands called Las Tres Marias after a big storm. *El Niño* again. I suppose a small boat wouldn't stand much chance out in the Pacific.'

'He was drowned?'

'Yes.'

'Too good for the bastard.' He gave an evil smile. 'Y'know, when she was in the nick out there, Nikki said he'd originally planned to fake a sailing accident in the Bristol Channel to cover his disappearance, but funked it because he thought it might go wrong … serve him right to go that way in the end. He's no loss. Waste of space. Suppose it's ironic in a way? Second time lucky.'

She kissed him. 'Second time lucky, George.'